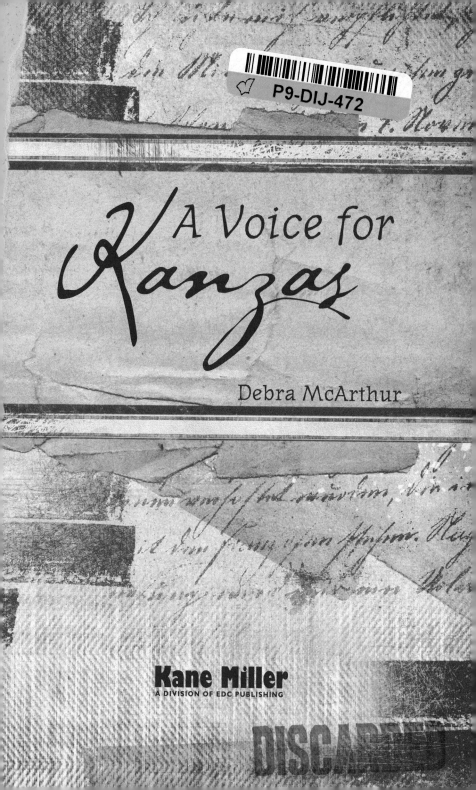

P9-DIJ-472

A Voice for Kanzas

Debra McArthur

Kane Miller
A DIVISION OF EDC PUBLISHING

True, This! –
Beneath the rule of men entirely great,
The pen is mightier than the sword.

Edward Bulwer-Lytton

First Edition
Kane Miller, A Division of EDC Publishing

Jacket design: Kat Godard, DraDog, LLC

Library of Congress Control Number: 2010942301

Printed and bound in the United States of America

ISBN: 978-1-61067-044-9

1 2 3 4 5 6 7 8 9 10

A Voice for Kanzas

Debra McArthur

For George and Norma Roberts,
who always loved to tell good stories.

For Lucy Catherine McQuitty McArthur,
for lending me a great name
for a character with great heart.

For Russell McArthur,
who would have liked this story, I think.

And, as always, for John. For everything.

1

Harrisburg, Pennsylvania,
March 12, 1855

The latch clicked softly as Lucy Thomkins eased the front door shut. The afternoon sun projected the "T" from the stained-glass window in the door onto the white marble floor of the entryway.

Dancers in rustling silk gracefully twirl to the harpsichord's magical spell ... The line had swirled through Lucy's brain all afternoon at school, and she was desperate to get a new poem on paper before it dissolved. She hung her cloak next to Papa's overcoat on the brass rack by the door. Folded pages stuck out of Papa's coat pocket. Had he brought home another copy of *The Democratic Review*? The last issue had several poems, and Papa had let her keep it. She took the booklet from his pocket:

INFORMATION FOR KANZAS IMMIGRANTS

Prepared by THOMAS H. WEBB

Secretary of the New England Emigrant Aid Co.

Boston, Mass.

No. 3 Winter Street,

Head of the Second Flight of Stairs,

On the Left

Ugh. Another political paper. "Kanzas" surely meant Kansas Territory, but it seemed odd that it used the old spelling. All the newspapers now referred to the territory as "Kansas."

Lucy had certainly heard plenty about it. It was Papa and Grandfather's favorite argument. Papa's temper – his "righteous anger," as Mamma called it – always came out when they talked about slavery. No one knew yet whether Kansas would be a slave state or a free state. The voters in the new territory would have to decide that. Lucy shoved the booklet back in Papa's pocket and tiptoed toward the wide, curved staircase. She had a poem to write.

"Lucy Catherine!" Grandmother stood at the parlor door.

She held her locket watch open. "Your needlework is waiting upstairs in the sewing room. Yesterday's stitching must be taken out. It's atrocious."

"Can't it wait just a minute? I need to write something."

"Another poem, I'm sure. I don't know why your mother allows it. By the time I was thirteen, I had a full set of embroidered table linens in my hope chest. You can't clothe your family in poetry."

"At least in my *verses*, the flowers are beautiful." Lucy climbed the steps as Grandmother followed, scolding all the way about Lucy's poor needlework skills. The patterns in *Godey's Lady's Book* called it "crewel embroidery," but "cruel" described it better.

The poem would have to wait.

Lucy paused outside Grandfather's study. The door was open a crack, and he sat at his desk, shuffling papers. The top of his bald head was red, a sure sign of anger.

Papa's voice was quiet. "It's a legitimate business opportunity. If you can look at it reasonably ..."

"You want me to invest in foolishness, Marcus," Grandfather said. "This isn't business, it's politics, and I won't be a part of it."

Grandmother pulled the study door shut. No eavesdropping allowed. Unless Grandmother was doing it.

The afternoon was as monotonous as the ticking of the pendulum clock in the sewing room. Lucy picked out stitches and replaced them with new embroidery as Grandmother sat nearby, glancing at Lucy's work and shaking her head. When

4

the clock chimed four, Lucy put her needle down. Instead of flowers and leaves, tangled loops of thread covered her sampler. She sighed. "This isn't how *Godey's* meant it to look."

"Oh, for heaven's sake." Grandmother took hold of Lucy's embroidery hoop, but it was stuck fast. Lucy had stitched it to her skirt ... again. "That's the third time this week," Grandmother complained. "Hand me your scissors."

Lucy reached into the sewing basket, but came up empty-handed. "I can't find them! I'm hopeless!"

The sewing room door swung open, and Papa stepped in. "Who's hopeless?"

"I am, Papa. I can't even find the scissors to cut myself loose from this awful thing."

Papa's gray eyes twinkled. He reached into his vest pocket and pulled out his penknife. When he opened it, he bowed deeply, his thick auburn hair nearly brushing Lucy's shoulder. "Allow me to release you from your needlework bondage, my lady," he said, and lifted the sampler enough to cut the threads that held it to her skirt.

"Thank you, kind knight." Lucy rose and curtsied. "I am forever in your debt." She leaned close to Papa's ear and whispered, "Please find something else for me to do."

Papa looked at the sampler in his hands and smiled. He handed it back to her with a wink. "Then, fair lady, you must accept the quest of going to the kitchen to speak with Eliza about a homecoming dinner for your mother and brother."

Lucy threw her arms around his neck. "That's wonderful!

When will they be here?"

"Tom is hitching Penny to the wagon now to go to the train station."

"Can I ride to the station with Tom, Papa?" she asked.

"Certainly not!" said Grandmother. "I'll not have half the town talking about my granddaughter riding alone across Harrisburg with the stable boy!"

Lucy whirled to face Grandmother, but Papa caught her arm and squeezed it gently. She knew the signal; this wasn't a battle worth fighting.

"Lucy, go talk to Eliza about dinner, please."

"Yes, Papa." She stuffed the sampler into the sewing basket.

Grandmother pointed at the basket. "After dinner, you must take all that stitching out and begin again."

"But I have lessons to finish!"

"Now, Mother," said Papa, "can't you commute the prisoner's sentence until tomorrow?"

Grandmother stiffened. "Make light of it if you wish, Marcus, but I am teaching the girl practical skills to be a fit wife."

"Lucy is a bright girl," Papa replied. "Whatever her family lacks in embroidered linens will be made up in a thousand other ways." Papa turned to Lucy. "Now, go see Eliza, Lucy Cat. And ask her to make Joseph's favorite chocolate pie."

<hr />

Lucy was setting the table with Grandmother's good china

when the wagon clattered into the side yard. Papa bounded out the door, and Lucy hurried behind him.

"Papa!" Joseph jumped off the wagon and ran to Papa for a hug. His mop of red hair was nearly as high as Papa's shoulder. How could he be so tall at only ten years old? Had he grown in the month they'd been away?

Joseph climbed back on the wagon to help Tom unload the luggage, and Papa helped Mamma down.

"Lucy, look!" Joseph stood on the back of the wagon, a large box balanced on his head. It slid sideways and hurtled toward Lucy.

Mamma looked over Papa's shoulder. "Joseph!"

Papa put up his hands just in time to catch the box by the brown string that encircled it. "Joseph, stop playing," Papa said. "Help Tom unhitch the wagon before you come inside."

Joseph jumped down from the wagon and ran to catch up with Tom.

Lucy looked at the box that Papa held. A label was stamped with the name of a Pittsburgh dressmaker. It looked expensive and not the sort of place Mamma would normally shop.

Mamma stretched her arms toward Lucy for a hug.

"How's my poet? It's good to hold you again." Despite her smile, there was sadness in her eyes. Lucy wished again she had been able to make the trip with Mamma to bury Grandfather Cameron. It must be hard to be an orphan, even for a grown-up woman. Joseph could not comfort Mamma at a time like that.

"I'm so glad you're back." Lucy lowered her voice. "Grandmother's been impossible."

Mamma smiled and glanced toward the house. "Was she really so bad?"

"Just don't mention poetry or sewing to her. She'll give you an earful about both."

Mamma nodded. "I'll avoid the subjects. I'm sure she'll have plenty of other complaints for me."

"My mother, complain?" Papa asked. "Never!" They all laughed.

Eliza stepped out of the side door. "Good to see you, Miz Thomkins!" she said. "Half an hour till dinner."

"I must freshen up." Mamma took Papa's arm as they climbed the steps. "I have some news for you."

"And I have some for you," Papa said. "Come to the parlor when you've changed." He hung her cloak on the coat rack and took the booklet from the pocket of his coat that still hung there.

Grandmother was examining one of the silver serving spoons when Lucy returned to the dining room. "I'm certain I told Eliza to polish this silver last week." She held it out. "Disgraceful." She shook her head.

Lucy took two crystal goblets from the hutch. They made a gentle ring as their rims touched. "Do be careful," Grandmother scolded. "You and your brother have chipped nearly every piece in the set." She picked up one of the pale-green linen napkins Eliza had set out on the sideboard. "And put out the burgundy linens to go with the good china!"

Mamma came down the stairs a few minutes later. She had changed into a fresh dress, but it was one Lucy recognized, not a new one from a fancy dressmaker. Still, Papa reached out his hand to her as if she were royalty. They disappeared into the parlor.

The back door banged open, and Joseph burst through. "Joseph Alexander!" Grandmother pointed at his feet, and Joseph stopped where he was. "You've been in the stable. Wipe your feet before you go running across my clean rug!"

"Yes, ma'am," Joseph said, inching backwards and shuffling his shoes on the mat by the door.

When Grandmother was satisfied he had done a proper job, she nodded. "That's better. Welcome home." She went back to the kitchen, carrying the tarnished spoon.

Joseph wrinkled his nose and stuck out his tongue behind her back.

Lucy pulled the burgundy napkins from the sideboard and handed her brother some forks. "Come help, and you can tell me about Pittsburgh."

Joseph went first around the table, placing the forks next to the china plates. "We spent hours and hours in the lawyer's office. We went back every day for nearly two weeks before Mamma was finished there."

Lucy followed him around the table, arranging the folded napkins at each place. "But what about the city? What was it like?"

"It was smoky from all the factories. And there were so many riverboats and barges, you could have walked across the river on them. You should have seen it!"

"I wish I could have," Lucy said. She placed the folded linen napkin next to Grandfather's fork and sighed. "Someday I'll get out of Harrisburg."

Joseph laid a fork by the next plate. "Not if Grandmother has anything to say about it. Boys have adventures; girls get to sew. Sorry!" He grinned – the grin he knew Lucy hated.

Eliza emerged from the kitchen with a steaming dish of mashed potatoes. Her face glowed with perspiration. "You children watch out for the hot dishes," she warned. "If your grandmamma is finished fussing over her silver spoon, I'll bring the rest of the food out." Eliza rolled her eyes, and Joseph laughed. She wouldn't have dared that expression in front of Grandmother. As it was, Grandmother threatened at least once a week to fire her. "Ya'll can go tell the others to wash up for supper."

Joseph took the stairs two at a time to fetch Grandfather from his study. Mamma and Papa emerged from the parlor, smiling and holding hands. Papa laid the booklet on the marble-topped table in the hall.

When they were seated, Grandfather said grace. Before the "Amen" was out, Joseph had his hand on the spoon in the mashed potatoes. They passed bowls around and waited for Grandfather to begin the conversation.

"Mary Margaret, I trust you had a successful trip." He

steadied a chunk of roast beef with his fork, sliced a piece from it and took a bite.

Mamma paused with her water glass lifted halfway to her mouth. "Successful? I successfully buried my father, if that's what you mean."

Lucy could hear the irritation in Mamma's voice. Anyone else would have said "I'm so sorry for your loss," but Grandfather measured everything by success or failure.

Grandfather went on without apology. "Not at all. I merely meant to ask if my friend Jenkins was helpful in settling your father's affairs."

"Yes, he was quite helpful. Father's assets were more than adequate for the funeral and headstone." Mamma glanced across the table at Papa. "And now that the estate is settled, Marcus and I are ready to start a new business."

"Now, that's good news," said Grandfather. "The import trade is picking up. How about trying your hand at that?"

Papa smiled at Mamma. "I think a retail store may be more profitable."

Profitable. A good word. Lucy thought of the house on Maple Street they'd sold when Papa's business failed two years ago. According to Grandfather, they were paupers now, surviving only because Grandfather let them live in his house.

Grandfather scowled. "You can't be serious, Marcus. You've already closed two stores in the last ten years in this town."

"Which is why we want to try our luck in Kansas Territory."

Lucy's fork dropped from her hand and clattered onto the

china plate. The booklet – *Kanzas Immigrants* – surely not!

"Papa, no!" she said.

"Oh, boy! Kansas!" said Joseph. "Can I get my own horse, Papa?"

Grandfather set his fork down and glared at Papa. "Why do you persist in this foolishness?"

"It's not foolishness," said Papa. "Settlers are leaving Boston next week for the territory. We can join the group at the depot in Erie."

"Kansas Territory!" Grandfather nearly spat the words. "Have you lost your mind? You can't take your family into that unsettled country of wild animals and savages!"

"Indians?! I could be an Indian fighter!" Joseph held his knife as if he were staring down the barrel of a tiny rifle. "Pow! Pow!"

Mamma snatched the knife from his hand and gave him a stern look.

"Kansas is not unsettled," Papa continued. "They have a town there called Lawrence. They need more settlers to vote in the elections to make Kansas free."

Lucy clenched her fists in her lap. "But, Papa, it's not even part of the United States! Miss Collins says that people live in houses made of dirt!"

Mamma raised her eyebrows. "This is adult conversation."

Lucy pressed her lips together to keep quiet. It wasn't fair. She was a poet! She could not live in the middle of the wilderness!

Grandmother turned to Mamma. "Mary Margaret," she

said, "surely you don't approve of this ridiculous idea."

"It's the very opportunity we've been waiting for. Our chance to start over."

"And you'd leave Pennsylvania and your family?"

"My family will go with me." The words hung like icicles in the air.

Grandmother's lips stretched into a straight, thin line. But she had never made Mamma feel like family.

"You're doomed to fail, Marcus," Grandfather continued. "You couldn't run a mercantile here in Harrisburg! I paid off your debts – twice – because you couldn't!"

"There was too much competition here to make a profit. The Aid Society agent says there's great opportunity in Lawrence."

"Hah!" Grandfather tossed his napkin on the table. "Great opportunity for them to find gullible fools to support their political cause."

"Their cause is just, Father." Papa's voice was rising. "We can't allow Kansas Territory to become a slave state."

"Why is this your fight, Marcus?"

"Because too many people won't accept it as their fight," said Papa.

Grandfather rose and stood very straight. "I promised to provide you with the funds to begin a new business, but I will not invest my money in this folly in Kansas."

Lucy's fists relaxed. That would be the end of it, then.

But Papa just smiled. "Maggie, tell him the discovery that Jenkins made."

Mamma held her chin a bit higher. "My father invested in the Philadelphia and Reading Railway years ago. Mr. Jenkins sold Papa's shares for me. It's not a fortune, but it's enough to begin our business."

Grandfather pounded his fist on the table. "It's insanity, and I forbid it!" The clatter of silver on china rang briefly, then died.

Papa pushed back his chair and stood to face his father. "We don't need your permission. We leave next week for Kansas Territory."

Lucy looked up at Papa. "Next week? What about the cotillion?" It was the first dance for the girls of Miss Delia's School with the boys of Westside Academy. Mamma said she would buy Lucy a new dress for it. She turned to Mamma. "You promised …"

Mamma placed her hand on Lucy's. "We'll talk about it later, Lucy."

Lucy's head spun as thoughts whirled through her brain. Her stomach felt queasy, and she rose from the table. "Please excuse me," she muttered. "I can't eat any more." She picked up Papa's Kanzas booklet from the hall table and climbed the stairs to her room.

2

Time of Departure.—The first Spring Party will leave Boston for Kanzas as early in March as practicable. Subsequently, Parties will for the present leave here weekly, at least.

Fare.—The passage fare for each adult, from here to Kanzas City, Mo., will be about $40; for children between the ages of 14 and 5, half price.

—Information for Kanzas Immigrants

Lucy couldn't concentrate at school the next day. No matter how she tried, she couldn't get Kansas out of her mind. *Unsettled country of savages and wild animals. Great opportunity for business.*

At the end of the day, Miss Collins returned everyone's composition book but Lucy's.

"Lucy, please wait after class," she said.

Lucy's stomach lurched. She should have known better. She had written poetry instead of essays for her assignments last week. Was Miss Collins angry? She had tried to write the essays, but the words would not come out that way.

She waited at her seat while her classmates gathered their

books and cloaks. They chattered as they filed through the door, talking about their dresses for the cotillion and the boys they hoped to dance with. The room was quiet as the door shut behind them, and Lucy walked to the front of the room.

Miss Collins held Lucy's composition book.

"Miss Collins," Lucy began, "I'm sorry for the poems."

"Yes … the poems. That wasn't exactly the assignment you were given, was it?"

"No, ma'am."

"I assigned a composition about women's role in society, and you wrote about Mrs. Sarah Josepha Hale's ideas of female education in a sonnet with the title, *Shall Godey's Book Be Yet the Death of Me?*"

Lucy's face grew hot with shame. "I'm sorry, Miss Collins. I tried to write essays, but my thoughts just seemed to come out best in verse."

The teacher's frown melted into a smile. "Don't be sorry. I enjoyed the sonnet."

Lucy looked up, surprised. "Really?"

"Yes, really. Your words bring both humor and serious thought to your subjects. Despite your dislike of Mrs. Hale's magazines with their needlework patterns, you make some excellent points about her public support of education for women. We can both hope that Mrs. Hale's ideas will lead to educational opportunities for more women."

"It seems that women don't get credit for having good ideas." Lucy looked at the composition book her teacher held.

"But you didn't like the other one?"

"Your reaction to Mr. Thoreau's *Resistance to Civil Government* was a ten-stanza rhyme that began … let me quote …" Miss Collins opened the composition book to the page she had marked. "Yes, here it is. 'Henry built his Walden home/ With boards he cut by axe./ He spent a night in jail because/ He would not pay his tax.'" Miss Collins removed her spectacles and looked up from the book. "A friend from Massachusetts sent me a copy of Mr. Thoreau's essay, and I found it worthy of consideration. That's why I shared it with the class."

"It seems silly to me. He spent the night in jail to protest taxes that support slavery. He wrote an essay about it, but it didn't help even one slave. What good is that? It was just words."

"You make a point. Couldn't you have said that with a bit more dignity? I think Mr. Thoreau deserves better treatment than a poem set to the meter of *Mary Had a Little Lamb*. I present my students with relevant writings so they will consider the issues, not make fun of them." She closed the composition book and returned it to Lucy.

"Yes, ma'am."

"You have a special talent, Lucy. Don't waste it. You will be a poet of note when you find your own voice."

Lucy returned her teacher's smile. "Thank you, Miss Collins."

"But remember that a good writer should be versatile. Essays are appropriate in some circumstances." Miss Collins winked. "In the future, you must try the essays as assigned."

The future … Kansas! "Miss Collins, I won't be able to!"

"Of course you will be able to write essays."

"No … I mean … I won't be here to write them!" Lucy swallowed hard to keep the tears from coming. "Papa is taking us away from Harrisburg. He wants to start a new business."

"Oh, my," said Miss Collins. "I'm sorry you're leaving. Are you going far?"

Lucy nodded and took a breath. "He's taking us to Kansas."

"Kansas!" Miss Collins paused a second. "Kansas Territory," she said. "Why, that's wonderful!"

Lucy stared at her teacher. "What?"

"You are off on the biggest adventure of your life! How I envy you!"

Lucy looked into her teacher's face. "You envy me?"

"Think of your own words about Mr. Thoreau. That social commentary was useless if it did not change even one life."

"But what has that to do with Kansas?"

"You are not simply making a gesture in protest, as Mr. Thoreau did. You will be a part of the movement to make a real difference."

"But I can't vote in the elections. I won't have a voice in Kansas."

"You may not have a vote, but Lucy Thomkins has a voice. You must find that voice and use it for more than just words. Words alone are only noise. To make a difference, they must be proven by action."

"What kind of action?"

Miss Collins shook her head and smiled. "I can't answer that question for you, but I think you will know what to do when the time comes. I will miss you, but I have every faith that Kansas will be good for you, and you will be good for Kansas."

"Thank you, Miss Collins. I'll miss you, too." Lucy gathered her things and pulled her cloak from the coat rack.

Miss Collins put the papers and books from her desk in her satchel. "When do you leave?"

"Next Thursday."

"Before the cotillion? You must be disappointed."

"Yes, ma'am. I was looking forward to it." Now Lucy really felt like crying.

Miss Collins patted her arm. "Perhaps your father would delay the trip for a week. Surely a few days would not make a big difference."

Lucy considered it. Mamma had said they would talk about it, but they hadn't been able to last night. Maybe there was hope. "I'll talk to my mother about it," she said. "Maybe she can convince Papa to wait a little longer."

"I hope so," Miss Collins said.

They parted as Miss Collins locked the outer door of the school. "Let me know when your last day in class will be."

Lucy hurried home, trying to frame her argument in her head. Mamma had promised, after all. Could she persuade Papa to delay the trip? She would just have to.

Lucy burst through the front door. "Mamma!" she called out.

Mamma stood at the top of the stairs. "I'm glad you're home, Lucy. Come help me sort Joseph's clothes. We can't take much with us – the baggage fees are outrageous."

Lucy hurried up the stairs and followed Mamma into the bedroom. "Do we have to leave so soon? The cotillion is next week. You said I could go." She paused for a breath and lowered her voice. "You promised me a new dress for it."

Mamma put down the shirt she held. "I'm sorry, Lucy. I know you were looking forward to the dance. I thought of it when I was in Pittsburgh." She reached into the wardrobe and pulled out a box, the one Joseph had balanced on his head yesterday. "I bought this for you."

Lucy slid the string from around the box and opened the lid. Inside she found folds and folds of ruffled silk, the shade of summer sky. Unfolding the fabric, Lucy gasped: a beautiful gown with three tiers of flounces over a stiff crinoline petticoat. The ruffled sleeves fell gracefully over full, white lace-edged undersleeves. "Oh, Mamma, it's the most beautiful dress I've ever seen!"

"It was an extravagance, but I had just learned of the inheritance when I saw it in the dressmaker's window. I couldn't resist," said Mamma. "Here, you must try it on."

Lucy slipped out of her school dress and stepped into the new dress. Mamma fastened the hooks on the center back seam.

Lucy stood in front of the long mirror. "It's beautiful," she whispered. "Please, can't we stay until the dance?"

Mamma sighed. "Papa surprised me, too. When I bought this dress, I wasn't expecting we'd be headed for Kansas Territory. I'm sorry you won't be able to wear it." Then, she brightened and pulled out the vanity chair. "Here, sit down and let me do up your hair. I want to see how you look."

Lucy watched in the mirror as Mamma's nimble hands worked, brushing Lucy's wavy brown hair. She parted it in the middle and drew back both sides before twisting the hair into a bun. With their faces nearly side by side in the mirror, Lucy noticed how much she looked like Mamma. Their hair was nearly the same color, except for a few strands of early gray that brushed Mamma's forehead. They had the same hazel eyes, and both their smiles turned up a little on the right side.

Mamma opened the top drawer of her dresser and pulled out a pretty silver comb to secure Lucy's hair. "There now, let's see you." She reached out and took hold of Lucy's hands as she stood. "You look so grown up!"

Lucy gazed at her reflection in the long mirror. She *did* look older. She turned to face Mamma again. "Please let us stay until the cotillion," she begged.

Mamma shook her head. "I'm sorry, Lucy. Papa needs to be in the Territory in time for the election. He's already made the arrangements."

"Can't Papa have a store here?"

"This is a chance for your father to start fresh," Mamma said.

"He can do that here!"

"He's tried." She paused. "And he cares about the freedom of the territory."

"More than he cares about us? I don't want to leave my

school! Miss Collins praised my poems and said I will be a 'poet of note' someday."

"There's a fine school in Lawrence. The Emigrant Aid Society has hired a New England teacher to work there."

"But it's not *my* teacher! What if the Kansas teacher doesn't like poetry?"

"There are other things in life than poetry, Lucy. Besides, we will all have to work together in the store. You won't have much time for writing."

"I'll never be too busy for poetry. Even Grandmother can't keep me from it."

Mamma shook her head. "That's enough, now. It's settled. I'm sorry about the dance, but –"

Lucy didn't wait to hear more. She ran from the room, her satin flounces rustling as she hurried out to the hall and down the stairs to the dining room. The lamps weren't lit yet, and the twilight made the room dark. She sat on an extra chair in the corner by the china hutch and buried her face in her hands.

Eliza's low singing came from behind the kitchen door. "*Swing low, sweet chariot … Comin' for to carry me home …*"

Home. What would home be like now? Kansas. Dirt houses. Working in a store. No time for poetry. No Miss Collins to guide her, and she'd probably never see any of her friends again in her life. And it didn't matter to anyone.

"*A band of angels comin' after me … Comin' for to carry me home …*" The kitchen door swung open. Eliza peered through the half-darkness of the dining room. "Who's there? Miss Lucy?

Is that you?" She struck a match and lit the nearest lamp, then she saw Lucy's dress and smiled. "Why, child, don't you look just like a princess?" Her smile turned to concern when she saw Lucy's tears. "What's the matter?"

"Oh, Eliza." Lucy caught her breath. "It's too awful."

Eliza pulled a cloth from her apron pocket. "Here, now, wipe those tears before you stain your pretty dress. What's so awful?"

Lucy dabbed at her face. "Papa is making us go to Kansas Territory. All he cares about is the elections. He doesn't care that I have to give up everything."

Eliza straightened. "I heard about your papa's plan, Miss Lucy, and you got no reason to feel sorry for yourself. Your papa's a brave man. He's working for freedom."

"Oh, I'm so tired of hearing about freedom!" Lucy wiped her hand across her face. "I don't have any freedom! I have to do what everyone else tells me to. Sometimes I feel like a slave."

As soon as she'd said it, Lucy knew her mistake.

Eliza's voice shook. She took a breath. "Don't ever let me hear you say that."

Lucy's face burned with shame. She sometimes forgot that Eliza had been a slave. She'd married a freed slave who worked five years to buy her freedom, then was killed in a railroad accident just days after she left the plantation in Virginia. She had worked for Grandmother as long as Lucy could remember.

"I'm sorry." Lucy took Eliza's hand. "I didn't mean to upset you, but the territory is uncivilized."

Eliza's voice was low, but firm. "Missy, you just look at

yourself sitting there all gussied up in that fancy dress. You haven't worked barefoot in a cotton field with a whip at your back. You haven't been sold to the highest bidder. Now, go along and get ready for dinner 'fore your grandmamma skins us both."

Lucy climbed the stairs to her room. Kansas. Freedom. Elections. Too much to think about. And she could only dream about the cotillion.

The Sorcerer's Voice

Summer sky wraps me in billows of silk,
And the harpsichord waltzes my feet.
Dancers with pink cheeks gracefully bow
As gloved hands and sweaty palms meet.
The dancers revolve, their motion a blur
Bright tunes through enchanted air whirl.
Till the sorcerer's voice-can it be Papa's voice?-
Freezes the scene with one word:
Kansas.

———◈———

On Thursday morning, Lucy's upstairs window was full of gray sky. In front of the house, Penny was hitched to the wagon, her breath steamy in the cold morning air. Two large trunks and two small ones rested on the wagon bed. Everything was loaded and ready to go. Grandfather had not spoken to any of them for three days, and he had left the house early without saying goodbye.

"Lucy!" Papa called up the stairs. "It's time to go."

Lucy pulled on her cloak and went downstairs. Joseph, Mamma, and Papa stood by the door. Grandmother stood with them. She spotted Lucy first.

"Lucy Catherine, what are you wearing?"

Mamma turned and saw the blue satin flounces of Lucy's skirt below the hem of her cloak. "Lucy, what are you thinking? You can't wear that on the trip!"

Lucy stood a little straighter. "Why not?"

"It's too dressy for traveling." Mamma frowned. "If you only knew what I'd paid for it …"

"But you said yourself that I wouldn't have the chance to wear it in Kansas."

"Yes, but it will surely be ruined on the trip," Mamma said.

"Then at least I'll have worn it." Lucy said. "Otherwise it will go to waste, and I'll never wear it."

"Lucy, be practical."

"I *am*." Lucy smoothed a satin ruffle. "I can wear plain dresses when we get to Kansas, but this may be my only chance to wear this one. Besides, the trunks are already on the wagon. If I change now, we'll have to dig another dress out, then pack this one."

Mamma shook her head and sighed. "Oh, very well. It's not worth the fight. You have your father's stubborn streak."

"I'll take that as a compliment," Papa said with a smile.

Grandmother shook her head. "What a waste of that beautiful dress," she said. She turned to Papa. "You can still change your mind. You can have a business here."

"There's more at stake than just a store," said Papa. "Kansas must be free."

Grandmother turned to Mamma. "Mary Margaret, at least think of your children," she pleaded. "What kind of education can they have in the territory?"

"I'm sure the children will get an education we can't even imagine," said Mamma.

Grandmother hugged Joseph. "You don't want to go to Kansas, do you?" Her voice shook with emotion.

He pushed away from her. "I'll have my own horse and maybe even a gun!"

"A more stubborn bunch of Thomkinses I've never seen," said Grandmother. She held Lucy at arm's length for a moment. Then picked up a small bag and gave it to Lucy. "I have made up some sampler projects and put in thread, needles, and scissors for you. At least you can keep your hands busy on the trip west." Lucy and Mamma exchanged looks.

"Thank you, Grandmother. I'm sure Kansas Territory will be sorely in need of some of my needlework," said Lucy. Even Grandmother chuckled a bit at that.

When Grandmother came to Mamma, she leaned over as if to kiss her cheek, but instead, she muttered, "We will keep your rooms ready for when you come back."

Mamma pulled away from her. "Thank you, Mother Thomkins, but that won't be necessary. We shall not be returning to Pennsylvania."

Grandmother frowned. "We'll see."

Tom appeared at the door. "The wagon is ready, Mr. Thomkins," he said.

"Then it's time," said Papa. He hugged Grandmother and kissed her cheek. "Goodbye, Mother. We'll write to let you know we've arrived safely."

Grandmother stood on the porch as they walked to the wagon. Papa helped Mamma up while Lucy and Joseph got on the wagon behind them.

Tom climbed onto the front seat next to Papa, touched his whip to Penny's rump, and the wagon jerked into motion. As the horse's hooves clomped on the cobblestones, Lucy looked once more at the three-story red brick house with its elegant black shutters. Grandmother stood on the porch for a moment, then turned and went inside, closing the door behind her.

Smoke curled from the chimneys of the houses on Third Street, and picket fences lined the road. Would Lawrence, Kansas, have picket fences? Would it have a church with a tall steeple like the Presbyterian Church in Harrisburg?

Even in the early morning, the train station was full of activity. As they stood on the wooden platform, conductors called out boarding instructions, babies cried, and porters loaded trunks from carts onto the railroad cars. The steam engines puffed, and the whistles of departing trains made Lucy jump.

While Papa made sure their trunks were safely loaded, Joseph touched the sleeve of the conductor.

"When will the train get to Kansas?" he asked.

The conductor laughed. "The rails only go as far as St. Louis," he said. "From there, you'll take a steamboat to Kansas City and a wagon the rest of the way."

Joseph grinned. "A steamboat!" He climbed aboard, pulling Mamma by the hand.

Just as Lucy put her foot on the step, she heard a familiar voice.

"Lucy! Lucy Thomkins!" Miss Collins was running on the platform, her bonnet ribbons fluttering behind her. Lucy stepped back from the train as her teacher caught her in a hug. "I was afraid I had missed you!"

"Miss Collins! I didn't expect to see you here."

"Could I let my most promising poet go away without even a goodbye?"

Lucy smiled, but shook her head. "They won't have much need of poets in Kansas Territory. Papa says it is rough country. There will be few babbling brooks to write of and little time for poetry."

"And you think those are the only worthy subjects of the poet?" Miss Collins pulled a small package from her cloak pocket and gave it to Lucy. "This is for later."

Lucy hugged her teacher again.

"Last call, miss," said the conductor. When she was seated on the train, Lucy tore the brown paper from the package.

Inside was a book. Most of the pages were blank, but the first page was edged with hand-colored violets and held an inscription in Miss Collins' familiar flowing handwriting. "For a gifted poet, Lucy Catherine Thomkins, who must find her own voice. Bring this book back some day with all your Western verses in it. With best wishes and fondest thoughts, Martha Collins."

Lucy looked up from the book and stared out the window as they left the Harrisburg rail yards and started across the long bridge over the Susquehanna River.

She imagined what the open spaces of Kansas Territory would look like and thought of Miss Collins' wish for her. *My own true voice. A voice for Kansas.*

3

Lawrence, Kansas Territory
March 30, 1855

Those immigrants who go out early in the Spring will enjoy the right of exercising the glorious privileges of freemen, at the first election; *a matter of great moment to them, and of vast moment to all who may subsequently become citizens of the Territory.*

—Information for Kanzas Immigrants

Her own shivering shook Lucy awake. The hard floor reminded her that she was not in her cozy bed in Grandfather's house; she was huddled on the floor of the sleeping room of Litchfield's boarding house. She pulled the rough blanket tighter around her shoulders. Three days in this horrible place, and she was still not used to the icy wind that blew between the boards of the building.

The cloth partition that hung from the rafters overhead did little to muffle the snores from the men's side of the room. At least three of the men kept up a steady symphony. Lucy guessed the trombone sound was from Mr. Casey, whose large nose resembled one. Despite her discomfort, Lucy giggled at the thought. Then Mamma was kneeling next to her, even though it was barely light enough to see.

"Lucy, come help with breakfast." Mamma nudged her gently.

"But it's so cold, Mamma."

"Don't act like a child. You are old enough to work with the women, and we need your help. This is Election Day. The men will want to eat soon."

Mamma hurried outside, and Lucy dressed quickly, shivering as she pulled on her dress. She wanted to cry every time she looked at it. Her beautiful Pittsburgh gown was dirty and burned from brushing the ground between the cooking fires. The trunk with her other clothes had been stolen from the steamboat somewhere between St. Louis and Kansas City. Lucy had carefully packed away the crinoline petticoat that had made the dress so full and beautiful. It was completely impractical here, but without it, the limp dress hung so long that the hem caught on the heels and buttons of her shoes. It looked worse every day, but this dress was all she had until they could move into their own home, and Mamma could make her a new one.

As if that weren't bad enough, she had also lost the few books she had been allowed to bring. Her beloved volume of poems by Edgar Allan Poé and her book of *Twice Told Tales* by Nathanial Hawthorne were both gone. Thank goodness she had not lost the poetry journal from Miss Collins, though she had not been able to write one poem since they had left Pennsylvania. She had kept it with her though, along with Papa's

Kanzas Immigrants booklet, in the sewing bag Grandmother had given her.

Lucy tried to comb her long hair, but it was no use – it was too tangled. She pulled the hair back and twisted it into a knot at the back of her neck. She was glad she had no mirror to see what she looked like. An indoor cookstove and decent bathtub were luxuries in Kansas, and this boarding house had neither. And even if there had been a bathtub, there was little privacy. Every room was so crowded that they had to eat outdoors, at tables made of boards laid across stumps and sawhorses.

Lucy stepped carefully over the eight children asleep on the floor nearby, then hurried outside to join Mrs. Litchfield, her mother, and the other women who were building the cooking fires.

Mamma handed her a bucket. "Fetch the water for coffee, please."

"Yes, Mamma." Lucy started down Massachusetts Street toward the well. The wind whipped at her skirt and bit at her legs through the tears in her stockings. She tightened her chapped fingers around the cold metal handle of the bucket. There was just enough water in the bucket to prime the pump, so she dared not spill it. She clutched her cloak under her chin with her free hand and stepped across the frozen ruts in the dirt road.

Lawrence was not like any place she had imagined. About fifty buildings made up the town. They were mostly A-shaped structures, framed with long wooden poles lashed together at the top and covered with thatched hay on the sides. A few stone buildings and some log cabins stood here and there. Papa said fifty buildings was not a bad start, since the town had been staked out only last August. But the one thing Lucy had looked forward to – the school – was a pile of burned rubble, destroyed after the stove caught fire a month earlier.

On her way to the pump, Lucy passed the lot where their general store would soon be built and imagined the store that would stand there. She stopped, picked up a stone and threw it through an imaginary window. Lawrence already had a store. Why did they need another? Papa said the town would grow, but Lucy could not see one good reason why anyone in his right mind would want to come here. Miss Collins had made it sound like a great adventure, but it was even worse than Lucy had imagined. She didn't dare say it, but she hoped the store would fail, just like Papa's other businesses. Maybe they could be back in Pennsylvania at Grandfather's house before Christmas.

She poured the water from her bucket into the top of the pump to prime it as she pumped the handle, down then up, again and again. Before the bucket was full, her arm ached, and she paused to rest and looked around. Was there anything of beauty here? Anything to inspire verse? The Kansas River, the Kaw, ran along the north edge of town, but it was low and choked with chunks of ice. Delaware Indians lived on the north side of the river. She looked eastward toward the horizon. Dr. Robinson, the Emigrant Aid Society agent and leader of the town, had said the Kanza and Shawnee tribes had occupied this land before the settlers came. Lucy would gladly give it back to them.

Even Ralph Waldo Emerson couldn't find inspiration in this place. She had memorized an Emerson poem about a flower. How did it go?

> *Rhodora! if the sages ask thee why*
> *This charm is wasted on the earth and sky,*
> *Tell them, dear, that, if eyes were made for seeing,*
> *Then Beauty is its own excuse for being:*

What would Emerson write about Kansas? Would he see beauty here that she was missing? Or would his journal be as empty as Lucy's?

The smell of campfire smoke brought Lucy back to her task. The women would be waiting for her to come back with the water. But wait – this smoke was not coming from the direction of the boarding house. She left the bucket and ran across the street and around the back of the *Herald of Freedom* office. The morning haze had lifted. Hundreds of tents, wagons, and horses huddled in the ravine just east of town. Smoke rose from dozens of campfires. The north wind had been carrying it away from town, but now it drifted up toward them. Lucy hurried back to her bucket, finished filling it and lugged it back to the boarding house. She took it to Mrs. Litchfield, who was waiting to make the coffee.

"Where did all the new settlers come from, Mrs. Litchfield?"

"Most all the folks in the boarding house came from Massachusetts and New York." Mrs. Litchfield held a coffee pot and nodded toward Lucy's bucket. "Fill the pot about half full."

Lucy poured water from the bucket into the pot. "No, I

mean all the ones camped just outside town. You can see the smoke from their fires over there." She pointed east.

Mrs. Litchfield looked where Lucy pointed. "Lewis!" she called to her husband, "Come see this!"

Mr. Litchfield broke away from his conversation with Papa and Mr. Brown, the editor of the *Herald of Freedom* newspaper. He strode across the street, looked over the ridge, then shouted to the men, "Thomkins! Brown! Looks like the Border Ruffians have come to join our little Election Day party!"

Papa and Mr. Brown joined Mr. Litchfield. "Where did they all come from?" Papa asked Mr. Brown.

"Missouri. They've come to take over the polls to keep us from voting, just as they did last November. We'd best let Robinson know there'll be trouble. We need to be ready for a fight."

Mrs. Litchfield, Mamma and the other women hurried to finish breakfast. Lucy went over to the fire where Mrs. Nichols was cooking bacon. Grease splattered into the flames and sizzled on the coals. "Who are all those people, Mrs. Nichols? Why are they here?" Lucy held the plate while Mrs. Nichols transferred the browned bacon from the skillet.

"To elect our legislature," Mrs. Nichols answered. "The Border Ruffians rode over from Missouri last fall to vote in our first election and put their own candidate in as delegate to Congress. Now they want to fill up our new legislature with proslavery men. Step back while I take this skillet off the fire."

"But they can't vote here, can they?"

37

"Guns and knives give men more rights than the laws do out here."

By the time all the men were ready, Dr. Robinson had arrived. "No time to eat," he told them. "The Ruffians will be at my office any minute. We need to get there first."

If there was to be a commotion at the election, Lucy wanted to be there. As she helped set out food for the women and children, the men hurried past her toward the Emigrant Aid office. At last Lucy slipped away from the boarding house.

By the time she reached Dr. Robinson's office, hundreds of men crowded the street. They were unshaven and covered with grime, as though they had traveled several days on horseback. "Watch out, gal," said a rough voice behind her. A large man pushed past her, and Lucy caught her breath when she saw a pistol stuck in the waist of his trousers. He wore a white ribbon in the buttonhole of his coat. She suddenly realized she was surrounded by men with white ribbons – and weapons. Was this ribbon how the Border Ruffians identified each other? Lucy eased toward the edge of the crowd, but stayed near enough to watch.

Mr. Blanton, the election judge, climbed onto a wooden box.

"Gentlemen!" he shouted. "I am the appointed judge of this poll, and I have been ordered by Governor Andrew H. Reeder to see that it is carried out in proper order."

"Then get out of the way so we can vote!" someone shouted.

"In accordance with the Kansas Nebraska Act of 1854, only

legal residents of Kansas Territory may cast votes for its legislature," continued Mr. Blanton. "Every voter must swear an oath as to his legal place of residence."

A man near Lucy shoved forward. "I don't have to swear any oath!" he shouted.

"Then, sir, you shall not vote," answered Mr. Blanton.

"That's right!" one of the Lawrence men said.

A Ruffian approached Mr. Blanton with a gun drawn. "I think my pistol will disagree with you," he said. "We can vote in Kansas, and we intend to do it! In fact, we'll vote instead of you abolitionists."

Cheers went up from the crowd. A cry of, "You tell him, Colonel Young!" came over Lucy's shoulder.

Mr. Blanton stood firm. "Congress declared that the settlers of Kansas would decide her policies on slavery. You have no right to vote here!"

"We hold our slaves according to the law," Colonel Young growled. "But if Kansas is free, they'll take off over the state line, and you New Englanders will help them." He stepped forward and pointed his gun at Mr. Blanton's nose. "Now open the door so we can get to that ballot box!"

The crowd pushed forward, and Lucy was pushed along with them. As Colonel Young went through the door, other armed men stood outside. They formed a double line, and the voters had to walk between them to cast their votes. They allowed several Ruffians to go in, but stopped the first man not wearing a white ribbon. Lucy's heart froze. It was Papa!

A tall man with a heavy beard blocked the door. "You don't want to go in there, do you?" he asked.

"Yes, sir, I do," Papa answered calmly.

"And how will you vote?"

Papa held his head high and his gaze steady. Lucy knew that look. He would not hide his intention. "I will vote for the Free State Party."

"Well, look-y here, boys!" said the Ruffian. "We got us an a-bull-li-shun-ist right here in front of us. I believe he needs to go back home and think about his vote some more. What do you think, Mr. A-bull-li-shun-ist?"

"I know my vote, and I intend to cast it!"

"I think you need some more time to think about it," answered the Ruffian. "Maybe a bullet in your head will help you think better!" The Ruffian raised his pistol.

Papa ignored him and pushed toward the door. The Ruffian pulled back the hammer on the gun and brought it level with Papa's temple.

"Papa!" Lucy screamed.

Papa turned toward her voice, along with everyone else in the crowd. Lucy rushed forward, straight toward the Ruffian with the gun. Rough hands reached out from the crowd and caught her. A man in a filthy buckskin jacket gripped her arms and pinned them to her sides. She struggled, but he gripped her tighter. The sour smell of whiskey caught in her throat, and she swallowed to keep from vomiting.

Papa stood motionless, the gun still pointed at his

head. "Lucy Catherine," Papa said calmly, "get back to Mrs. Litchfield's. Your mother will be looking for you."

Lucy couldn't speak, but she shook her head.

"Well, now," said the Ruffian with the gun. "You got yourself a fine gal there, don't you, Mr. A-bull-li-shun-ist? You don't want your Lucy to see her papa with a hole in his head, do you? How about you just step away from that door?"

"I came to Kansas to vote," said Papa.

"And I came to Kansas to stop you," said the Ruffian.

Papa stood his ground, the pistol still held at his temple.

The Ruffian looked across the street at Lucy, then back at Papa. "If I shoot you dead in this street, who will see your gal safely home?"

Papa looked through the crowd at Lucy. She felt hundreds of eyes on her, and her heart thumped so hard it felt like it would leap up into her throat. She struggled to break free of the hands that held her, but they only tightened more.

The Ruffian grinned and nodded toward the man holding Lucy. "I'll bet my friend Otis would take care of her."

The man who held Lucy now spun her around and put his face close to hers. "You're dressed up for a party," he said. Lucy turned her head away. The man's left earlobe was scabbed and partly torn away, as if an animal had bitten it. He pulled her closer and pressed his body against hers. "We're havin' a big party right after this election, Miss Lucy. You could be my dancin' partner." The men around him laughed. He looked up at the Ruffian who held the gun and said, loud enough for

41

them all to hear, "Yessir, I'd take *good* care of this gal."

Lucy cried out, and Papa stepped away from the door.

The Ruffian lowered his gun. "Any more of you want to vote?" No one moved. "Just as I thought," he said. "Bunch of cowards. You don't deserve to vote."

The Ruffians swarmed toward the door. Lucy's captor released her with a shove, and Papa caught her. He held her tight while the Ruffians pushed past them, then turned her gently to walk back to the boarding house, his arm still around her shoulders.

Finally, he spoke. "This was no place for you to be, Lucy Cat. You should not have left the boarding house."

Lucy looked up at Papa. "They were going to kill you!"

"I don't think they would have shot me." He looked away.

"You didn't vote today because of me."

"I wouldn't risk your safety." Papa's hand smoothed her hair. "There will be other days to work for the cause."

"Other days? What do you mean? Surely we're not staying here now!"

"Of course we must stay. We can't let the Territory fall into the hands of men like that."

Lucy pushed his arm away. "Papa, you're putting the Territory above your life. What will happen at the next election? If they shoot you next time, what will happen to us?"

"It's about freedom, Lucy."

"Not *my* freedom! If I had any freedom, I would go back home! Let the stinking Ruffians have this place!"

Papa looked back down the street where the Ruffians were lined up to vote, and the Lawrence men stood helplessly by. "No! It's about the freedom of a human being to belong only to himself."

"We don't have slaves!" Lucy said. "Slaves live in the South. Even if you make Kansas a free state, people in the South will still do what they want!"

"Someone has to help those who cannot free themselves," Papa answered. "And someone has to preserve the right of men to cast their votes without intimidation. I can't stand aside and do nothing."

"What would Mamma say, if she knew what happened here today?"

"Mamma mustn't know." His voice became stern. "You should not have come here," he said again.

"Why can't we go home, Papa, and let the Kansans settle it?"

"Because we are Kansans now. This is our home, and it will be a home without slavery."

Lucy stepped back from Papa, out of his reach. "I hate this place! Kansas Territory will never be my home!"

4

The Company, it should be distinctly understood, is desirous of seeing the Territory peopled with good men and true, who will maintain their own rights, and respect those of others; who, save in extreme cases, will rely for victory upon the teachings of the Bible and Ballot-box, instead of the bottle and musket.

–Information for Kanzas Immigrants

The day after the election began a bit warmer. Lucy and Mamma helped with breakfast again, and the sunny morning made sitting at the outdoor tables almost pleasant. Lucy tried to put yesterday out of her mind. The air was filled with the steady buzzing of Lawrence's two sawmills and the smell of freshly cut wood. Hammer blows echoed through town as workers constructed houses and stores. Wagons rattled by, loaded with building stones for the new hotel.

At most of the tables, men bitterly discussed yesterday's election and the Ruffians who had taken over the ballot boxes. At the Thomkins table however, the talk was about the new store. Mr. Wynn, a carpenter from New Hampshire, had helped Papa draw the plans for the building.

"Gather round, Thomkinses," Papa said. "Have a look at our future enterprise in the territory of Kansas." He unrolled several large sheets of paper in a stack and placed coffee cups on the corners to hold them flat.

The top drawing showed the front of the building, a two-story frame house with a centered door, a large window on either side on the first floor, and two windows overlooking the street on the second floor. A sign across the front of the building proclaimed, "Thompkins General Store."

"Oh, Marcus, it's beautiful!" Mamma said. "How long will it take to build it?" Her voice held a cadence of excitement that Lucy hadn't heard for a long time.

"Wynn says it should take just a few weeks. He's arranging the order for the lumber, and the Aid Society has brought out more than twenty carpenters who will be working in teams to help people build their houses and businesses." Papa smiled. "I'll be there every day, working on it with my own hands."

Joseph stood at Papa's elbow to get a closer look at the papers on the table. "Can I help build it?" he asked.

As the rest of her family huddled around the table, Lucy looked away from the plans. Papa's words from yesterday still echoed in her brain: *We are Kansans now.*

"The windows in front will have displays of our merchandise," said Papa, pointing at the drawing.

"What will we have in the store?" Joseph asked.

"We'll have all the supplies that settlers need," Papa said.

"Food, tools, material for clothes, dishes, building supplies …
all kinds of things."

Joseph pulled one of the coffee cups aside to peek at the
pages below. "Show me the barn, Papa. How many horses will
we have?"

Papa laughed. "We won't have any horses, son."

"Why not? We'll need a wagon to get supplies," Joseph said.
"We have to have horses."

"We can rent a wagon from the livery stable when we need
one."

Joseph frowned. Papa put a hand on his shoulder. "It will
be a struggle just to feed ourselves. We can't afford to feed animals, too."

Joseph sat down next to Lucy.

Papa pulled the next drawing out and turned it so Mamma
could see it better. "This is the main floor." Papa pointed to the
drawing. "Most of it will be for merchandise, of course. The
kitchen is here – in the room at the back." He pointed to one
side of the kitchen. "That cookstove you want will go here."

"What about furniture and fixtures?" Mamma asked.

"Thaddeus Burke – he's a cabinetmaker from Rhode Island
– is going to teach me how to build shelves and cabinets," Papa
said. He pointed to the right wall in the drawing. "The stairs to
the living quarters will be along the wall over here."

"Oh, it looks wonderful!" Mamma said. "We'll have our
own house again." She looked up. "Isn't it wonderful, Lucy?"

Lucy managed a smile. "Yes, wonderful."

Mamma lifted the corner of the drawing. "Show us the upstairs plan."

Papa moved the first-floor drawing aside to show the upstairs rooms.

"Look, Lucy," he said. "Your room and Joseph's room both have windows that look out over the front of the store onto Massachusetts Street. Mamma and I will have this room on the side of the house." Papa pointed to Lucy's room. "Over here by the window, I'll build a writing desk for you, Lucy Cat." He looked up at her for a reaction.

A writing desk in her own room. Lucy imagined sitting at a desk facing the window, but she could not imagine any words on the page. "Thank you, Papa," she said, looking down at her hands.

"That's not fair!" Joseph said. "If Lucy gets a desk and Mamma gets a stove, I should get a horse."

"We can't afford to keep a horse, Joseph," Papa said. "Maybe you can learn to ride one that belongs to someone else."

"It's not the same."

Mrs. Litchfield came over to the table and laid a hand on Mamma's shoulder. "Maggie," she said, "will you and Lucy stay and help for a bit? Dr. Robinson has called a meeting for all the men. They'll want more coffee."

"Of course we'll help," said Mamma. "It's the only way to really know what goes on in this town, isn't it?"

"It's certainly the best way," replied Mrs. Litchfield. Papa rolled up the plans and cleared the table, while Mamma and

Lucy followed Mrs. Litchfield to get the coffee pots.

It only took a few minutes for a crowd to gather. In addition to the Lawrence men, there were many others who came to town from the surrounding countryside. Some were nearly as rough-looking as the crowd at the election yesterday, but none wore white ribbons. Lucy decided to keep a keen eye, just the same.

Mrs. Litchfield brought out all the brown crockery cups and even some tin ones to serve the crowd. Lucy made her way from table to table to pour coffee, catching bits of conversations as she went. The men raised their cups toward her coffee pot, but they hardly seemed to see her.

"I tell you, it's got to stop!" said a man at a table near the edge of the crowd. "Grover and Jacob are behind this operation, and everybody knows about it."

"The Ruffians are just waiting to catch a load of runaway slaves," said another man, as Lucy poured his coffee.

"That's right, and if they bring in a federal marshal to enforce the Slave Act, they'll get a posse from Atchison or Weston to back him up. We can't let this get out of hand. The proslavers are hungry for a reason to burn this town to the ground."

Lucy stepped back from the table, her head filled with images of a burning Lawrence. She spotted a man at another table holding up an empty cup and hurried over. She poured coffee as he and the man across from him continued their conversation. Their heads were close, and their voices low, as though they shared a secret.

"Shipment coming through tomorrow night," the first man said.

"How many?" his companion asked.

"Six. Can we bring them out your way, John?"

The man leaned in. "Bring them."

A shipment? Lucy walked away from the table, puzzled. Were they talking about supplies or people?

Dr. Robinson stepped up on a bench, and the conversations stopped. "The election news is bad. A rider came from Topeka this morning and said the Ruffians invaded their polls, too."

"How did our count figure out, Doc?" asked Mr. Miller, the editor of the *Kansas Free State*.

"One thousand thirty-one votes in our ballot box," he answered.

"But we have only 369 eligible voters, according to our census," said Mr. Casey.

"How many Free State Party votes?" asked Mr. Brown, the editor of the *Herald of Freedom*, the newspaper sponsored by the Emigrant Aid Society.

"Two hundred fifty-three votes for the Free State candidates," the doctor answered. "Cast at the end of the day, after the Ruffians left town."

"The Ruffians will fill up the Territorial Legislature," said Mr. Miller.

"I've drafted a letter of protest to Territorial Governor Reeder," said Dr. Robinson, pulling a paper from his vest pocket.

"I need every man to sign it. It's a petition to throw out the election results." He placed the paper on the table in front of him.

A man standing at the edge of the group stepped forward. "What good is a petition to the governor? Reeder's a puppet of President Pierce! The whole lot of them wants Kansas to be a slave state!"

"Calm down, Willis," said the doctor.

"And not a one of you New Englanders is willing to stand up to these Ruffians, even when they threaten our homes and families!"

Dr. Robinson looked squarely at Mr. Willis. "And what do you propose we do?"

"We've got to arm ourselves!" Willis answered.

Mr. Casey spoke up. "That's right, Willis, we'll send you with your horse and wagon over to Westport to pick up a few dozen rifles from our Ruffian friends who run the stores there. How many bullet holes will your wife have to sew up on your corpse?"

A few men laughed.

Lucy thought about Papa with a gun to his head. She couldn't see anything funny about that.

"You Emigrant Aid men think you have all the answers," Willis challenged. "What do you think we should do?"

Papa rose and faced Dr. Robinson. "Perhaps Mr. Thayer and Mr. Lawrence in Boston would help us out," Papa offered.

"Thomkins is right," said Mr. Miller. "Surely Amos Lawrence, the founder of the Emigrant Aid Society, would supply arms to defend the town that bears his name." He glanced at his rival, Mr. Brown. "Maybe he could get some of those new Sharps rifles to send us. They would sure out-fire anything those Ruffians have."

"Are guns really necessary?" asked Dr. Robinson.

"What do you mean 'necessary'?" asked Mr. Miller. "They were armed to the teeth yesterday, right here in our town!"

Lucy remembered the man with the torn earlobe and shuddered.

"No one fired a shot. They have threatened us since the day we arrived here, but they haven't committed any acts of violence. Their boldness comes from the whiskey they tote in and the guns they fire in the air. They have never fired at any man, woman, or child. I believe their bark is worse than their bite."

Lucy poured coffee for a man at a table next to Papa's. "Bark or bite, they're still dogs," she said to herself quietly.

"You know the Ruffians board every steamboat that carries freight bound for the Territory," Dr. Robinson continued. "Do you think they won't notice boxes of Sharps rifles? And suppose we do acquire some of these weapons … the first time a proslaver is killed, the newspapers in Missouri and the South will lay the fault on the Emigrant Aid Society and on our cause. That won't win us any friends in Congress."

"Nobody said anything about attacking the Ruffians," said Mr. Willis. "Don't we have the same right to defend ourselves that any American has?"

Many men in the crowd murmured their agreement. Dr. Robinson held up a hand to quiet them. "All right. It's against my better judgment, but perhaps the presence of weapons will inspire a measure of respect from our enemies. I'll send your request to Mr. Thayer and Mr. Lawrence."

As many of the men turned to leave, Dr. Robinson called out, "Gentlemen! You must still sign the protest letter to the Governor before you go!"

While the men gathered around the table to sign the letter, Lucy, Mamma, and Mrs. Litchfield gathered the cups from the tables.

"I don't like it one bit," said Mamma. "Guns in the hands of these angry men … it's bound to bring more trouble."

"But, Mamma," said Lucy, "the Ruffians all had guns yesterday!" The words were out before she could stop them. Mamma frowned. "Papa told me," she added quickly. "If we don't arm ourselves, we will be at their mercy."

"I hope you don't count yourself in that 'we,' Lucy Catherine," said Mamma. "It's bad enough that the men feel the need to carry guns. We may soon have a hard time knowing who the enemy is."

The gun pointed at Papa's head, the rough hands holding her, the smell of the Ruffian's breath on her face, the fear she had felt – it was all still fresh for Lucy. She knew exactly who the enemy was. If Papa was really determined that they would stay here, they would – she would – have to be ready to fight.

5

Religion and Education.–At Lawrence there are several regularly constituted religious societies of various denominations. A free school is established there, in which the ordinary branches are taught, and measures are in train to found an Academy for instruction in the higher branches. *In behalf of each and all, the Secretary earnestly solicits contributions in money or books.*

–*Information for Kanzas Immigrants*

By the middle of April, Lawrence was bright with sunshine and spring. The melting snow had turned the streets to mud, but the spring winds soon dried them to rock-hard surfaces, deeply rutted with wagon tracks. Buildings were springing up on every street as men worked in teams to construct new homes and businesses. The noise and activity created a feeling of new life in Lawrence, and even Lucy could not resist the combination of springtime weather and optimism that infected the citizens of Lawrence.

Papa was helping rebuild the school. When it was finished, the next project would be the Thomkins' store. "They say the new school is twice as big as the last one," Papa announced one night at dinner. "But with all the new families in town, it should be nearly full."

Papa loved to talk about his work with the builders. His smile came easily when he talked about the pine, maple, and oak boards that came in on the wagons from Missouri. "When will we start class?" Lucy asked.

"We varnished the benches and desks today," Papa said. "The school should be ready by Monday. By then, we'll already be at work on the store."

Joseph had already met several boys near his age, but Lucy spent most of her time helping Mamma and the other women at the boarding house with the huge wash pots hung over the fires outside the boarding house. School would be a welcome change.

On Saturday, they heated water all day for washing clothes – and children. Every child at the boarding house endured a scrubbing. Lucy toted kettles of hot water to the tubs all day. After each child was finished, she emptied a little of the used bath water and added more hot water to the tub. As the day went on, the water in the tubs became as muddy as the rising waters of the Kaw. When at last it was her turn, Lucy could not bear to put herself in the dirty water that remained.

"All the hot water pots are full of clothes now. There isn't any hot water to refill the tub," Mamma explained. "We can only add a little more to warm this."

Lucy shook her head. "I can't get into this!"

"You don't want a cold bath, do you?"

"It would be better than coming out of the bath dirtier

than when I went in."

"Suit yourself," Mamma said. "But you'll have to make the trips to the well."

"But …"

"If you want clean water, pump and carry it." Mamma handed Lucy one of her old dresses. "Put on this dress of mine so I can wash yours. It looks awful." Before she closed the door, Mamma added, "And when you're finished, I'll still need your help with the laundry."

Lucy put on Mamma's dress. She used the bucket to empty the dirty water out of the tub and pour it outside. Then she made four trips to the well. But even with four bucketsful, the water in the tub was just a few inches deep, and Mamma had left her only one kettle of hot water. At least it would help take the chill off. She undressed quickly and thought of how good it would feel to be clean.

Lucy put a foot into the tub and gasped. She swallowed hard and put her other foot in. Icy coldness. She squatted and picked up the rag and soap Mamma had left for her. Each time she splashed the water to rinse her body she gasped again, until at last she was clean. Shaking from head to toe, she stepped out of the tub. Her skin was red from the cold and the scrubbing. Still shivering, she knelt beside the tub, bent forward over it, and used a pitcher to pour the cold water through her hair. She dried herself quickly, twisted her hair back and put on Mamma's dress.

By the time she had emptied the water from the tub and joined Mamma at the laundry, Lucy had returned to almost normal temperature.

Mamma was tending to two large kettles of steaming water. "Feel better?"

"Oh, yes." Lucy forced a smile.

Lucy watched as Mamma stirred clothes in one of the pots. She caught a glimpse of a blue ruffle. "Will my dress survive the wash?"

"It will never look new again, but it will surely look better than it did. I wish you would just wear one of mine. That one looks fine on you."

"Fine? It doesn't fit me at all, Mamma. It was made for you, not for me."

Mamma poked the wooden paddle into the pot. "Does it really matter?"

"Yes! If I wear this one, you'll say, 'It's good enough,' and I'll have to wear it for months. I need a new dress of my own. Grandmother says a proper lady should never accept a hand-me-down."

"Your grandmother's pride is not her best quality, nor yours. But I suppose you can choose to look foolish if you want to."

By mid-afternoon, all the clothes were washed, but Lucy's dress was still damp when she went to bed that night. Surely it would be dry by Monday.

As Lucy and Joseph left the boarding house for their walk to school, Mamma handed Lucy two parcels wrapped in paper.

"Here are lunches for you both," said Mamma. "Now, Joseph," she said sternly, "you must sit still in school and pay attention to the teacher so you can help Papa run the store. You will have to be able to add up all the money we will make." Mamma smiled and kissed each of them on the forehead. "Lucy, don't let him dawdle."

As they walked toward the school, Lucy's stomach burned with nervousness. What would school in Lawrence be like? Certainly nothing like her school in Harrisburg. The girls at Miss Delia Abernathy's School for Young Ladies all came from the best families in town. They would never be dressed like the children here.

Lucy looked down at her blue dress. It was ragged, but it was cleaner than before. And it was certainly prettier than the calico and muslin things that most of the women here in Kansas wore. She would have to wear one of those plain dresses soon enough, but for now she still had her Pittsburgh gown, tattered as it was.

Lucy and Joseph walked past the new store, where Papa and other men of the building crew were hard at work. They were stacking building stones for the foundation, and the outline of it looked much larger than Lucy had imagined. Papa waved as they walked by, and Joseph ran over to greet him. "Let me help you build the store," Joseph pleaded. "I don't want to go to school."

Papa laughed. "But you have to go with Lucy. You have an important job to do."

Joseph looked at her. "I do? What is it?"

Papa winked at Lucy. "You have to keep the boys at school from fighting over your pretty sister."

Joseph grimaced.

Lucy shook her head, but smiled a little. "Come on, Joseph," said Lucy. "We can't be late on our first day. Bye, Papa."

As they crossed the street, Joseph declared, "I really don't need to go to school, you know."

"You heard what Mamma said," Lucy told him. "You have to be able to help run the store."

"I'm going to be an Indian fighter!"

Lucy laughed. "The tribes around here are peaceful. We don't have to fight them."

Joseph looked serious. "They may say they're peaceful, but how do you know you can trust them? I wouldn't trust one as far as I could throw him."

"You'd better not let Papa hear you say that. Besides, we all have to work in the store. It's a family business, remember?"

Joseph looked across the street at a horse tied outside the blacksmith shop. "One of these days I'll get a horse, ride out to Fort Riley, and join up with the cavalry. I won't be stuck behind a counter in a store." He ran ahead of Lucy toward the school, leaving her to walk alone. Should she tell Mamma what he had said? Probably not. He wouldn't be getting a horse anytime soon, and he'd surely come to his senses before then. Mamma had enough to worry about.

"Hello," said a voice behind Lucy. She felt a tap on her right shoulder. Lucy looked to her right, just as a giggle came from her left.

"Over here!"

A smiling, blonde-haired girl walked beside her. "Oh ... hello," Lucy said. The girl looked about Lucy's age and wore a plain brown dress that hung loose on her slender frame.

"I haven't seen you before," the girl said. "New in the territory?"

"We came three weeks ago," said Lucy.

"With the Aid Society, I'd guess," she said, looking at Lucy's dress. "I'm Annie Jacob." She offered her hand. "What's your name?"

Lucy put her hand out to shake. "Lucy Thomkins. Have you been in Kansas long?"

"Since last summer. We came from Indiana, right after they opened up the territory. My pa's a preacher, but he came here to stake a claim on a farm." She pointed toward the south end of town. "We live out by the Wakarusa. How come your pa came to Kansas?"

Lucy pointed down the street behind them. "He wants to run a store. That's it back there."

"You don't sound too sure about it," said Annie.

Lucy shrugged.

A boy rang the bell in the schoolyard, and Annie walked a little faster. "C'mon, Lucy. Mr. Fitch gets awful cranky when we're late."

At the edge of the schoolyard, several horses stood patiently, tethered to a hitching post. Joseph lingered there, talking to a boy who stood by a spotted horse. As the ringing stopped, the children filed through the door.

The building smelled like newly-cut pine and varnish. Rows of benches sat in the middle of the room. Several desks with rough-cut stools were lined up along each side wall. Lucy started toward a bench, but Annie put a hand on her arm.

"Those are for the younger ones," she whispered. "We sit at the desks."

Lucy and Annie took desks near each other as the rest of the children found places in the room.

Lucy ran her hand along the sanded edge of the desk in front of her, thinking about Papa's hands at work. A new stove stood near the center of the room. Thankfully, its heat wouldn't be needed for the next few months. Maybe this schoolhouse would last longer than the last one. Empty bookshelves lined the front wall. She scanned the room quickly – where were the books?

"Good morning, students," said the schoolmaster, a slim young man with a stern expression and a dark suit. He adjusted his spectacles as he looked around the room. "My name is Mr. Fitch. The Emigrant Aid Society employs me as your teacher. I insist on cooperative behavior in this school, and I have been known to enforce that rule with a hickory switch." He fixed a stare on a dark-haired older boy who was gazing out the window. "Isn't that correct, Mr. Willis?"

At the mention of his name, the boy startled and turned

toward the teacher. "Yes, sir," he mumbled, as the other boys snickered.

"We'll begin with introductions. Please stand, tell us your name and your age," he instructed, taking up a pencil and a ledger book.

One by one, each student stood and said his or her name and age. The newer and tidier clothes of the newly-arrived Lawrence children contrasted with the worn, homemade garments of those who had come in from the country around the town.

The four older students were last to speak. The dark-haired boy, Samuel Willis, was fourteen. A tall twelve-year-old boy named Matthew Curtis was next. Annie announced her age as thirteen.

At last, it was Lucy's turn. Everyone in the room was looking at her, and the blue dress suddenly seemed hopelessly out of place. One of the smaller children giggled, and Lucy remembered why she was standing. "Lucy Thomkins," she said, "thirteen." She sat, her face burning in embarrassment.

"We usually begin the day with recitations from our readers," Mr. Fitch said, "but our books were lost in the fire, and we have no replacements." Some of the younger children exchanged smiles, but Lucy could only think of her old classroom, with its shelves of books on all subjects. No books? What kind of school was this?

"But not to fear," he continued. "We will have our reading lesson. Mr. Brown has provided us with copies of this week's

Herald of Freedom newspaper. We will begin by reading from it. Miss Jacob, will you please begin with the item on the left side of page two entitled *Thoughts*?" Lucy looked for the article then smiled when she spotted it. A poem! A poem in the newspaper in Kansas!

Annie stood.

> *"The snow-clad hills of old Vermont*
> *Now wear a gloomy brow;*
> *The sons that shone to cheer them once,*
> *Shine far, far distant now …"*

Annie continued to read the verse about settlers from eastern states coming to Kansas to fight for freedom.

Matthew stood to read the middle part of the poem:

> *"Then Kansas! Love the generous men!*
> *Who own all men are free.*
> *And love their wives, who far from them,*
> *Do love and pray for thee …"*

Mr. Fitch asked Lucy to read the last few lines. She stood.

> *"That iron bands and clanking chains*
> *Poor slave may never wound.*
> *And honest blood, through slavery's veins,*
> *May never curse the ground."*

Lucy sat when she finished. It was a good poem, and the last thing she expected to find in the territory. Perhaps there would be some pleasant surprises here, after all.

Mr. Fitch smiled and looked around the room. "I know we

can all appreciate the prayers of those we have left behind as we came West for the cause of freedom." He held up the newspaper again.

"Mr. Willis, please begin the other poem on that page," Mr. Fitch said.

"No, sir," said Samuel. Every student in the room looked up in surprise.

"You refuse to read?"

"Yes, sir," replied Samuel firmly. "My pa doesn't want me reading poetry."

"And why is that?" asked Mr. Fitch.

"Because poetry is for sissies, and he doesn't want me growing up to be a sissy." Samuel didn't add "like you, Mr. Fitch," but everyone in the room heard it anyway.

Mr. Fitch spoke slowly and evenly. "Elegant use of the language, Mr. Willis, is one of the highest forms of art. I will speak to your father. In the meantime, perhaps you could choose an article to read for us."

Samuel looked at the paper in front of him. He put his finger on a place about halfway down the second column. "Yes, sir," he said, with a little smile. "I found one I can read."

"Please go ahead," said Mr. Fitch.

Samuel began, "'The lazy, lousy, worthless Negro-stealing members of the Boston Emigrant Aid Society – the mean, dirty, scrapings of gutters who ...'"

"Samuel, you may stop," said Mr. Fitch.

"'... come West as the hired e-mis-sar-ies ...'" continued

Samuel, sounding out the words.

"That will do, Samuel," said Mr. Fitch more firmly.

"'... of such de-spic-a-ble traitors as Eli Thayer and Amos Lawrence ...'"

Mr. Fitch slammed his hand on the top of Samuel's desk. "Stop!" He looked around the room at the faces of the confused children. "Mr. Brown reprints some stories from the proslavery papers, so that we may be informed of their sentiments. It is not," he looked at Samuel, "suitable for reading aloud in this classroom, Mr. Willis."

The rest of the morning was taken up with math lessons. Mr. Fitch asked Lucy to help two of the younger girls who were working on their multiplication tables. Annie worked with a little girl who was learning to count. Matthew helped two boys practice writing their numbers on their slates. Joseph and some other children had a lesson on division with Mr. Fitch.

By the time they had finished, all the children were fidgety. Mr. Fitch dismissed them for lunch.

The younger children ran to the door first. Lucy walked with Annie. Samuel and Matthew followed them.

"Yep, Matt," said Samuel. "You sure have to watch out for those 'lazy, lousy, worthless Negro-stealers.'"

Annie turned to face the boys and put her hands on her hips. "Sam Willis," she said, "you can go away and mind your own business."

"I will mind whatever business I want to, and it won't include hiding any runaway slaves, and asking the Ruffians to come burn our town down!"

"You know she wasn't a runaway! She was sent here by those Ruffians just to stir up trouble!" said Annie.

"My pa says …"

"Your pa doesn't know anything about it, and I wish he'd quit talking like he does," said Annie. "My pa just wants to farm his land and get along. Why can't your pa do the same?"

"That's just what he'd like to do, but until your kind gets some sense and quits stirring up trouble with the Ruffians, we have to sit up nights with our rifles ready."

"If you keep causing trouble, you won't have to worry about Border Ruffians coming after you because I'll do it myself!" said Annie. She turned and walked away from them.

Lucy turned too, but Samuel caught her arm. "You should be careful who you choose for your friends, Insider."

She jerked her arm free. "I don't know what you mean, but I think you should keep your hands to yourself!"

6

Sources of Information. Newspapers.— Those who are desirous of procuring a large amount of information at a small expense, and of being kept posted up on Territorial affairs, should subscribe to the Kanzas *Herald of Freedom*, published weekly at Lawrence, K.T., by Mr. George W. Brown, editor.

–Information for Kanzas Immigrants

She caught up with Annie when they were out of earshot of the boys. "What was that about?"

"Oh, those two just like to make people mad," said Annie. "They'll do anything to poke fun at the Insiders."

"Who are the Insiders?"

Annie giggled. "Why, you are! All the folks who came out here with the Aid Society."

"Why Insiders?" asked Lucy.

"The Aid Society took the land along the riverfront for the town," explained Annie. "Some folks don't like it that the Society forced squatters off their claims and gave the best land to their own people. That's why you got a lot in town." Annie nodded toward Samuel and Matthew. "The folks not with the Society – the Outsiders – had to find another claim. There was a fuss about it, but they finally settled it, and everybody got a claim, even if it wasn't the one they wanted."

"But why did the article say 'Negro-stealing traitors' of the Aid Society?"

Annie glanced over her shoulder. "Shhh," she whispered. "It was just a big mistake. The Border Ruffians planned it to make trouble, that's all."

Then she sighed. "I guess I might as well tell you the truth, since you're going to hear a lot of lies about it anyway. Last month a Negro girl knocked on our door. She told Pa she had been freed by her master and was on her way to Iowa. It was almost dark, and she said she was afraid to go on alone. Pa said she could stay until dawn. In the middle of the night, some men came pounding on our door. They said if we didn't give her up, they would have Pa arrested for stealing her."

"Oh, that's awful! What happened to her?"

"They treated her pretty rough while they were at our place, but the whole thing was a trick: They forced her to help them. They wanted to make a stink and get it in all the papers, so they could say that the people in Lawrence were stealing slaves. The Leavenworth and Atchison papers are still talking about it, so I guess the plan worked."

"Do people in Lawrence think your father tried to steal her?"

"Most everybody knows the truth now, but some folks, like

Sam Willis' pa, like to keep things stirred up." Annie looked around. "Come on. We'd better eat before Mr. Fitch calls us back in."

They found a shady place at the side of the school, away from the others. Annie unwrapped a paper parcel. Inside was a piece of corn bread about the size of her fist.

"Where's the rest of your lunch?" Lucy asked.

"What do you mean?" Annie broke off a piece of the bread and ate it.

"Don't you have some meat or something to go with that?"

"No. We have meat for supper, but not for lunch."

Lucy opened the paper parcel her mother had given her. Inside were several slices of ham, some cheese, and a handful of dried apples.

Annie was looking at it too, but she looked away when Lucy saw her. Lucy had been hungry, but she didn't feel right eating all this when Annie had so little. Still, Annie had not asked for anything. Would she be insulted if Lucy offered her food?

"Oh, my," said Lucy.

"What is it?" asked Annie.

"Mamma must have given me Papa's lunch by mistake. I can't eat all this."

"What will your pa do?"

"Oh, I'm sure he'll go back to Mrs. Litchfield's and get something," said Lucy. "Would you eat part of this so I don't have to carry it home?"

Annie hesitated, looking at the ham slices. "If you don't want it."

"Could I trade you for some of that bread?"

"Sure," said Annie, trading half of her corn bread for the ham and cheese that Lucy offered. She bit eagerly into the ham.

Lucy broke off a bite of the corn bread. "I'm surprised I haven't seen you in town before," she said. "Where is your farm?"

"It's a couple miles south of town."

Lucy couldn't imagine living outside of town. "Why so far?"

"Pa wanted farmland with some timber, so we had to be close to the river." Annie shrugged. "Besides, we're Outsiders – we couldn't get a place any closer."

"Are the Outsiders still angry?"

"Not so bad now. Most everybody around Lawrence is on the same side about slavery. But some folks, like the Willises, seem to like being mad."

Lucy remembered the man from the meeting who was so eager for guns. Willis.

Annie was as good a listener as she was a talker. By the time they finished eating, Lucy had told her all about Harrisburg and even about her poetry. It felt good to have a friend.

When Mr. Fitch rang the school bell, Lucy and Annie rose to go back in.

Matthew poked Samuel when he saw the girls and pointed in their direction. The boys stepped in front of them, blocking their path. Samuel looked at Lucy and ran his gaze from her head to her toes. "Get lost on the way to the ball, Cinderella?"

Lucy looked down, but didn't respond.

Annie stepped forward. She pointed at his bare feet. "Why? You looking for some new slippers?"

Matthew snickered, and Samuel frowned at him.

He stepped closer to Lucy. "What'd you say your name is?"

"Lucy," she answered.

"Ought to be 'Lucky,' just like all you Insiders."

"Well, it isn't," said Lucy.

"You look like it to me, *Lucky*," said Sam. He used the same tone of voice that Joseph did when he called her Lucy Cat. "You may think you're pretty smart, but you and your Insider friends better watch your step, or you won't be so lucky, Lucky!"

Annie looked over Samuel's shoulder. "We're coming, Mr. Fitch!"

Both boys whipped around. Annie grabbed Lucy's hand, and they ducked past them. Mr. Fitch was nowhere in sight.

The afternoon dragged, with a history lesson that Mr. Fitch read from Washington Irving's *Life and Voyages of Christopher Columbus,* and penmanship practice as Mr. Fitch read sentences such as "Speak truth, or be silent" and "Master your passions or they will master you." Lucy was never so eager to be released from school as she was that day. She wondered if perhaps she should sign up for the cavalry with her brother.

When Mr. Fitch dismissed them that afternoon, Joseph ran off with the other boys for a game of tag in the schoolyard. Lucy and Annie were finally free of Samuel and Matthew so they could talk as they walked home. Even though Lucy was an Insider and Annie was not, Lucy was glad they could still be friends. And they had one thing in common: They both disliked Sam Willis.

"Why does he make so many threats?" Lucy asked.

Annie shrugged her shoulders. "Don't worry about him. He's more talk than anything. He just likes to sound tough."

Lucy smiled. "Thanks for sticking up for me."

"You'd do the same for me, I think." Annie turned toward the road to the edge of town. "See you tomorrow," she said, as she waved. "I'm sure it will be another adventure."

Lucy continued on alone and thought about her first day in her new school. Insiders. Outsiders. Rumors and gossip and slaves. On top of everything else, a school with no books – whoever heard of such a thing?

As she approached the boarding house, Mrs. Litchfield saw her coming and ran out to greet her. She held an envelope.

"I'm so glad you're here, Lucy!" she said. "Dr. Robinson asked me to mail this letter for him, and I forgot all about it until just now. Can you take it to the post office for me? It needs to get in the mail to Westport tomorrow."

"Yes, Mrs. Litchfield. I'll take it right now." Lucy glanced at the letter. It was addressed to Amos Lawrence in Boston, Massachusetts. It was the same address as the one on the *Kanzas Immigrants* booklet she still kept. Was this the letter asking Mr. Lawrence to send guns? And would he send them? Just because he cared about the town that bore his name?

Lucy considered that. If he cared enough to send guns, wouldn't he also care enough to send books so that the children of Lawrence could get an education? The booklet said the Aid Society planned to build a college in Lawrence. Surely they would think that books were as important as guns, if they knew the school had none. Lucy walked to the post office considering what she might say to Mr. Lawrence. Would Papa be angry with her if she wrote a letter to such an important man? And how could she write a letter, since she didn't even have a pen or paper, let alone postage? She thought about the day at school with the newspaper, Mr. Fitch reading to them and the penmanship lessons with the list of sentences. How different would school be if they had some proper books to use? Maybe Mr. Lawrence wouldn't send them, but Lucy would have to find a way to ask.

———⟫◈⟪———

After dinner, Lucy walked over to the *Herald of Freedom* office, next to Papa's new store. The door was open just a little, and Mr. Brown was bent over his desk. Lucy knocked lightly. Mr. Brown looked up.

"Yes … come in, young lady."

"Hello, Mr. Brown. I'm Lucy Thomkins. My father is building the store next door."

"Thomkins, yes, of course. What can I do for you, Lucy?"

"I'm sorry to bother you, Mr. Brown, but I need to write a letter, and I have no paper or pen. Could you spare a sheet of paper, please?"

"I guess so. Writing to some handsome young man back East?"

Lucy blushed, and Mr. Brown smiled. "And I suppose you'll need an envelope as well?"

"Yes, please."

"Come sit, then." He pointed to the chair on the other side of the desk. Lucy sat. "There is a pen and an inkwell on the shelf behind you." He gave her a quick smile. "And I'll pay attention only to my own work and won't peek at your letter."

"Thank you, sir," said Lucy. She took the sheet of paper Mr. Brown offered and dipped the tip of the pen's nib in the ink. The words came quickly.

April 15, 1855
Lawrence, Kansas Territory
Dear Mr. Lawrence:
My name is Lucy Thomkins. I am thirteen years old and a student at the Lawrence Free School. Mr. Fitch works hard to teach us, and the citizens of Lawrence have built a new school for us. But we are still missing one important part of our education: books. Our books were lost in the fire and have not yet been replaced. Although Mr. Brown has

kindly provided us with copies of the **Herald of Freedom**, the children need proper books. I know you want the best for all the citizens in Lawrence, including the children. Please, sir, would you send books for us? We have young children who need primers and older children who would like books of stories, such as the fine work of Nathaniel Hawthorne. If you could also send along one or two books of poetry, perhaps by Henry Wadsworth Longfellow or William Cullen Bryant, it would be very kind of you, sir.

Sincerely,
Miss Lucy Thomkins

Lucy put the pen down and read her letter to be sure it had no mistakes. She blotted a few small drops of ink and blew lightly on the paper to be sure it was dry.

Mr. Brown looked up. "Are you finished?"

"Yes, sir."

"Not quite as long a love letter as I might have expected," he teased.

"No, sir."

"Here is an envelope for you. If you get to the post office

early, you may still get it in with Babcock's mail for this week."

"Thank you very much, sir." Lucy took the envelope, but paused.

"Is there something else?"

"I hate to ask it, sir, but … could you spare a pen? I may need to write some more later. Papa has supplies coming soon, so I'll return it."

"I suppose I can spare a pen for a neighbor. I would hate to discourage anyone who wants to write."

"Thank you, Mr. Brown!" said Lucy.

She walked home, carrying the borrowed pen and ink and the envelope with the letter to Mr. Lawrence. She would take the letter to the post office on her way to school tomorrow. She could ask Papa for postage money and tell him she was writing to a friend. That was mostly true, wasn't it?

Her head was filled with questions. How long would it take for the letter to reach Boston? What books would Mr. Lawrence send? Did she dare to hope for some volumes of poetry? If only she had books, Kansas might be tolerable. She thought about her journal, carefully tucked under her sleeping pallet. A poem was at last forming in her head, and she hurried home. It was still early, and no one else was upstairs when Lucy opened her journal and began to write.

While some may yearn for piles of gold
And others silver long to hold,

These riches to my eyes seem pale
When measured 'gainst a well-told tale.

Though diamonds draw the gaze of kings,
And rubies fashioned into rings
May cost a courtier's hefty purse,
None move the heart like lovely verse.

Mere paper bound and stitched to boards
Outweigh the pirates' treasure hoards,
When thought and voice conspire to hook
A reader to a best-loved book.

Lucy smiled as she closed the journal. Perhaps it wasn't the best poem she had ever written, but it was a poem. Her first poem in Kansas.

7

The large number of loaded teams almost constantly in our streets gives Lawrence the air of a business place of considerable importance. As soon as steamers shall commence arriving and departing daily from our Levee–which will probably be within a day or two, judging from the present state of the river–our town will present a commercial aspect superior to any other point in the Territory.

–*Herald of Freedom*, May 19, 1855

Once the foundation was laid, the store went up quickly. Papa spent his days there, and Joseph helped when he could. Mamma worried about everything: the cost of it, the size of it, the number of windows. The day Papa and the men put the roof on she was nearly frantic with worry.

After six weeks of living in the boarding house, Lucy was eager for the store to be finished. One day in mid-May, she passed by on her way home from school. "Lucy, come inside," Papa said. "I have a surprise for you."

The rest of the workmen had quit for the day, so the house was quiet. Lumber and tools were scattered everywhere, but Papa led her through the mess to the kitchen. In the center of the small room sat a table. No, not a table.

She smiled. "My desk?"

He nodded. "What do you think?"

She ran her hand along the top of the raw wood surface. It was sanded as smooth as silk. "It's wonderful," she whispered. There was an indentation on the flat top panel to hold a bottle of ink. Two small brass hinges secured a slanted top that closed over a compartment where she could keep her journal and pens.

She put her hand on the edge of the lid to lift it. The edge felt rough. She touched it lightly. "I think you need to sand it here," she said.

"It's not quite finished yet, Lucy Cat." He picked up a rag that was dark with brown stain. As she watched, he rubbed the rag back and forth across the surface of the slanted lid. The rich color soaked into the wood. He followed with a clean rag, wiping the stain away and revealing the grain of the wood.

He dipped the staining rag into the color again and wiped it across the rough edge. When he followed with the second rag, the stain stayed in the notches, and Lucy could read the words that Papa had carved there: *The pen is mightier than the sword.*

"I want you to remember how powerful words can be, Lucy Cat," he said. "You have a gift you can use for good."

She hugged him. "Thank you, Papa. I'll remember."

"Now, get back to the boarding house before your mother starts to worry. And not a word to her or your brother. After today, no one gets to see the inside of the store until it's ready."

On the first sunny morning after a week of springtime rains, Lucy, Mamma, and Papa stood in the mud of Massachusetts Street in front of the store, waiting for Mr. Litchfield and Joseph to bring the wagon from the boarding house with their belongings. It was finally moving day.

Mr. Garrett, one of the carpenters, had promised to paint the store's sign for Papa, and he had kept it hidden in his barn as he worked on it. Now he perched on a ladder, holding the edge of a tarp that covered the newly-hung sign over the door of the store.

"Everybody ready?" he called to them.

"Yes, sir!" answered Papa.

Mr. Garrett yanked the cloth. The tarp fell, revealing the sign:

Thomkins Family Store

The letters were painted in red on a white background. Curly flourishes edged the borders of the sign, and in the lower right-hand corner were the words "M. Thomkins, Proprietor."

"Oh, Arthur! It's just perfect," Mamma said, and Mr. Garrett beamed with pride as he stepped down from the ladder.

Mr. Garrett stepped back to admire his work. Papa gave his hand a vigorous shake. "Handsomest sign in the territory, Arthur!"

"I hope it will bring you success, Marcus. If the Border

Ruffians will give us half a chance, we may yet make a life out here," he said.

As Mr. Garrett walked away with the folded tarp under one arm, a mule-drawn wagon approached, jouncing along the rutted road, splattering mud as it came. Mr. Litchfield sat next to Joseph on the driver's seat, and Joseph held the reins. The Thomkins' few trunks and bags, all their belongings, rode on the wagon bed.

Joseph pulled the reins. "Whoa, Daisy," he yelled to the mule, and she stopped. Joseph jumped down from the wagon, landing with both feet in a puddle. "Mr. Litchfield let me drive!" he announced.

"And you did a fine job, young man," said Mr. Litchfield.

Papa and Mr. Litchfield unloaded the trunks.

Joseph jumped up both porch steps in one bound and grabbed the door latch. It wouldn't budge.

"We can't get in!"

Papa reached into his coat pocket and pulled out a large brass key. "Yes, we can, but you'll have to wait for the rest of us," said Papa. Joseph pushed on the door, but Papa put a hand on Joseph's shoulder. "Just a minute, partner. First things first." Papa turned to Mamma, bowed low and picked her up. "My lady, you must be first through the door," he said.

He swept her over the threshold and set her gently on her feet. Joseph and Lucy followed them inside. Papa reached for the edge of the brown paper covering one of the front windows. He pulled it loose, and sunlight filled the room.

"Well?" he asked. "What do you think of it?"

"It's wonderful …" Mamma said, "but since it's so empty, it doesn't feel like a store yet."

"What? Empty!? What do you mean *empty?*" Papa paced toward the vacant corner nearest the front window. "Why, just look at the crates of nails and boxes of tallow candles." He strode across the room, pointing at the shelves on the opposite wall. "And here are jars of canned peaches and pickles." He walked toward the other front window, pulled the paper from it, and pointed at the wall. "And bolts of calico of all colors – just right for a new dress, right, Lucy Cat?"

"Right, Papa! And look at the boxes of tea and coffee beans, Mamma! And tins of lamp oil and molasses."

Joseph pulled Mamma by the hand, leading her toward the back wall of the room. "Look back here, Mamma!" he said. "The sales counter where you will keep your cashbox with all that money!" They all laughed together.

Mamma led the way past the sales counter and through the door at the back of the store. She swept her arm toward the empty back room "And back here is my kitchen and my fine new cookstove!"

"That's it, Maggie girl!" said Papa.

"Do you want some help with these trunks, Marcus?" Mr. Litchfield stood in the doorway, one of the smaller bags in his hand.

"Oh, my goodness!" said Mamma. "We forgot all about them."

"Sorry, Lewis," said Papa. "I'll come right out."

At the wagon, Mamma picked up a bundle of blankets. Papa and Mr. Litchfield took opposite ends of one of the biggest trunks. Joseph struggled with another, dragging it up the steps of the porch. Lucy took one of Mamma's bags and the tapestry bag Grandmother had given her.

Joseph left the trunk inside the front door and bounded up the stairs to the second floor. He disappeared for a few seconds, then came back to the top of the stairs. "Lucy! Come up and see our rooms!"

Papa had not put boards on the front of each step, so Lucy could see between them. The room nearest the stairs would be Mamma and Papa's. She set Mamma's bag near the door of that room and crossed the open area that would be their sitting room.

"Over here, Lucy," said Joseph. "Your room is right next to mine."

The room was almost bare. No bed, yet, but that could wait. Near the window, her new desk waited. Papa had even made a stool for her to sit on. Lucy reached into the tapestry bag and pulled out her pen and ink bottle. She placed the ink bottle in the round hole and laid the pen next to it. She reached again into her bag, pulled out her poetry journal and the *Kanzas Immigrants* booklet, lifted the lid of the desk and placed them inside.

Sunlight streamed through the window. She saw Lawrence differently from here, and it was buzzing with activity. On the corner across the street, builders worked on the new hotel. The

Eldridge brothers were using concrete for the construction, and the hotel would be big enough to shelter many people and even withstand an attack by Border Ruffians, if necessary. Today, though, with the smell of new wood around her, Lucy could hardly imagine such a thing.

On the street, Papa took the last of the bags and boxes from the wagon. As Mr. Litchfield snapped the reins and the wagon clattered away, Lucy saw a familiar figure coming across the street. Annie! Lucy ran down to the porch to meet her.

"I went to the boarding house to see if you were sick since you didn't come to school today. They told me you were here."

"It feels good to be out of the boarding house."

Annie looked up at the sign. "Is your pa ready to open the store?"

"Not yet. We don't have any merchandise. The supplies are coming, but the river boat is stuck in Kansas City. The river should be high enough in a few days." Lucy took Annie's hand. "Come in. You can see the house."

"Sure is big," said Annie. "How many people are going to live here?"

"Just our family, but it's really not so big. Most of it will be the store." Lucy pointed at the back of the room. "Our kitchen is back there, but our rooms are upstairs. Come see."

Lucy stood at the door to her room and let Annie go in first.

"A room all to yourself! We only have one room in our house. Pa says heaven has rooms for all of us, and until then, we can be happy with what we've got. Where do you sleep?"

"Papa only had time to build one bed, so for now, Joseph and I will just sleep on blankets on the floor. I've been doing that for weeks anyway, so I won't mind it for a while until I get a bed. Look – Papa made me a desk!"

"That's nice, but I think I'd rather have a bed." Annie reached for Lucy's pen and held it up. "This is a fancy pen. A metal tip and everything. All I've ever used is a quill." Annie replaced the pen carefully on the desk and looked around. "You never told me your pa was rich."

Rich? The idea seemed strange. But at this moment, standing in her room, Lucy did feel rich. And she felt a little bit ashamed of the complaining she had done for the last few weeks.

"What happened at school today, Annie?"

"Oh, gosh, I nearly forgot. That's what I came by to tell you! Mr. Fitch is leaving!"

"Leaving? Why?"

"Sam and Matthew were after him again. They found a dead rattlesnake and brought it in and put it under the stove. The smell was awful, but no one could figure out what it was. Little Dora May found it and let out an awful scream. Mr. Fitch said it was the last straw."

"Where will he go?"

"He says he's going back East to get a position in a proper school. Said he couldn't see how anyone could expect him to teach under these conditions, with children who act like animals."

"What will we do for school?"

"He'll have to stay until a new teacher gets here. The Aid Society says so."

"How long will that take?"

"I don't know, but I'm sure the boys will make it seem like forever to him." They both laughed.

"Maybe they will be too busy to bother us," Lucy said.

"They'd never be too busy for that." Annie looked around the room again, and then moved toward the door. "I'd best get home. Ma will be wondering what happened to me. Thanks for showing me your house, Lucy. It sure is fine."

"Thanks, Annie. Maybe sometime you can stay in town and spend the night."

"I don't think so. Ma needs me at home. Anyway, I'll see you." Annie walked down the street, toward the road that led south out of town.

Mamma came out on the porch and laid a hand on Lucy's shoulder. "Come on, Lucy. Let's get over to the boarding house and help with dinner. Mrs. Litchfield said we could take our meals there until our stove and other supplies come. We should at least help out."

"Yes, Mamma." Lucy was reluctant to return to the boarding house, but at least they would not be spending the night there. They would be back home after dinner.

<hr>

The rest of the family had gone to bed when Lucy sat at her

desk and opened her journal. She worked by the light of the small oil lamp Papa had let her take to her room. "Just be sure to put it out before you go to bed," he had warned. "We don't want to burn the place down!" As she looked past the small reflection of her lamp on the window glass before her, lightning flashed to the west of town. A few seconds later, thunder rumbled across the prairie and caused the window to rattle. Soon, a few drops splattered against the glass, and then a steady drumming began on the roof.

The view through the window was spectacular. The blackest black of night was crisscrossed by bright-white skeleton fingers of light. At Grandfather's house she had sometimes been frightened of storms, but tonight she stared out the window in fascination. In the bright flashes, she could see for miles before everything was swallowed up again in darkness. It was beautiful. She heard footsteps, then a soft knock at her door.

"Everything dry in here, Lucy Cat?"

"Yes, Papa; no leaks." She glanced toward the window. "Come look."

Papa stood behind her and looked out at the show on the prairie. "It's magnificent, isn't it, Lucy Cat?"

They stared together for a few minutes, then Papa squeezed her shoulder. "Good night. We have lots of work to do tomorrow. And be sure to put out that lamp."

Lucy turned to a fresh page in her journal and began to write.

Outside, a roar 'tween earth and sky is raging;
As thunder rolls and raindrops pelt the ground.
But inside, peace and safety, rest and slumber,
As father, mother, sister, brother
Love and comfort one another
Home at last; their destination found.

Could it be? Was this really their home? Lucy read through the words one more time. She closed the book, extinguished the lamp, and curled up in her blanket on the floor to watch the storm a little longer before sleep came.

8

The steamer *Emma Harmon*, Capt. J. M. Wing, was made fast at our Levee on Sunday last, at about five o'clock p.m., *it being the first steamer which was ever at our wharf,* and the first on the Kansas River which was sustained wholly by private enterprise. On her arrival she was greeted by three hearty cheers from the citizens, which were as cordially responded to by the officers, passengers, and crew. She had on board about fifty passengers besides a large quantity of freight.

–*Herald of Freedom,* May 26, 1855

Getting the store ready took nearly every daylight hour for the next few days. While most of their neighbors rested after church, the Thomkinses worked together. "The Lord will forgive us a few hours of labor on the Sabbath," Mamma said.

Joseph stood on the stairs, brushing white paint on the handrail. Beneath him, Papa nailed wood panels to enclose the area underneath the stairs, leaving space for a hinged door to create a small closet.

Mamma sanded the top of the table Papa had built for measuring fabric. She rubbed the sanding block in short, quick strokes on the flat surface, then swept her left hand across the spot to be sure there were no splinters to snag material.

Lucy wiped the front windows with a rag. Each window had twenty-four panes of glass. No matter how much she wiped, she just couldn't get rid of all the streaks. She pushed back a damp strand of hair with her forearm, then stepped outside to clean the other sides. Mr. Brown rushed out of the newspaper office when he saw her.

"Lucy!" he called to her. "Tell your father that *Emma Harmon* is coming in. He'd better get down to the river!"

Lucy went back inside. "Papa, who is Emma Harmon? Mr. Brown says that she is down at the river, and you should go."

"It's the steamboat!" said Papa. "Our merchandise is here! Come on, Joseph, we'll need to borrow a horse and wagon from Wyman's stable." Joseph ran out the door, with Papa right behind.

Mamma hurried up the stairs and came back with her black handbag. "Someone has to pay for the merchandise," she said. She and Lucy ran all the way to the river.

Everyone in Lawrence stood at the levee. Horses, mules, and wagons crowded the street, ready to haul the freight that would soon arrive. Mr. Litchfield brought Daisy and the wagon to meet the passengers who would be staying at the boarding house. Lucy joined the crowd at the edge of the river and looked toward the east. A shrill whistle went up from a stern-wheeled steamer making its way up the river swollen from the previous night's rain. As the boat neared the levee, the men on shore raised a cheer of "Hip, hip, hooray!"

An answer of "Hip, hip, hooray!" came from the boat's crew

and from the passengers who stood near the railing, waving to the citizens of Lawrence.

The crewmen tied ropes to the dock and extended the gangplank so the passengers could come across. The ship's crew stacked trunks and luggage on the shore, and Mr. Litchfield loaded his wagon. Papa and some of the Lawrence men boarded the boat to help unload the cargo. They sorted the boxes according to the names on them, and within a few minutes, the pile of crates and barrels marked "Thomkins General Store, Lawrence, K.T." was as tall as Lucy. Mamma and Lucy inspected each container. Lucy read the labels as Mamma made a list.

"Here's a barrel of nails, Mamma."

"Good!" Mamma wrote it on her list.

"This box says hammers, saws, and axes."

"Those will sell quickly!"

"Candles, lamp oil, tallow …"

Papa brought a large wooden box out. "Here's some flannel and calico, Maggie," he said, setting the box down. "Looks like you'll be getting that new dress soon, Lucy."

"Thank goodness," said Lucy. She continued to read labels. "Here are some food items, Mamma. Sugar, cornmeal, flour, coffee."

Joseph called out more labels. "Brass hinges, door knobs, locks, keys."

Papa went back to the boat for more boxes, and Mamma's list grew. At last, they were all unloaded, and Captain Wing brought the bill of lading for Mamma and Papa to check against their list.

"You're sure this is all?" asked Mamma.

"Yes, ma'am," said Captain Wing.

"No cookstove?"

"Sorry, ma'am. There should be another boat in a few days."

When they were sure that everything was accounted for, Papa signed the bill, and Mamma reached into her bag for the money. Captain Wing counted the money and shook Papa's hand.

"Good luck with your store, Thomkins. It looks like you're ready to do business in Kansas Territory," he said.

"Thank you, Captain," said Papa. "I'm sure we'll see you again."

Lucy watched while Papa and the other men piled the cargo onto the waiting wagon.

"Maggie," Papa said. "Why don't you take the children back to the store? " Papa said. "I'll bring the wagon shortly."

Mamma paused. "Yes, I suppose that's a good idea." She looked around. "Where is Joseph?"

Lucy spotted her brother with several boys, playing amongst the piles of crates. "I'll get him, Mamma. We'll meet you back at the store."

Lucy made her way through the crowd toward her brother. "Joseph!" she called.

He looked up, then ducked behind a pile of crates. He clearly did not want to be called away from his game.

Lucy tried to sneak around to catch him by surprise, but nearly tripped over a long, low box. It was marked with a stenciled word: "Books." Two more crates just like it rested nearby. Mr. Lawrence had sent them! Lucy imagined all her favorite stories and poems neatly stacked inside the crates. The boxes were labeled "Charles Robinson." He would have to open them.

Dr. Robinson stood with a group of men nearby. Lucy did not want to interrupt, but she just had to get Dr. Robinson's attention; she needed to see what was in those boxes.

Mr. Farris was waving his fists angrily as he talked. "It's less than a week until the next election, Doc. If we don't have some protection, the Ruffians will take over the ballot box again! You told us Thayer and Lawrence would send those Sharps rifles by now!"

"I'm sure they haven't forgotten us. But you know the Ruffians are watching all shipments of goods to us," said the doctor.

"Wing said some Ruffians came aboard at Kansas City," agreed Mr. Abbott, "but he said they didn't take anything."

"The next boat is due in a few days," said Dr. Robinson. "Maybe they will come then." The men grumbled and began to walk away.

Lucy touched Dr. Robinson's arm. "Dr. Robinson, would you please look in these boxes? I think they are for the school."

"Which boxes, Lucy?"

She pointed to the three wooden crates. "These," she said, leading the way. "I think Mr. Lawrence sent us some books."

Lucy revealed her secret: "I wrote to him and told him we needed books. I hope you don't mind, sir."

"Of course not. Let's see what we have." He picked up a crowbar from the ground and loosened the lid on one of the boxes. He inched it up carefully, then grabbed the edge to pull it loose.

When the lid came free, Dr. Robinson stepped back. Lucy gasped when she saw the contents of the crate.

"Farris! Abbott!" called Dr. Robinson. "Over here! You need to see this!"

The men gathered around and edged Lucy out of the way. Mr. Abbott was the first to step forward and put his hands into the box. He lifted out a rifle and held it high. "Ha! Look here, boys! Our friends in Massachusetts have sent us some books to use in the education of our Missouri neighbors!"

Mr. Grover reached into the box next. "Sharps slant breech carbine," he said. "Fifty-two caliber."

Papa stepped back from Mr. Grover. "It isn't loaded, is it?"

Mr. Grover shook his head. "You have to make your own cartridges. You'll learn how."

Mr. Farris took up the crowbar and pried the tops from the other crates marked "Books." Each crate held dozens more rifles, aligned in neat rows.

"Prettiest books I've ever seen!" said Mr. Abbott. Now all the men held guns, examining the dark wood stocks and fingering the breech-loading mechanisms.

"Can load and fire it three times before your enemy can

load a musket once," said Mr. Farris, pulling back the hammer and inspecting the firing chamber.

"And just in time for the election," added Mr. Abbott. "We'll elect a Free State representative this time!"

"Darned clever, packing them as books," said Dr. Robinson, shaking his head.

"That explains why the Ruffians didn't disturb them," said Papa.

Lucy could barely hold back her tears. They had tricked the Ruffians, but they had also tricked her. Couldn't they have sent even one box of books? She turned to go, but stopped short.

Papa turned a rifle over in his hands, examining the dark wood of the stock. Lucy watched as he lifted it to his shoulder and looked down the barrel. His mouth tightened into a hard frown as his index finger curled around the trigger. Still aiming the rifle, he swung his body away from the rest of the crowd. Lucy stood a few feet behind him, but he hadn't seen her. She watched as Papa pivoted slowly, the barrel of the Sharps sweeping horizontally. "Papa!"

He lowered the gun. "Lucy –"

"I'm going home."

"Lucy," Papa called after her.

Behind every house, every building, she imagined one of her neighbors aiming a gun at her.

Should she be *glad* that Papa had a rifle to defend them?

9

We came here to work, not to fight; to plant fields & build up towns, to erect schools & Churches & live peaceable & happy in the enjoyment of the finds of our industry. The proslavery party did not understand us. They mistook our quiet disposition for cowardice. How widely they were mistaken, the history of our battles will prove. We do not like to fight, but we can & will fight desperately when there is no other alternative.

–John E. Stewart, Kansas settler

Every afternoon, the pounding of hammers and the buzzing of Lawrence's two sawmills fell silent as the men gathered to practice marching and military drills. Papa joined the new militia unit, the Lawrence Defensibles, and they set up a firing range at the edge of town for target practice. No matter how often Lucy heard it, each volley of gunfire made her jump.

When Papa wasn't at the firing range, he was busy making ammunition cartridges. Mamma shouldered the burden of tending the family business. She tolerated his absence from the store, but she refused to allow him to roll the ammunition cartridges inside.

The black powder *was* dangerous. Nearly every one of the Defensibles had powder burns on his hands and face. Behind the store, Papa set up a small table. Making the cartridges was a time consuming task, and Papa sometimes didn't even stop for meals. One evening while Mamma and Joseph were at the boarding house, Lucy brought Papa's dinner to him. He was seated on a wooden keg, hunched over his little table.

Lucy set a plate with chicken and dumplings near his elbow. "You'd better eat now, Papa. Mamma wants me to bring the plate back right away so they can finish cleaning up."

"I need to finish these," Papa said. He placed the flat end of a lead bullet against the end of a short wooden dowel and rolled a cartridge paper around them both to make a paper tube with the bullet inside. A neat row of about fifteen finished cartridges lined the edge of the table.

"You have enough, Papa."

He reached for his glue pot. "I'll need twice this many for shooting practice tomorrow." He brushed glue on the edge of the paper and held it in place with his finger.

Papa frowned as he removed the wooden peg from the paper tube and dipped a small scoop into the pouch of black powder. He poured the powder into the paper tube, then looked up. "You understand, don't you? You know why I have to do this?" He twisted the paper at the end of the cartridge, and reached for the glue brush again.

"I don't know, Papa. I'm scared of the Ruffians, but I'm also scared of you shooting someone."

"When I think of Election Day, and that man …" Papa stopped.

"I feel like I would shoot him myself if I got the chance."

Papa glued the twist of loose paper at the end of the cartridge. "Promise you'll never say that in front of your mother. She'd never forgive either of us."

"I promise, Papa."

<hr />

Gun fever came in the open schoolhouse window on the wisps of blue smoke from the firing range. Whenever the men practiced, the boys were too fidgety to pay attention. The third time Mr. Fitch caught Willy Parsons pointing his finger like an imaginary gun at Jake Cuthbert, he sighed, then shouted.

"Mr. Parsons!"

Willy and Jake both jumped and turned to face the teacher.

"I don't know your reason for acting out Mr. Cuthbert's demise, although I'll admit that I have considered murder in this classroom on occasion."

Lucy stifled a giggle.

Mr. Fitch glanced out the window and sighed again. "Even the quiet of a prison cell sometimes seems appealing." He pulled his watch from his vest pocket, glanced at it, then slid it back. "No matter. The steamboat is due in a few hours, and on it, your new teacher." He smiled. "And I expect to be on that boat when it departs. You are all dismissed."

The front two benches fell over with a crash as children rushed for the door.

Mr. Fitch shook his head. "God help that poor woman."

Lucy and Annie waited while the others scrambled over each other. By the time they reached the schoolyard, the boys had already started their game. Samuel and Matthew divided the boys into teams of militia men and Ruffians for mock battle. Scrap wood from nearby building sites served as pretend rifles, and the shots echoing from the rifle range made the game seem even more real.

"Charge!" Samuel ordered, and his militia men advanced. Gunfire exploded from the rifle range as four boy-Ruffians fell.

Lucy stepped backward as Joseph ran past to stand over one of the fallen, his friend Thomas.

"Say your prayers, Ruffian," he snarled, as he pointed his stick-rifle at Thomas' head.

Lucy rushed forward and pulled the stick from his hands. "Stop it!"

"Gimme that!" Joseph reached for it, but Lucy tossed it aside.

"What's the matter, *Lucky*?" Samuel stepped between Lucy and her brother. "Don't like it that your brother wants to shoot a Ruffian?" He turned to Joseph. "I'll bet your pa has one of those fancy Sharps rifles, doesn't he?"

"Yeah, we've got one!" Joseph said. "It's a beauty!"

"I figured as much. They gave them all to the Insiders." Samuel spat into the dirt, inches from Lucy's shoe. "Your pa know how to shoot it, Joe?"

"He sure does," Joseph answered. "He's out there practicing right now."

A crowd of boys began to gather around them.

Samuel stepped so close his face was just inches from Lucy's. He grinned. "So, who do you think he's planning to shoot, *Lucky*? Prairie dogs?"

The boys laughed.

Lucy would not step back. "My father didn't come here to shoot anyone; he came here to run a store and to vote."

Samuel's smile was gone. "In Kansas, a man's got to be able to shoot to get a chance to vote!"

He slapped Joseph on the back. "I'll bet you know how to shoot that Sharps, don't you?"

Joseph hesitated. "I …" He looked at Lucy. "I haven't fired it yet."

"You haven't? Why not? If my pa had one, I wouldn't let him sleep until he took me shooting!" He frowned at Joseph. "You scared of it?"

"No! I'm not scared! Papa doesn't want … he … hasn't had time to teach me yet, that's all."

"I see how it is. You just need somebody to show you how to use that rifle. My pa hasn't got a Sharps yet – supposed to get one when the next shipment comes." He put a friendly arm around Joseph's shoulders and started to walk him away from Lucy. "I'll tell you what, Joe. I'll come over to your place later. Would you like to ride my horse Jasper?"

"Sure!" Joseph said.

"I thought so. I'll bring Jasper. We can take that Sharps out."

"No!" Lucy grabbed Joseph's arm. "You can't take Papa's rifle!"

"Who asked you?" Samuel frowned and looked at Joseph. "You gonna let your sister tell you what to do?"

Joseph pulled free of her grasp. "No."

"It'll take men who can shoot to kill to defend this town," Samuel said. "Tell your pa to keep practicing. I hear most of those insiders couldn't hit a Ruffian if he was arm's length from them." He turned toward Matthew. "Come on. Let's go to the range. We *men* can do some shooting."

Joseph watched as the boys walked away.

Lucy put a hand on his shoulder. "Let's go. If another boat is coming, we need to help get things ready at the store."

He shrugged free of her and frowned. "I'm going to the firing range. I'll come when Papa is finished shooting." He hurried after Samuel and Matthew.

Lucy watched as Joseph caught up with the two older boys. Samuel looked back at her and grinned.

"Aren't you going after him?" Annie asked.

Lucy turned toward the store. "I have to go home and help out. Mamma will need me even more if Joseph's not there."

Annie fell in step beside her. "Maybe I could help at your store for a little while. Ma's not expecting me home yet."

"Thanks. Mamma won't be happy to hear that Joseph ran off to rifle practice."

Mamma was busy when they arrived, and Joseph's absence did not sit well. "I don't trust that Willis boy," she said. "And we still have merchandise to organize."

Annie and Lucy worked on displays. They used shipping barrels and crates for shelves and followed Mamma's plan for arranging merchandise in the store. Hardware and building supplies took up one side of the room. Household items like blankets and dishes lined the opposite wall. Mamma put the food at the back of the store. She hoped that on their way to the back for the food items, shoppers would find other things they needed.

Mamma wrote out a list of the prices for each item: $1.25 for an axe, $2.00 for a pair of blankets, $1.25 for a gallon of lamp oil. Next, she showed Lucy how to use the scales to measure items sold by the pound, like sugar, raisins, and coffee. Annie wrote a sign announcing "Tallow candles, 15¢ per lb."

Mamma pointed out the last crate to unpack, a box marked "Domestics," with the word "calicoes," added below. "Lucy, bring a crowbar and help me open this."

Lucy's pride had made her refuse to wear Mamma's dresses, but her poor blue gown was hopelessly tattered, and she was tired of the teasing from Samuel and the other boys. Now Mamma would be able to make her a new dress.

Lucy pried the lid loose, and they pulled aside paper wrapping to reveal bolts of cloth. Small printed flower buds contrasted with the red, blue, green, and yellow background colors.

"Oh, pretty!" said Annie.

As they removed one bolt of fabric after another, the girls admired the colorful assortment.

"Lucy is a bit overdue for a new dress, don't you think, Annie?" Mamma asked.

"Yes, ma'am," Annie said, looking at Lucy's dress. "That one never seemed quite right for Lawrence."

"Which one do you like best, Lucy?" Mamma asked.

"I'm not sure. Maybe this one," Lucy said, pointing to a bolt of red material.

"This one brings out your eyes." Mamma held up a piece with blue background and tiny red rosebuds.

"How soon could you make it?"

"I just can't imagine when I can find the time, with all I have to do here. A tailor has set up a shop over at Hornsby's store, but I hear he's expensive."

Lucy looked at Annie's faded dress. Even though it was worn, it was neatly sewn. "Does your mother make your dresses?"

Annie laughed. "She sure couldn't pay someone else to do it."

"Would she make a dress for me? We could pay her with enough material, thread, and buttons to make you a dress, too, couldn't we, Mamma?"

"Yes, we could do that," said Mamma. "Do you think she would, Annie?"

Annie reached to touch a bolt of yellow calico, then smiled

at Mamma. "Oh, that would be so ..." she hesitated. She drew her hand back from the fabric. "I don't know. Ma is pretty busy with things at home."

"Would you ask her? It would be a big help to me," said Mamma. "You may choose the calico you like best. Some muslin, too, if your mother can use it."

"I'll ask her, ma'am," said Annie. "I'd better go now." She hurried out of the store before Lucy could even say goodbye.

Lucy and Mamma took the rest of the bolts of cloth out of the crate. Mamma held each one up to Lucy to see which one suited her best. She lifted the end of the blue calico again. "Here, hold this one next to your face," she said.

"No, not that," said Papa, as he came through the door. "We'll have every young man in the territory at our doorstep if you wear a dress made of that."

"But she wouldn't look so much like Cinderella," Joseph said. "Sam says ..."

"I don't care what Samuel Willis says," Mamma interrupted. "You should have come straight home. I needed your help here. I don't want you anywhere near that firing range. It's bad enough we have one family member risking life and limb."

Papa hung his hat on the peg by the door. "Now, Maggie, the boys just came to watch."

Mamma crossed her arms. "I don't like it, Marcus. It's dangerous."

Papa put the gun in its usual spot inside the cabinet below the stairs. "They stayed well out of the way. Besides, Joseph

110

knows he is not to handle this gun. Right, son?"

"Yes, Papa," Joseph said. "I know."

"Good boy," Papa said. "You can help me make cartridges to-night. We'll need plenty to be ready for the election tomorrow."

"Why is there another election so soon?" Lucy asked.

"The governor threw out the results of the last election, so we'll have to vote again. This time we'll have a fair vote."

"Will you shoot the Border Ruffians if they come?" Joseph asked.

"I don't think we'll shoot anyone," said Papa. "If the Ruffians know we can defend ourselves, they'll back down."

"But what if they don't?" asked Lucy.

"Then we will do what we must," Papa said. He looked at Lucy. "They won't threaten us again."

"I don't like it, Marcus," Mamma said.

"I came here to make Kansas a free state, and we need a fair election to put Free State delegates in the legislature," Papa said.

The shrill blast of a steam whistle split the air. "But now, I believe there is a boat about to dock, and I'll bet there's a new cookstove on board."

"Oh, thank goodness!" said Mamma.

Papa clapped a hand on Joseph's shoulder. "We'll need a wagon from Mr. Wyman's stable."

Joseph scowled. "If I had my own horse, we could have a wagon, too. Then we wouldn't have to pay Mr. Wyman to use one of his every time a shipment came in."

"When you make enough money to feed a horse, you can have one," Papa replied. "But today, we'll borrow one from Mr. Wyman. Now, go."

Joseph ran across the street as the rest of the family hurried toward the river. Lucy couldn't help thinking about the new teacher. Mr. Fitch said it was a woman. Maybe this teacher would stay long enough to help Lucy with her poetry – if Samuel and his friends didn't run her off first.

They reached the river just as the crew put out the gangplank. Another whistle went up from the boat, and cinders rained down on the crowded dock. As the deck hands secured the heavy ropes, passengers stood along the railings.

"Thomkins!" called a deck hand. "Shipment for Thomkins!"

Papa stepped forward. "Here, sir!"

"You'll need some help with this," the man said, pointing to a large wooden crate on the deck.

"There you are, Maggie!" Papa said proudly. "Ohio Patent Number 4 cookstove! Only the best for you!" He looked up the street. "Now, we just need that wagon."

Mamma and Papa went on deck to see what other merchandise they had on board, and Lucy waited by the road for Joseph and Mr. Wyman to arrive with the wagon.

"Hey, *Lucky*!" Lucy knew that voice. She wouldn't respond.

"Think Prince Charming is coming in on the boat?" Lucy could feel the heat rising in her cheeks. Sam Willis was driving a wagon toward the dock, and her brother sat on the driver's seat next to him.

Joseph jumped down from the wagon. "Sam works at Mr. Wyman's stable!"

Sam sat on the driver's seat, the reins still in his hands. "Yep. He even pays me."

"Sam says I can help him, too."

"You already have a job at our store," Lucy reminded him.

"I could do this, too." He patted the neck of the spotted horse tethered to the wagon. "I might even make enough money to get a horse of my own."

Lucy looked up at Sam.

He shrugged. "You never know."

Lucy shook her head. Mamma and Papa wouldn't allow that. "Right now, Papa is looking for this wagon," she told him. "You'd better go help him."

Joseph edged through the crowd toward the boat.

Sam jumped down from the wagon. "Hope the next shipment of Sharps is on this boat," he said. "My pa is still waiting to get his hands on one. I thought maybe your brother would let us practice with your pa's gun, but he's still too scared."

Lucy turned to face him. "Joseph's not waiting for courage," she said. "He's waiting for permission."

"If he had enough of one, he wouldn't need the other."

Lucy didn't reply. Samuel Willis was trouble. No doubt about that.

Several men stepped forward to help Papa and Joseph with the crate, and they loaded it onto the wagon.

A shout went up around some of the other cargo. Mr.

Abbott and Mr. Bowles used a crowbar to attack one of several crates marked "Books." Was this the next batch of rifles Samuel said was coming?

"Stop that!" called a woman's voice. "How dare you open those boxes?"

A tall, older woman hurried down the gangplank. Her gray hair was pulled tightly into a bun, and her back was straight as a rod. As she reached the foot of the gangplank, the lid of the crate came free. The men stepped back in surprise. The crate contained books!

Lucy tried to see between the men to read the titles on the brown cloth covers. She couldn't be sure. Was she seeing *Evangeline* and *The House of Seven Gables*?

The men just stared at the crate. "Well, I'll be …" said Mr. Abbott.

"Punished is what you'll be!" said the woman. "That crate is mine, and I expected it to arrive unopened." Mr. Bowles snatched up the lid, put it back on the crate and hastily tapped at the nails to secure it.

Mr. Abbott looked up and removed his hat. "I'm sorry, ma'am," he said. "We thought this box contained some goods we were expecting."

"And just what were you expecting?" she demanded.

"Guns, ma'am," Mr. Abbott said, reddening with embarrassment.

"Guns! I was informed that this town needed books. I have brought them for the education of the children. Those boxes are clearly marked. Perhaps we need reading classes for adults as well."

"No, ma'am … we can read just fine … I'm sorry, Miss …"

"Elma Kellogg, the new school teacher."

Lucy smiled. Mr. Lawrence had sent books and a new teacher. And she seemed like a teacher who would not stand for the foolishness of Sam and his friends.

10

The *Philadelphia Ledger* states that Theodore Parker told them in his antislavery address in that city last week that 200 Sharps rifles had been sent from Boston in boxes, labeled "books," to arm the New England settlers in Kansas territory against the attacks of the Missourian incursionists.

If all the reports are true about "Arms for Kansas," we think that our neighbors in Missouri have just cause to "expect to see sights" if they attempt again to override the popular will and law of Kansas.

–Herald of Freedom, June 1855

Papa was up before dawn on Election Day, ready to defend the ballot box with the Defensibles. Lucy came downstairs to watch him getting ready. He packed cartridges in a small wooden box to keep them from getting torn. The box went into a leather pouch with a strap to hang over his shoulder. As he inspected his rifle for the third time, Lucy spoke. "Do you think the Ruffians will come?"

"They've come twice before. But this time, we'll have armed men surrounding the polls."

"They'll be surprised when they see those rifles."

Papa put the rifle down, his face serious. "Lucy, promise me that you will not leave this house."

"I didn't mean …" Lucy began.

"I need to hear you promise that you won't leave this house."

"I promise, Papa. I'll stay here."

"I'm trusting you," said Papa.

Lucy hugged him. "And you promise you'll be safe, no matter who is there today."

"I promise," said Papa.

Joseph came to the top of the stairs. "Wait for me! I want to go with you!"

"No. You stay here," Papa said. "It may be dangerous."

"Why do I have to stay here with the women? I'm almost a man."

Joseph sounded just like Samuel Willis.

"That's exactly why," Papa told him. "Lucy and Mamma need you here."

"But I won't have a rifle to defend us!"

"You don't need one. You have a store full of weapons."

"Like what?" Joseph looked around. "A hatchet or a hammer?"

"Even simpler than that." Papa pointed at one of the pottery crocks of spices. "Pepper."

"Pepper? What good is that?"

"You toss a handful of pepper into a Ruffian's eyes, and I guarantee you will slow him down."

Joseph scowled. "It's not the same as a gun."

Papa picked up his rifle. "I have to go now. The polls will open soon."

Mamma stood by the door. "Marcus, please be careful!"

"You know I will, Maggie. We'll let them know we take our voting seriously. When I come home, I'll put that stove in for you."

"I'll take that as a promise," said Mamma.

Papa kissed Mamma and opened the door. "If there is trouble, latch the door and stay upstairs."

As Papa left, Lucy looked out the window. In the early morning light, she could make out other men in the street. She couldn't be sure, but they all looked like Lawrence men.

As she lined up the colorful bolts of fabric on the shelf, Lucy kept watch for signs of Ruffians. Mamma arranged and rearranged her display of crockery dishes. Joseph fed peppercorns into the grinder until Mamma told him to stop.

But the election was different this time. There was no encampment outside town, no strangers with white ribbons. One by one, the Lawrence men voted.

Papa came home after the votes were counted. This time, there were no proslavery votes in Lawrence.

"Abbot heard that the proslavery papers in Atchison and Weston called the new elections illegal," Papa said. "They urged the Ruffians to ignore it."

"Well, thank goodness, it's over," Mamma said. "Maybe things can finally settle down."

Lucy was certainly ready for that. She hardly knew what she believed anymore. She could still see the gun held at Papa's head on that first Election Day, and then Papa with his gun on the dock … The Emigrant Aid Society said it stood for freedom and justice. The Ruffians used intimidation to force their will on others.

The people of Lawrence needed to be able to defend themselves. But even good men like Papa could be moved to violence, and having a deadly weapon in hand could bring disaster. With so many guns and so much anger on both sides, how long would it be before threats turned to actions?

The longer Lucy thought about it, the more it troubled her.

Lessons for our Children

How can we teach them to love their neighbors?
How can we teach them to mind the law?
How can we teach them that all men are brothers,
And justice and freedom the birthright of all?

Do we teach them love with our hatred?
Do we teach them truth through our lies?
Do we teach them freedom through bondage,
Or justice when fairness has died?

If hatred cannot teach a child to love,
Or lies teach him falsehoods to shun,
Why try to teach him that peace could be won
If only we had enough guns?

Lucy blew lightly on the page before her. She had written

the title *Lessons for Our Children* at the top of the page only after she had finished the poem.

Yes, the children in town were certainly learning a lot of lessons by watching the men with their Sharps rifles. Lessons about killing. It was so clear to her.

She had written dozens of poems in her life, but this poem was different. It had a purpose beyond the pages of her poetry journal. In fact, Lucy was certain that she had a duty to bring this poem to the citizens of Lawrence. If it were read by others, perhaps they would see what the guns were doing to their town. Of course, some people wouldn't like the message, but that was all the more reason why they needed to hear it. But how could she get anyone else to read it?

And then she knew.

She carefully removed a blank page from the back of her journal and copied the poem in her neatest handwriting. She wrote her name at the bottom of the page.

Yes, this poem would reach readers in Lawrence. She extinguished the flame in the oil lamp and crawled into bed.

11

Miss Kellogg, late of Massachusetts, has opened school in Lawrence. She has a very respectable number of students, and more are coming in daily. Miss Kellogg has adopted the books used in the schools of this place last winter, to wit: Town's Speller and Definer, also Town's Series of Readers from No. 1 to 4; and also Watson's Mental Arithmetic.

–Herald of Freedom, June 1855

Lucy was awake early the next morning. She dressed quickly and looked again at her poem. Yes, it had to be today. School would begin with the new teacher tomorrow, and she might not have another chance. She could hear Mamma and Papa in the kitchen.

She folded the paper, picked up the pen and ink bottle Mr. Brown had lent her, and went down the steps. From the stairs, she could see into the kitchen, where the new stove was out of the crate. Papa was measuring the stovepipe while Mamma hovered nearby.

Lucy slipped out the front door without either of them noticing and hurried next door.

At the *Herald of Freedom* office, the door was open. Lucy took a deep breath for courage and knocked lightly.

Mr. Brown looked up and smiled. "Good morning, Lucy. How is business at the store?"

"Very good, sir," she replied. "I have my own pen and ink now, so I've brought yours back. Thank you very much." Lucy placed the pen and ink on the desk.

"You're quite welcome. I'm glad you could use them." He smiled politely and went back to his reading. She stood still until he looked up again. "Is there something else?"

She clutched the folded paper tighter to keep it from shaking. "Yes, sir … well, I think so. I've noticed that you often publish poetry in your newspaper."

"Yes, I think it adds a bit of culture to the *Herald.* Do you enjoy it?"

"Oh, yes, sir. I enjoy poetry very much." She held out the folded paper with her poem. "In fact, I write poetry myself."

"You do? Well, that's excellent." He nodded and smiled, but didn't reach for it. "Maybe someday when you're older you will write something I can put in my newspaper."

"Actually, sir, I have a poem here that I think your readers would like." She placed it on the desk. "I came to ask if you would consider printing it in the newspaper."

Mr. Brown leaned back a bit in his chair. He still smiled, but now he tilted his head forward and looked over his spectacles at her. "I appreciate your offer, young lady, but I can't accept your poem. I'm sure it's a lovely piece for a person your age, but the *Herald of Freedom* has readers all across the country. We send it to New York, Massachusetts, and many other places."

"Yes, I know that, Mr. Brown." She didn't want to plead, but he was dismissing her so quickly. "Perhaps if you would only look at my verse ..."

"I can't publish the writing of a child. I must protect the credibility of my newspaper." He picked up her poem and handed it to her. "I really must get back to work now."

Lucy stepped backward toward the door. She felt her cheeks burn hot, but Mr. Brown didn't notice. He didn't even look up at her again. She could hardly believe it.

She struggled to control the tremble in her voice. "I understand, sir. I'm sorry I bothered you with it."

She turned and hurried out the door. She was too angry to go back in the store, so she sat on the back stoop, fuming. *The writing of a child.* He wouldn't even look at it. She should run back there and tell him his high-and-mighty newspaper wasn't good enough to print her poetry! She should make him beg her to let him read it! She should ...

"Lucy!"

She nearly jumped out of her skin. Mamma stood at the back door. "I've been looking for you. I need –" Mamma stopped. "What's wrong? You look feverish. Are you ill?"

"No ... it's just ..." Mamma might think she'd been foolish to take her poem to Mr. Brown. She wasn't ready to admit her failure. She stood and forced a smile. "I'm fine."

"Come inside then," Mamma said. "I need your help in the store."

Lucy tucked the poem into her pocket. She would not give up so easily.

⇒◆⇐

When Lucy came out the front door on her way to school the next morning, she refused to look in the direction of the newspaper office as she passed.

"Lucy!" Annie ran to catch up with her. The stiff breeze made them both clutch at their skirts as they walked. "Ma said she'll make your dress!" Annie announced. "And she'll make me a new one, too!"

"Thank goodness," Lucy said. "I'll be able to throw away this poor old thing." One of the blue flounces on Lucy's dress had come loose, and it waved like a flag in the wind. Just a few weeks ago she had hated the simple calico the other girls wore. Now she would welcome it.

Annie skipped along beside her. "Could we stop at your store this afternoon to tell your ma?"

"Oh, yes. Mamma will be glad to hear it." Lucy wished she could be as excited as Annie, but her feelings still stung from yesterday's disappointment.

Annie spun around, as though dancing. "Do you think she will let me choose the material today?"

"I'm sure of it," Lucy said. "You can choose whatever color you like."

"I like the yellow with the blue flowers. It's like a sunny day." Little puffs of dust rose from behind their feet as they walked. "Have you met the new teacher?" Annie asked.

"Not really. I saw her at the boat when she arrived. She seems very practical, and she brought books for us. I just hope the boys will behave."

"Sam and Matthew behave?" Annie giggled. "I'm sure they'll be behaving – like animals!" Both girls laughed as they hurried to school.

Miss Kellogg was in the schoolyard. She pulled the bell rope with one hand and held tight to her skirt with the other.

They took their chairs, and Lucy smiled when she saw the neat rows of books on a shelf at the side of the room. As she smoothed her skirt to sit, she felt a bulge in her pocket. The poem was still there. Should she show it to the teacher? Best to see what she was like first.

Miss Kellogg stood at the front of the room. She did not smile, but nodded an acknowledgement to each child who greeted her with, "Good morning, ma'am."

When everyone was seated, she adjusted her high lace collar, folded her arms across her dark blue dress, and addressed them. "Good morning. I am Miss Kellogg, your new teacher. Mr. Fitch left me a list of students. Please answer when I call your name."

She called the names down the list, studying each child's face. When she finished, she laid down the list and removed her spectacles.

"Mr. Fitch was kind enough to leave me a lengthy commentary on each of you, regarding his estimate of your intelligence and the quality of your upbringing, as well as a summary of your school behavior." Across the room, Sam poked Matthew with his elbow. Lucy could guess the nature of Mr. Fitch's comments about that pair. Miss Kellogg continued. "I was kind enough to destroy that commentary without reading it. And now you have learned one thing about me: I like to form my own opinions."

Lucy smiled. Yes, she would show her poem to Miss Kellogg.

The rest of the morning passed quickly, with students grouped by age reading from the *Town's Readers*, beginning with Number 1 for the youngest children. By lunchtime, all the students had been placed into groups for reading. Lucy and Annie were both in the highest group, but so was half the class.

By the middle of the afternoon, Lucy's enthusiasm had dimmed. Even in the highest level book, the readings were simple and uninteresting. She touched the folded poem and hoped for a chance to talk to Miss Kellogg.

When school was dismissed, Lucy touched Annie's sleeve. "I need to talk to the teacher. I'll meet you at the store," she told her. "Mamma will be glad to hear your news about the dress. Tell her I'll be there in a few minutes."

Annie nodded. "I'll see you there – I hope she still has some of that yellow calico!"

Miss Kellogg carried books back to the shelf and sorted

them by reading level. Lucy picked up several from the benches near her.

"Thank you for your help," Miss Kellogg said, as Lucy put the last book in place. "We had a busy day, didn't we?"

"Yes, ma'am. It's nice to have books. The newspaper was hard for the little ones."

"I'm sure it was. They will do better with proper readers." Miss Kellogg's smile softened her stern appearance.

How could Lucy ask about the other books without being too bold? She couldn't say that she had looked in Miss Kellogg's personal belongings at the dock. "Miss Kellogg, the fourth level readers seem very simple. Do you have any for older students?"

The teacher took a small step back and looked at Lucy. "How old are you?"

"Thirteen, ma'am." Lucy looked down at her dirty, tattered dress. She surely made a poor first impression.

Miss Kellogg nodded. "I mistook you for younger. What kinds of books do you enjoy?" She walked to the front of the room, and Lucy followed.

"Poetry," she answered. "But I lost all my books when we came West. My trunk was stolen."

Miss Kellogg turned to face her. "That must have been a bitter disappointment."

"Yes, ma'am, but at least I didn't lose my poetry journal," Lucy offered. "My teacher in Pennsylvania gave it to me as a parting gift."

"A poetry journal?" The teacher smiled. "I didn't expect to

find a poet in Kansas. I'd like to read your verse sometime, if you'd like to share it."

It was just what she had hoped for. "I have a poem with me." Lucy unfolded the paper and offered it to the teacher.

Miss Kellogg placed her spectacles on her nose and began to read. She looked up from the paper. "You wrote this yourself?"

"Yes, ma'am." She hesitated, then added, "I asked Mr. Brown if he would put it in the newspaper, but he said he couldn't use it."

"I see," Miss Kellogg said. "You'd like an audience for your verse. Tell me the point of this poem, please."

The point? Surely that should be obvious. "Ma'am?"

"What is it you want the reader to think? That guns are evil? That the citizens of Lawrence don't need to defend themselves and their families?"

"The men in town think that guns will solve their problems." Lucy thought about Papa the day he picked up that rifle the first time. "When the rifles arrived, it was like a disease had infected most of the men in town! They forgot about everything else."

"I see." Miss Kellogg looked at the paper again. "Why did Mr. Brown dislike the poem?"

"That's just the problem – he didn't even look at it!" Lucy's anger flared as she remembered Mr. Brown's rejection. "He said he wouldn't use it because of my age."

"That was a mistake on his part. A poem should be judged on its own merits."

Lucy smiled. "You think it has merit?"

"It has some merit." Miss Kellogg handed the paper back to Lucy. "But I'm unclear about your intent. Do you mean that guns are the main problem in this territory?"

"Well, I …" Lucy didn't know how to end the sentence.

"Answer the question, Miss Thomkins." Her voice was stern. "Is it the guns or something else?"

Lucy nodded, but her answer was quiet. "It's the guns, ma'am."

"Then you have missed the point of the struggle." Miss Kellogg's voice softened. "You are right in a way. The territory is infected with disease." She pointed at the paper in Lucy's hand. "But guns are not the disease – they are only a symptom."

"I don't understand." Lucy refolded the poem.

Miss Kellogg reached for Lucy's hand and led her to the front of the room. She pulled a slim book from a carpetbag there. "If I lend you a book of poetry, will you read it?"

Lucy nodded. "Oh, yes."

"I won't guarantee that you will like what you read, Lucy." She placed the book in Lucy's hands. "But you might begin to recognize the real disease we fight."

Lucy examined the book. On the cover, the handwritten title announced *Voices of Freedom* and below it, "J. G. Whittier." At last, a book of poetry. "Thank you, Miss Kellogg. I promise to take care of it and return it."

"I trust you with it," Miss Kellogg said. "And I trust you to read it well. You will soon see what Mr. Whittier stands for. I hope it will help you decide what *you* stand for, as well. When you know that, I think you will find a new purpose in your poetry."

12

What, ho!—*our* countrymen in chains!

  The whip on WOMAN's shrinking flesh!

Our soil yet reddening with the stains,

  Caught from her scourging, warm and fresh!

What! mothers from their children riven!

  What God's own image bought and sold!

AMERICANS to market driven,

  And bartered as the brute for gold!

–John Greenleaf Whittier, "Stanzas"

When the bell on the store's front door tinkled, Lucy looked up from the poetry book. Mr. Burris, a young father whose claim was just outside town, came through the door with his four-year-old daughter, Amelia. Lucy marked her place with a bit of ribbon and laid the book aside. The young father stood near the front door, looking around and shifting nervously from one foot to the other. Amelia sucked the middle two fingers of her left hand while her father held her right hand. The little girl's dress was dirty, and her matted hair had not been combed in a long time.

"Hello, Mr. Burris. Can I help you?" Lucy asked.

"Yes ... well, I hope so," he stammered. "Is your father here?"

Papa was adjusting the stovepipe in the kitchen, and the clanging there suggested that perhaps it wasn't going well. Mamma was there, too. Lucy came around the counter.

"He's busy right now, but maybe I can help you find something." She patted Amelia's shoulder, but the child buried her face in the side of her father's trousers.

"No," Mr. Burris said. "I … I need to talk business." He turned to go.

Mamma came in as Mr. Burris pulled Amelia toward the door. "Mr. Burris, wait, please."

He took off his hat and stood awkwardly.

She approached and spoke softly to him. "I'm so sorry about baby Nathan," she said. "The measles have taken so many. How is Rebecca?"

"Rebecca … she just can't get over it." He paused to control his shaky voice. "She can't even bring herself to look at the three girls – seems to think she'll lose them, too, even though they all came through the sickness." He put a hand on Amelia's head. "If we stay here, Rebecca's going to just wither up. We're going back to her folks' place in Illinois."

Mamma nodded. "I'm sorry to hear that. What can we do?"

He looked down at Amelia. "I need to talk with your husband, ma'am."

"Marcus and I run our business together. He'd approve of our talking about it."

Mr. Burris cleared his throat. "I don't hardly know how to begin, except just to say it outright – we're broke. We spent all we had to file our claim and build the house. We don't even have money for the train tickets."

Poor Mrs. Burris. Poor Amelia. Lucy spoke softly to the child, "Here, Amelia, I have something you'll like." Lucy led the little girl to the back counter and broke off a bit of a peppermint stick.

Mr. Burris regained his composure a bit. "I'm ashamed to ask for your charity, but I just don't know what else to do. We need food and supplies to get us by until we get back East."

"I understand," Mamma said. "Do you plan to sell your household goods?"

"Yes, ma'am, but we won't get much. Everyone is struggling."

Mamma nodded. "Maybe we can help. We've been so busy with the store that Marcus hasn't been able to make much furniture for us. If you could trade yours for supplies and enough cash for your trip back, would that help you?"

"We could start over."

"Then the arrangement would be good for both of us," Mamma said.

Papa emerged from the kitchen, wiping his hands with a sooty rag. "Good afternoon, Michael," he said.

"I hope you don't mind me speaking business with your wife, but she said it was all right. If you agree to our plan, then I'll be grateful."

"If Maggie has made a bargain with you, then it's a bargain with me as well." He reached out to shake the younger man's hand.

Mr. Burris returned that afternoon, his wagon loaded with furniture piled high and secured with ropes. Papa helped him unload a table, four straight-backed chairs, two bed frames, two bureaus, and a rocker. At last, Lucy would have a bed in her room.

Mamma gathered some food and other supplies for the family, and counted out the rest of the trade in cash. "This should cover the fare for your family and even a night's lodging in Kansas City while you wait for passage on a boat. I'm sure you'll find a buyer for the wagon and team before you go."

Mr. Burris accepted the cash. "I'm thankful, Mrs. Thomkins," he said. "As soon as I told Rebecca we could go, she perked up a little. I think she'll be better – we'll all be better – when we get back to our folks."

Lucy helped Mr. Burris carry the supplies out to his wagon. As he placed a bundle in the wagon bed, he stopped. Lucy followed his gaze to a small wooden cradle that rested in the corner of the wagon bed.

"I nearly forgot about that." He looked at Lucy.

"We don't have any babies in our house, Mr. Burris."

"Please, I can't take it back there. It'll break Rebecca's heart all over again to see it."

When Mamma saw it, she shook her head. "I'm sure someone in town will need it soon enough," she said, "but I just don't think I can bear to look at it. Can you find a place for it, Lucy?"

As she sat at her desk that evening, Lucy's fingers found the scrap of ribbon and opened the book to the poem she had been reading that morning. *Mothers from their children riven ... God's own image bought and sold.*

She shifted in her seat, and her foot bumped the little cradle she had put beneath her desk.

13

Was awakened by a little tree-toad on my pillow this morning. I found a mouse in the tub, and a swallow came into the kitchen as we were at breakfast. I am wondering if all the "four-footed beasts and creeping things" have appointed a place of rendezvous upon our premises; and suggest, laughingly, that "the rattlesnakes will come next." Scarcely had we finished breakfast, before the cry from near the wood-pile was, "Here's a snake!" It measured about eighteen inches in length, was ugly looking, and had four rattles.

–Mrs. Charles Robinson, June 1855

Annie kept Lucy updated on the progress of the new dress. On Monday, she told Lucy, "Ma cut the pattern for your dress last night." On Wednesday, she told her, "Ma put the bodice together." On Thursday, "Ma sewed the skirt on. It sure looks nice." When Lucy came downstairs for breakfast on Friday, Annie was on the front porch of the store looking in the window. She tapped the glass urgently, and Lucy opened the front door.

"Ma's nearly done with your dress," Annie said, as she came through the door. "She wants you to come out to the house to try it on."

"Let's go ask Mamma. She's in the kitchen."

Mamma was taking biscuits from the oven. She looked up when the girls came in. "Good morning, Annie. Would you like some eggs?"

"Oh, I didn't come for breakfast, ma'am," Annie said, looking at the biscuits. "Ma's almost done with Lucy's dress. She needs her to come out to the house to fit it."

Mamma wiped her hands on her apron. "When?"

"Today after school." Annie couldn't look away from the food on the table.

Mamma gave a plate to Lucy, then set one in front of Annie. "Does it have to be today? I need Lucy and Joseph to help me sort new merchandise."

Joseph pushed his chair back and rose from the table. "I'm going to the stable with Sam after school today."

"I need you here," Mamma told him.

"But Sam's going to show me how to hitch a team to the wagon today," Joseph said. He opened the back door. "Papa said I could go."

"Well –" but Mamma didn't finish the sentence. Joseph was already gone.

Mamma picked up his plate from the table. "Annie, are you sure it can't wait until tomorrow?"

"No, ma'am. It must be today. Tomorrow Ma's expecting some …" She stopped. "She's got something important to do. It's got to be today."

"I suppose the sorting can wait. How will you get there?"

"We'll walk out to my house after school," said Annie. "Pa

can bring Lucy back in the wagon." She reached for a biscuit.

Mamma looked worried. "Is it safe for you girls to walk alone?"

Annie smiled. "I do it all the time, ma'am. It's just a few miles – not so far, really."

Mamma frowned. "I suppose not. Stop by here before you go. I'll pack some flour and sugar for your mother."

"Thank you, ma'am. She'll be glad of that."

By the time they finished eating, the girls had to hurry to school. They ran into the schoolyard as the bell was clanging.

Joseph and Sam were still outside the door when Lucy and Annie got there. They followed the girls inside.

"You sure you're gonna bring it?" Sam asked. "You been saying it for a week."

Joseph's voice was quiet, but Lucy heard one word.

"Today."

———⟫•⟪———

All day, the sky hung low and gray over Lawrence. Still, not a drop of rain had fallen to settle the dust in the streets of town when Lucy and Annie left school. They stopped at the store to pick up the parcel of food for Annie's mother.

Papa stood at the bottom of the stairs, a pile of boards balanced in his arms. He turned when the bell on the door jingled. "Good afternoon, ladies!"

"Hello, Papa. Not going to the rifle range today?"

"No, your mother has a list of chores for me. I told her I'd put up these shelves today. Need to keep the peace at home sometimes, too, right, Lucy Cat?"

"Right, Papa."

Papa put a foot on the bottom step, then stopped. "Is your brother on his way?"

"He left school with Sam Willis. He said you knew."

"Hmmm ... maybe he did mention that." Papa shook his head and started up the steps. "But I thought he was going to help me out," he said.

They found Mamma in the kitchen, wrapping the parcel for Annie's mother. "Those clouds worry me," she said. "I don't want you girls to be caught in a downpour."

"The rain won't come for a while yet, ma'am," Annie assured her. "It won't take long to get to our place."

"And your father will bring Lucy back in the wagon?"

"Yes, ma'am. He said so this morning." Annie took the parcel Mamma had fixed. "Thank you, ma'am. Ma will surely appreciate it."

"Maggie," Papa called from upstairs. "Come show me where you want these!"

"You girls be careful," she said, before she hurried up the stairs.

Lucy opened the door for Annie.

Joseph was outside, peering in through the window. "Is Papa home?"

"Yes. He's upstairs," she answered.

"And Mamma?"

"She's helping him with the shelves," Lucy said. "I thought you were going to the stable."

Joseph stepped forward to take the door before Lucy shut it. "I just needed something," he said. "See you later!"

"See you," Lucy said. Across the street, she saw Sam. He was in the shadow of the post office, but he was watching. Something was not right.

As they walked, Annie chattered away about all the things she wanted to show Lucy at her house. "We have kittens," she said. "And Mazie, our cow, had twins this spring. They're the cutest things!"

At the edge of town, the girls passed the Lawrence cemetery. They paused, and Lucy looked over the low stone wall. The flowers had wilted on Nathan Burris' small grave. "Poor little thing," Annie said. "Third baby this spring to die of measles." Nearly thirty stones marked the resting places of those who had not survived their first year in Kansas. Each one had left a family grieving. The thought of a stone with the name Thomkins made Lucy shudder.

Just outside town, the road turned to enter the wooded area along the river. Lucy thought about all the tales the boys at school told of Indians hiding outside of town to ambush settlers. They were just boy-tales and not true, but she still felt nervous. These woods could hold all kinds of secrets.

As they walked the three miles to Annie's house, the woods deepened. In several clearings, a few logs indicated the beginnings of new cabins. As they passed the fourth one, Lucy asked, "Are you getting new neighbors?"

"No." They went closer, and Annie pointed at the logs. "See

the moss on them? Some men set those out last summer and never came back."

"Did the Ruffians scare them away?"

Annie laughed. "They *are* Ruffians. They never wanted to live here. They just set out the claim and then rode back to Missouri."

"Why would they do that?"

"To keep Free State settlers out."

In the distance, thunder rumbled. Lucy looked up at the sky. "How much farther?"

"Oh, it's right up ahead." Annie followed some wagon ruts that veered off the road, but no house sat in the clearing. The girls walked around a grassy mound of earth. Something stuck out of the top of it. Was it a stovepipe? On the other side of the mound was the strangest thing Lucy had ever seen. The back side of the mound was cut away, and a house was dug out of it. The front wall was chinked logs with a door and one window. The grass-covered top of the mound served as the roof of the house. The sod roof extended from the front of the house on the right side of the door to make a kind of shed to hold a plow and a few other tools. The house was completely hidden from the road.

Behind the window, a checkered curtain moved, and a face appeared behind the glass. The door opened, and a woman with gray-streaked blonde hair stepped back to let them enter. "You must be Lucy! Annie's told me all about you!" Mrs. Jacob's blue eyes squinted when she smiled.

Annie held out the parcel. "Lucy's ma sent some flour and sugar," she said.

Mrs. Jacob took the package and turned to Lucy. "She's a generous woman. Please tell her I'm much obliged."

"Yes, ma'am, I will."

Mrs. Jacob opened the corner of the parcel. "White flour! We haven't had white flour in ages. That will make some fine biscuits. Annie, go out and get some wood for the fire." Annie went out to the woodpile, and Mrs. Jacob took the flour and sugar to a small wooden pantry near the stove.

The only light in the room came from the one window. As her eyes adjusted, Lucy looked around. The room was about twenty feet wide and went back about ten or twelve feet from the front wall. A cookstove, a table, two beds, and a few chairs filled the room, leaving little space to walk between the furniture. Wood planks were set into the dirt floor, and three walls were bare earth. Overhead, logs served as rafters to support the sod roof, and several vertical poles around the room helped hold them up. A garden hoe leaned against a wall. Why would they have a hoe inside the house? A damp and earthy smell settled into everything.

After Mrs. Jacob put away the flour and sugar, she stepped across the room and opened the lid of a trunk. "I can see why you chose this blue calico," she said, as she pulled the new dress out of the trunk and held it up to Lucy's shoulders. "It brings out the roses in your cheeks! You'll catch some young man's eye."

Lucy smiled. "That's what Papa said, too. I'll just be glad to get rid of this dress I brought from Pennsylvania."

Mrs. Jacob looked down at Lucy's dress. "I'm sure it was pretty before you came out here. Slip out of it and try this on. Careful of the pins, now."

Mrs. Jacob helped Lucy out of her dress and lifted the new dress up so Lucy could slip it over her head. The calico felt rough on her skin, but it was better than the ragged gown she'd worn all these months. The memory of trying on that blue dress in Grandfather's house was so different from this moment. Back then, she could never have imagined what she had been through the past four months.

Lucy's conscience poked at her, along with the pins in the dress. She had been stubborn, refusing to wear a dress of Mamma's. And now when Mamma had no time to sew, she was getting a brand new dress that Mamma had to pay someone else to make.

Mrs. Jacob pinned the back opening, then pinched the seams along the sides of the dress, pinning the fabric to make the dress fit closely, but not too tight. "I'll leave some extra in the seams so your ma can let it out later if you need more room."

Mrs. Jacob's fingers along the side seams tickled a little, but Lucy stood still. "Thank you, Mrs. Jacob. I'd like this dress to last a while."

As Lucy looked around the house, all her complaints about the hardships of their life in Kansas pricked at her, too. The mostly dirt floor, the damp smell of the earthen walls, the way Annie's mother looked at white flour as a luxury … Lucy had never even considered how the settlers outside of town lived.

Annie came in with firewood as Mrs. Jacob was pinning the sleeve hems. "Pa's coming up the road," she announced.

"Tell him to wait outside a minute while Lucy changes into her other dress."

Annie went back out as a horse and wagon clattered into the yard. Mrs. Jacob folded the unfinished dress carefully and put it back into the trunk, then helped Lucy fasten the hooks of her old dress. A loud crack of thunder rattled the window.

"Good heavens!" Mrs. Jacob said. "That was close!"

The door swung open, and Annie ran in, followed by her father. He dropped a cloth sack next to the door and leaned his rifle against the wall next to it. A few drops of rain fell from his thick beard onto his rough homespun shirt. "Whew! That's gonna be a toad strangler!" He shook the rain off his leather hat and tossed it onto the table.

"Oh, dear," Mrs. Jacob said. "Lucy was just ready to go home."

"I believe we'll have to wait a little while," he said, "but I got some squirrels. We can eat first, then I'll take her to town. I'll start the fire for you."

"Lucy brought us some flour. I'll make some dumplings for our stew. You girls can cut some vegetables while I skin the squirrels."

Mr. Jacob soon had the fire going, and he put a pot of water on top of the stove to heat. He lit two oil lamps to brighten the room. The rain was falling hard now. Annie set out some potatoes and carrots on top of the oilcloth covered table. She handed Lucy a paring knife, but glanced up at the ceiling. Lucy looked up, too, but didn't see anything there.

Mrs. Jacob came in with chunks of meat on a wooden chopping board. Lucy was glad Mrs. Jacob had cleaned the squirrels outdoors. Butchering was a chore she would rather not watch. Mrs. Jacob heated fat in a skillet and began to fry the meat. Outside, the rain came down harder. Lucy continued to cut up potatoes, until she saw Annie drop her knife and lunge to grab a bucket.

"Here it comes!" Annie said. "Lucy, get that wash pan!"

"Why?" Lucy had no more than asked the question when she knew the answer. Muddy water began running in streams through the ceiling and dripping onto the furniture and the floor. Mr. Jacob pulled tarps over the beds. Everyone grabbed a tub, pan, or basin to catch the muddy water. Lucy glanced at the trunk that held her new dress. Small wood blocks held it off the floor, and the lid seemed to be keeping the water out. When she looked at the ceiling above the trunk though, something long and black hung from it. Was that a vine hanging from the ceiling? She took a step nearer, just in time to see it fall onto the top of the trunk, then slither onto the muddy floor. Lucy screamed.

As the shape disappeared under the chair, Mr. Jacob grabbed the hoe that leaned against the wall, moved the chair aside with one hand and swung the hoe in an arc, all in one smooth motion. With a thud, the excitement was over. Mr. Jacob took the dead snake outside. Lucy sank onto a chair.

"It's okay now." Annie patted Lucy's shoulder. "It was just a bull snake, not a rattler." Lucy gasped as Annie continued. "I nearly jumped out of my skin the first time that happened. One thing about life in a dugout house – it's never dull."

In a few minutes, Lucy calmed down. When the storm ended, they emptied the pots and pans outside, then replaced the pans to catch the water that still dripped from the ceiling. The water in the kettle on the stove boiled, and before long Mrs. Jacob served up a pot of bubbling squirrel stew with dumplings. Mr. Jacob began, "Lord, we thank you for the bounty of our table …" A horse whinnied outside. Mr. Jacob got up from the table and looked out the window. "Joel Grover," he announced, and went out the door.

Lucy, Annie, and Mrs. Jacob began to eat as the men talked outside. The rider left, and Mr. Jacob returned. "I have to go," he told his wife, as he put on his hat.

"What about Lucy?" Mrs. Jacob asked.

"I'll take her home in the morning. Joel will let her folks know."

"Is it safe to do this now, John?" Mrs. Jacob asked. Mr. Jacob glanced across the table at Lucy, then back at his wife.

"Is it ever safe?" He picked up his gun on his way out the door. The horse's harness jingled, and the wagon clattered down the road.

They finished their meal, and Mrs. Jacob spooned the

leftover stew into a smaller pan that she covered and placed back on the stove to keep warm until Mr. Jacob returned – whenever that would be. By the time the dishes were washed, Lucy was exhausted. The walk from town, the rain, the snake …

"I think we're all about ready for bed," Mrs. Jacob said. "Annie will make room for you in hers."

"Come on, Lucy. I'll show you where our outhouse is." They went out, and Annie led Lucy around the side of the house. When they came back in, Mrs. Jacob held out a slightly tattered nightdress. "You can sleep in this, Lucy. We'll leave the coals going in the stove to keep the damp out. Thank goodness we got the tarps pulled over the beds before they got wet."

Lucy made Annie inspect the bedding. When Lucy was certain that no snakes were there first, she and Annie settled under the quilts. As Lucy closed her eyes, Mrs. Jacob nodded in her chair by the oil lamp, facing the front window.

14

I have spent a great portion of my time on this way, & have brought away from Mo. fourteen, including one unbroken family of which I feel rather proud & very thankful that I have been able to do so much good for the oppressed, & so much harm to the oppressors. At some future time I will write you some extract, from my diary, which I think will interest you for we have had many hairbreadth escapes, considerable fighting & some interesting conversation.

–John E. Stewart, Kansas settler

The house was dark when Lucy awoke, but a harness jangled outside. Mr. Jacob must be back. Mrs. Jacob lit the lamp and went out. Voices murmured outdoors, but Lucy stayed in the warm bed with Annie's steady, deep breathing beside her. The storm had passed, and moonlight filtered through the window, first bright, then fading as clouds lingered in the night sky. Mrs. Jacob's dark silhouette came in, crossed the room, took the stew kettle from the stove and went out again. A few minutes later, both of Annie's parents came in, extinguished the lamp, and settled into their own bed.

All was quiet, but Lucy could not go back to sleep. The longer she lay there, the more she needed to go to the outhouse. The bed was warm; the night was cool and damp. Surely she could wait until morning. No, she just couldn't. Soft snores came from across the room. She was the only one awake. She slid out from under the blanket and shivered. She put her feet into her shoes and laced them loosely. She would be quick about it. She opened the door as quietly as she could and slipped outside.

The moon was shrouded in clouds, but it cast enough glow to outline the shape of the open-sided shed to her left.

The leaves whispered in the cool night breeze. Lucy remembered the story of *Young Goodman Brown* that Miss Kellogg had read yesterday from Hawthorne's *Twice Told Tales*. Old Scratch with his walking stick that wriggled like a snake. No – it was a silly thought. There were no demons in these woods. But …

The outhouse had seemed just a few steps from the house when she was with Annie. Now it felt like miles. She hurried down the path, glancing nervously around her for moving shadows. She relieved herself quickly in the outhouse. As she stepped out, she held onto the door so it wouldn't close with a bang.

When she stepped around the corner of the shed, she was aware of eyes on her. Someone was near, watching her. "Annie?"

Quick breathing. More than one person breathing. A whimper. One of Annie's kittens? No. The breathing stopped. Lucy held her breath, too. The whimper again, but this time muffled. The breeze blew the clouds aside, and moonlight illuminated the shed and its occupants.

They huddled against the back of the shed: a man, a woman, and a baby. Even in the moonlight, their dark faces were barely visible, their clothing all black. The woman pulled the baby close to muffle its cries. Lucy froze.

The woman's eyes met hers. Lucy looked at the baby, but the woman turned away, as though to hide it. Whittier's line, *Mothers from their children riven*, came to her, as though whispered.

The man straightened and stepped forward in front of his family. He stood directly in front of Lucy, his gaze steady.

Her tongue felt wooden. She couldn't speak. She backed away from them toward the door. So this was Annie's secret. The puzzling looks at the dinner table, the sudden departure of Annie's father. Lucy was never supposed to know, but now she did. She slipped back into the house and carefully felt her way through the dark to the bed. It was warm there, but she still trembled.

Eventually, sleep overtook her, and Lucy's troubled dreams filled with sounds and images. Horses. A wagon. Voices. Clouded moonlight. Indians darting between the trees. Snakes.

"Hey, sleepyhead." Annie stood next to her. "Wake up." Sunlight streamed in the window, and something sizzled in a pan on the stove. "Pa wants to take you home right after breakfast. He's outside now, so you can get dressed."

Lucy blinked and sat up. "Last night … I …"

"Whew, that snake was a whopper, wasn't he?" Annie whistled. "We don't usually see them that big, even in the summer."

"No … I saw … outside …" She stopped.

"What?" Annie looked at her curiously.

What had she seen? Was it real? Had she dreamed it? "Nothing. Just crazy dreams, that's all." She shook her head, wishing she could shake the images from her brain. She wiggled out of the borrowed nightdress and reached for her old blue dress. Annie fastened the hooks for her.

"Breakfast is ready." Mrs. Jacob scooped some fried potatoes from a skillet onto tin plates. "Pa needs to get to town early today, so you girls eat quick now."

Annie took a plate and passed one to Lucy. "Can I go to town with Pa and Lucy?"

"Pa will get Lucy home," her mother said. "You have chores here."

Mrs. Jacob did not offer anything besides the potatoes, but they were fragrant with chopped onion, and the warmth helped quiet Lucy's uneasy stomach.

Mr. Jacob pushed the door open and stuck his head inside. "The team is hitched and ready to go," he announced. "Let's get you home, Lucy."

Annie and Mrs. Jacob walked out to the wagon with them. As they left the house, Lucy glanced into the shed. It looked just the same as it had yesterday afternoon. There was no clue that anyone had been there.

Mr. Jacob helped Lucy into the wagon bed. "Road might be rough from that storm. You'll be safer back here."

"I'll have your dress ready in a few days," Mrs. Jacob said.

"See you later, Lucy." Annie waved as the wagon pulled away.

They rode for a few minutes in silence, until Lucy was brave enough to ask the question that burned in her brain. "Were there people at the house last night?"

"Mighty stormy night for callers." He held the reins loosely and looked back at her. "Why? You expecting somebody?"

"No, sir, but I …" She looked at his face for his reaction. "I went to the outhouse, and someone was in the shed."

He laughed. "You had some powerful dream, didn't you?" The horses hurried their steps. "That old bull snake gave you enough of a fright to set you to mumbling all night. I expect you saw all kinds of things in your sleep, and I wouldn't blame you a bit." He cleared his throat. "No, there wasn't anyone around our place last night. I'd have seen them when I came in."

Was it just a dream? She was nervous when she went to the outhouse. Had she imagined it? When the wagon stopped in front of the store, Mr. Jacob got off and offered his hand to help her. As she stepped down, she felt a tug and heard a rip. The back of her dress was caught on a nail on the wagon. How much more could this poor dress endure?

When Lucy pulled her dress free, she saw something else: a damp shred of black fabric caught on the same nail. She yanked it loose and hid it in her fist.

Mamma stepped out of the door and came to put her arms around Lucy. "Thank you for keeping her through the storm, Mr. Jacob."

"No trouble. She had a scare last night and maybe a bad

dream or two, but I expect she'll tell you about it." He climbed back on the wagon and snapped the reins. He touched his hat and nodded in their direction, then clattered down the street.

Lucy followed Mamma through the door, but glanced down at the scrap of black cloth in her hand.

All day it troubled her. She couldn't get it out of her brain. The images in the dark, the faces, the child held half-hidden.

By the time she retreated to her room that night, Lucy was certain: Her experience last night was no dream.

She sat at her desk and picked up the book Miss Kellogg had lent her. The ribbon still marked the page with the line she had remembered: *Mothers from their children riven.*

She turned pages, finding one disturbing title after another: *The Hunters of Men, Clerical Oppressors, The Christian Slave,* and finally, *The Farewell.*

> *Gone, gone – sold and gone,*
> *To the rice-swamp dank and lone …*

She skimmed ahead to the next stanza, with the same repeating lines:

> *Gone, gone – sold and gone,*
> *To the rice-swamp dank and lone,*
> *There no mother's eye is near them,*
> *There no mother's ear can hear them;*
> *Never, when the torturing lash*
> *Seams their back with many a gash,*
> *Shall a mother's kindness bless them,*
> *Or a mother's arms caress them …*

Lucy opened her journal and struggled to write the words as quickly as they came to her.

The Empty Cradle

A mother cries out, "My poor babe, he is gone!
Carried by angels who took him away."
His fever is past, his suffering done,
Her prayers cannot alter the course of the day.
A stone marks the spot where he's laid to his rest,
A holy man brushes the dirt from his hands.
"Ashes to ashes" the grave has been blessed,
"Twas God's will to take him to Heavenly lands."

Another cries out, "My poor babe, he is gone!
Stolen by strangers who took him away."
His past life is gone, suff'ring only begun.
Her pleas cannot alter the course of this day.
No one will tell where his home will be next,
The slave master totals the cash in his hands.
"Owner to owner," he tells the unblest,
"Twas business to send him to work other lands."

Two mothers are grieving for babies the same,
Two tragedies: one tale of death, one of shame.

15

Arrangements having been made by the citizens of Lawrence to celebrate the coming 4th of July, notice is hereby given that the procession ... will march at ten o'clock ... to Clinton Park, where the Declaration of Independence will be read, an oration delivered, &c. At the close of the exercises, the procession will march to Pleasant Grove, where a public dinner will be served up.

—Kansas Free State, July 2, 1855

On the third of July, Lawrence buzzed with activity. All along Massachusetts Street, business owners draped bunting of red, white, and blue across the fronts of their buildings. Mamma propped the front door open with a wooden crate, hoping to lure a bit of breeze inside, despite the dust it would bring with it.

Lucy watched through the window as Papa and Joseph nailed the striped fabric to drape in swags along the porch rail. The school term had ended on the last day of June, but Lucy would rather have been in school than stuck in the store, checking each task off Mamma's long list. She had already wiped dust from every glass lamp chimney on the shelf, and now Mamma had her washing the front windows for the third time.

Even this activity did not block out the images of the past few days: the dark figures in the shed, the muffled cry of the baby. They echoed in her room at night; they crept into the space behind her thoughts as she worked in the store. The scrap of black fabric lay tucked away in her bureau drawer.

More than anything, she wanted to talk to Annie. *Slave stealers.* That's what the proslavery papers called people like Annie's parents. Helping slaves escape was dangerous. It was illegal. She thought of all the times Annie had stopped herself in mid-sentence. The times she looked away and made excuses.

She needed Annie to tell her the truth. But then what? What would she do about it?

Mr. Winston's wagon stopped in front of the store. He called to Papa and pointed to a box in the bed of his wagon.

Papa picked it up and brought it through the front door. "Here's some more merchandise for you, Maggie. Winston brought it up from the levee." He hoisted the box onto the back counter, and it landed with a heavy thump. Joseph came in behind him, carrying the hammer.

Mamma examined the label on the box. "Oh, my! I'd begun to think we wouldn't have this in time."

Joseph used the claws of the hammer to pry the lid loose. Mamma eagerly dug through shredded paper to reveal glass jars and tubes.

Lucy gasped and stepped closer to the box. "Jewels?"

Mamma laughed. "Almost." She gently lifted a glass tube

and removed the cork. "Glass trade beads. Hold out your hand." Mamma poured some of the beads into Lucy's palm. The tiny beads gleamed like pearls.

Joseph snorted. "Who's going to buy things like that out here?"

"The Indians will," Mamma said. "They decorate their clothes with them. I hear the women will gladly trade skins and garden vegetables for nice beads."

"Well, I'm not doing business with any Indians," Joseph said. "Sam says the Indians only come to town to steal and spy on us and to kidnap white babies."

No one said anything for a few seconds. Lucy looked up from the beads. The silence made Joseph blush. He scowled and crossed his arms.

Papa laid a firm hand on Joseph's shoulder. "I won't hear that talk. The tribes in our area are peaceful. They farm and hunt nearby and come to town to trade for supplies. We will do fair business with anyone who comes into this store."

"But Sam says …"

Papa interrupted him. "Samuel Willis needs some lessons in respect. If *you* need a lesson, I can supply one."

Lucy knew that tone. Papa meant it, and Joseph knew it, too.

He shrugged off Papa's hand and walked to the door. "I'll be back later."

"Joseph!" Mamma called after him. But Joseph was already halfway across the street. He and Samuel ducked around the side of the post office and disappeared.

Mamma shook her head. "I don't know why he spends so much time with that Willis boy. I'm sure they are up to no good."

Papa picked up the hammer from the table. "He wants to earn money by working at the stable, but Wyman says he can only pay for one stable hand."

Mamma wrinkled her nose. "From the smell of his clothes, he's doing his share of shoveling manure."

"That doesn't mean he's making any of the money. Wyman doesn't think Samuel is sharing any of the wages."

Mamma frowned. "Then why on earth does he keep going back?"

Papa shrugged. "To work with the horses, I guess."

Lucy held her tongue. Sam Willis had more in mind than help at the stable. He was still pestering Joseph about Papa's Sharps rifle. Joseph had been acting so sneaky lately that Lucy suspected he had already taken the gun at least a few times without asking. She thought of telling Papa, but it was still just suspicion. "Let's look at the rest of the beads," she said.

Mamma brightened and held out the tube so Lucy could pour the beads she held into it. "Yes, let's see what else is here." One by one, they lifted the tubes and bottles from the box. Some of the beads were as large as peas, others were as small as mustard seeds. They arranged them on the counter, and Lucy admired the iridescent shades of blue, pink, green, and yellow.

"Dr. Robinson has invited the Delaware and Shawnee to the celebration tomorrow," Papa said. "Maybe they will come into the store."

Lucy frowned. "Why don't we just close the store tomorrow?" she asked. "Other businesses are taking the day off."

"That's exactly why we can't close," Mamma said. "It will be our busiest day! Besides, maybe some Indians will come in."

Lucy heard Grandfather's voice in her head. "Savages," he had called them. Would they wear paint and feathers? "Do they speak English?"

Papa smiled. "Whether they do or not, I'm sure your mother will find a way to do business."

Mamma laughed. "That I will! Lucy, find some pretty bowls and make a display by the window. In the sunshine, these beads will sparkle like diamonds. I was hesitant to spend the money for them, but now I have a feeling it will be a good investment."

Lucy found some clear glass bowls and arranged them on a table where they could catch the afternoon sun. She was pouring the colored beads into the bowls when Mr. Jacob's wagon stopped in front of the store.

As her father tied the horses, Annie jumped from the wagon. She carried a bundle under her arm and waved at Lucy through the window. "I have your dress!"

Lucy met her at the door. She unfolded the dress and held it up. "Come upstairs with me while I try it on!"

Annie looked at her father. He nodded, and Lucy led the

way to the stairs. This would give them the chance to talk. But how would she start that conversation?

Annie chattered away as they climbed the steps. "Ma added some lace at the neck. She thought you'd like it. She worked extra hard to have it ready for you in time for the picnic tomorrow."

Lucy knew the adults could still hear them. "Won't everyone be surprised to see me in something new?" She led the way into her room and closed the door behind them.

Annie helped Lucy with the hooks on her blue dress, and Lucy stepped out of it and laid it on the bed.

"With the buttons on the front, I can get dressed easier now." Lucy pulled the new dress over her head, inhaling the fresh smell of the new fabric. She looked down as she pushed the buttons through the button holes on the front of the dress. She twisted a little to see the back of the dress. The hem brushed her legs a bit above her ankle.

"Ma made it a little shorter, just so it wouldn't pick up so much dirt."

Lucy turned to face Annie. "What do you think?"

"You look like a real Kansas girl, Lucy."

Lucy looked in the cloudy mirror over the bureau. *A real Kansas girl.* Hadn't she been a real Kansas girl for the past three months?

When Lucy turned, Annie was holding the old blue gown. "What will you do with this old dress?" she asked.

"That poor thing. Probably throw it away."

"Won't you be a little sorry to let it go?" Annie touched a frayed silk flounce. "It's kind of like a part of you. From your life before Kansas."

Lucy remembered the day Mamma had given it to her. It seemed like a million years ago, like another girl who had hidden in the dining room, crying. Another girl who had complained to Eliza about not having freedom. She wasn't that girl anymore.

"Lucy?" Annie touched her shoulder. "Are you all right?"

Lucy sat on the edge of the bed next to Annie. "I know about the slaves."

The dress slipped from Annie's hands. She bent quickly and picked it up. "What slaves?"

"The ones at your house. I went to the outhouse while you were asleep. I saw them hiding in the shed."

"Oh, Lucy, you're so funny!" Annie giggled, but her eyes searched Lucy's. "You just had a dream. You were pretty shook up."

"No, it was real." Lucy opened the bureau drawer and reached in. She found the scrap of black fabric she had pulled from the wagon and held it out.

"Oh, glory …" Annie's voice changed to a whisper. "Did you tell anyone?"

"No. I had to talk to you about it."

"You can't tell, Lucy. It'd cause such an awful lot of trouble. The Liberty Line is the only hope the slaves have." She looked into Lucy's eyes. "And Pa … they would hang him if they knew."

"No, Annie. The slave laws are harsh, but they couldn't hang him."

Annie nodded. "Pa says the new legislature's making its own laws now – laws for the Territory."

Lucy shook her head. "They can't do that! That's why we elected the Free State men to go to Pawnee for us. They won't let them make laws like that."

Annie looked anxiously at the door. "Shhh!" she whispered. "Pa says they threw the Free Staters out, Lucy. The folks who work for the Liberty Line risk everything now. *Everything*. Promise me you won't tell. I'll do anything if you'll only promise."

Lucy bit her bottom lip. She thought of Eliza. Thought of that family in the shed at Annie's house. Thought of the poems. Mr. Brown said she was just a child. Miss Collins said words without actions were just noise. Miss Kellogg told her to find out what she really stood for, and now, right at this moment she knew. "Let me help."

"What? You can't! It's too risky."

"I don't care. I want to be part of the Liberty Line."

Annie shook her head. "No. You can't."

"What do you mean, I can't?" Now Lucy's pride stung. "I want to help!"

"Sshh!" Annie scowled. "Hush … just be quiet."

"But I want to help them," Lucy whispered.

"Why?" Annie asked.

"Miss Kellogg gave me a book. It's a book about slavery, and I …"

Annie stood in front of Lucy's desk. "A book? Do you think

171

this is some adventure story?"

"No. It's just that I never really understood it before."

"And you think you can understand it from a book?"

Lucy reached for Annie's hand. "Please let me do something."

Annie frowned and pulled away. "I can't."

"Why not?"

"Because the Liberty Line doesn't need people who want to fight the idea of slavery. It's about real people."

"But, Annie …"

"Don't, Lucy." She paused and took a deep breath. "I have to tell Pa you know. I'll tell him you want to help and see what he says. Until then, you have to promise me you won't tell anybody. Not Miss Kellogg. Not even your ma or pa."

"I promise."

Annie brushed past her and hurried through the door. Lucy followed her down the stairs.

Mr. Jacob was still talking to Mamma and Papa when the girls came down the stairs. "Yep, word is that they threw the Free Staters out of the legislature in the first half-hour. A bunch of Ruffians had been staying up nights with jugs of bootleg whiskey and the Missouri legal code, crossing out 'State of Missouri,' and writing in 'Territory of Kansas.' Day after to-morrow, it'll be a crime to even carry a Free State newspaper under your arm."

Mamma's worried look gave way to a smile when she saw Lucy in her new dress.

"Look at you!" Mamma held Lucy at arms' length to inspect

her head to toe. "You look like a different girl!"

"I told her she looks like a Kansas girl now," Annie said. She smiled, but didn't look directly at Lucy.

"That's it, exactly," said Papa. "You look like a Kansas girl, Lucy Cat."

Mr. Jacob put his hat on and moved toward the door. "We've taken enough of your time, Mr. and Mrs. Thomkins. We'd best be going home, Annie."

"Wait!" Mamma said. "Don't forget the material for your dress, Annie." Mamma had already tied the fabric and notions into a bundle with string. "I put five yards of muslin in along with the calico, too. Tell your mother I'm grateful for her work on Lucy's dress."

Annie took the bundle. "Thank you, Mrs. Thomkins."

While Mr. Jacob untied the horses, Annie leaned close to Lucy's ear. "Remember your promise." She climbed up on the wagon, next to her father.

Lucy nodded, then waved goodbye as the wagon clattered away.

After dinner, Mamma took Lucy's old blue gown from the bed. "I can't think of a thing we could use this for," she said. "I guess I could give it to the quilt circle ladies at the church. They might be able to use some pieces from it."

"Can I keep it?" Lucy asked.

Mamma looked surprised. "Why do you want to keep it?"

"I don't really know." Lucy reached for the dress. "I just have a feeling that I may need it for something. Isn't that funny?"

"Yes, but we women learn to trust our intuition." Mamma spread the dress on the bed. "You really should mend it and wash it before you put it away, though."

That night, Lucy found thread in Mamma's sewing basket. It seemed like a lifetime ago that she had sat in Grandmother's sewing room and complained about her "cruel" needlework. On that day, she had been sure that if she ever escaped Grandmother's tedious embroidery she would never willingly pick up a needle again. How wrong she had been. Wrong about so many things.

Stitches

A simple thread, a single strand
Pulled by a needle, pulled by a hand.
A bit of floss can mend a tear.
A garment mended, ready to wear.

An easy task to mend a rip,
Till fingers fumble and needles slip.
Then blood may stain and make us ask,
"Must mending be a painful task?"

Our land is torn by hate and strife,
And blood pulled forth by gun and knife.
If Kansas is the cloak we wear,
Is blood required to mend the tear?

16

Choose ye this day which you shall serve, *Freedom or Slavery*, and then be true to your choice. I seem to hear the millions of freemen and the millions of bondmen in our own land, the millions of the oppressed in other lands, the patriots and philanthropists of all countries, the spirits of the Revolutionary heroes, and the voice of God—all saying to the people of Kansas "Do your duty."

–Dr. Charles Robinson, July 4, 1855

Lucy awoke to the sound of gunfire. Border Ruffians! Had they discovered the slave stealers? She sprang from her bed and ran into the hall, where she collided with Papa.

"I heard guns outside," she said.

"Some of our neighbors are firing blanks to celebrate," Papa said. "Happy Independence Day, Lucy Cat."

Lucy ran to the window. On the street below, men were greeting each other with shouts of "Ho to Kansas!" and "Liberty for all!"

Today she would wear the dress of a Kansas girl, but had she changed on the inside from the Pennsylvania girl she had been? Would Annie and her father trust her to help with the

Liberty Line?

Joseph was at the breakfast table when Lucy entered the kitchen. "I don't want to work today," he said to Mamma. "I want to see the parade and go to the picnic."

"The parade will pass by our front door," Mamma said. "We'll watch it from here. Then we'll close the store while we go to the picnic. You won't miss anything."

Joseph frowned. "It's not fair. Everyone else gets the day off."

"I don't get the day off," said Papa. "I have to march in the parade in this infernal wool jacket and listen to all the speeches of the day." Papa had on his new Lawrence Defensibles uniform. The stiff black jacket, with its high collar and double row of brass buttons, made Papa stand tall. Despite his complaints, he looked distinguished and proud in his uniform, and he was clearly excited about the parade.

"Hurry and eat," Mamma said. "We have work to do before the festivities today."

"Sorry, Maggie." Papa held a can of gun oil and a rag. "I need to clean my rifle then join the militia by the levee." He sat down in his chair and inspected the rifle. "I can't believe I put this gun away without cleaning it. I always clean it."

Lucy kicked Joseph under the table. He pushed a forkful of eggs in his mouth and looked back at her.

Mamma had her back to them. "It's been busy the last few days," she said. "You were probably distracted when you came in and just forgot."

Papa shook his head. "I suppose it's possible, but I thought I had made more cartridges after our last practice."

When he was finally satisfied with the condition of the rifle, Papa rose. "Well, I need to go. We have parade practice before everyone else arrives to line up."

"I'm going, too!" Joseph said, jumping up from his chair.

"No, you don't!" Mamma pointed at the broom. "You will sweep the store from back to front."

"Awww, I hate sweeping."

"And you'll do it carefully this time," Mamma added, "sweeping the dust out the door instead of stirring up a whirlwind and just spreading it all over the place."

Mamma knew him so well. Lucy hid a snicker behind her napkin, but that didn't escape Mamma's notice, either.

"And don't think that you're getting off easy, young lady," she said. "I promised to make cakes for the picnic, so I'll need your help in the store while I cook." The teakettle on the stove rattled as the water began to boil. "Good. The water's hot, so you can start by washing the dishes while I set up the ledgers for today. It's going to be busy, I just know it!" Mamma's voice trailed off as she bustled out of the kitchen.

Joseph smirked at her. "Yeah, *Lucy Cat*, get started on those dishes. I'll be long gone before you get out of here today."

Lucy rose from the table and picked up a towel to hold the teakettle handle as she poured hot water into the dishpan. "Sam Willis is going to get you into trouble."

He brought his plate over. "Mind your own business, and

I'll mind mine."

"Does your business have something to do with Papa's dirty gun?"

He set the plate down. "He just forgot to clean it last time, that's all."

"We both know that's not true." Lucy dropped the silverware into the hot water. "If Papa finds out …"

"What are you going to tell him? You don't know anything."

"I know that I don't trust Samuel Willis. He is only interested in himself."

"Sam knows a lot more than you do about who to trust in this town. It's your friend who's going to get you into trouble." He picked up the broom and walked out.

He was right, of course. She didn't have any proof about the gun, only suspicion. And Joseph was only repeating Samuel's suspicions about Annie, but he was right about *that*, too. And he didn't know the half of it. More secrets.

Mamma was right to expect a crowd in the store. It was all they could do to keep up, especially while Mamma hurried between the sales counter and the kitchen where she was preparing the cakes. Joseph and Lucy weighed flour, counted out hinges and door knobs, and measured cloth for people they'd never met in town before. It seemed that everyone was in Lawrence this morning, and they all needed supplies.

By ten o'clock, a crowd stretched all along both sides of Massachusetts Street to watch the parade. Mamma had Joseph take crocks of peppermint sticks and lemon drops out to the front porch to sell. It wasn't long before Sam showed up, and whenever Mamma turned her back, the two boys snitched bits of candies for themselves.

A cheer rose from the direction of the levee, and the parade was underway. The first rider sat atop a beautiful black horse and carried the flag of the United States. The crowd cheered as the red and white stripes and thirty-one stars waved proudly. How long would it be before more stars appeared on the flag, including one for Kansas?

The flag was followed by more riders, including dignitaries of Lawrence like Reverend Snyder, Mr. Babcock, and Dr. Robinson. Lawrence's band marched behind them, accompanied by the drum and bugle corps from Fort Riley. As they came nearer, Lucy caught her breath and felt her heart join in time with the drums' heavy beat. Samuel let out a whistle so loud Lucy winced and clapped her hands over her ears.

Mamma emerged from the store and stood next to Lucy just as the militia units passed. The Kansas Sharp Shooters came first, followed by the Lawrence Defensibles. Both units carried Sharps rifles on their shoulders as they marched by in perfect rank and file. Lucy pointed at the end of the third row. "Look! There's Papa!" Lucy waved, and Papa winked in her direction.

Families of settlers followed the militia. They rode in wagons decorated with wildflowers and banners.

A delicious smell came from the door behind them. "My cakes!" Mamma gasped, and hurried back inside.

A little boy near Lucy pointed down the street and tugged

his father's shirt. "Look, Pa!" he said. "Indians!"

The man looked up and said, "Yes, Delaware."

The Delaware men wore cloth shirts and leather breeches with fringe on the sides. Some had feathers tied in their hair, standing up from the backs of their heads. Their chief rode tall on a horse at the front of the procession, his feathered headdress flowing down his back. The men who followed him rode their horses in crisscrossed lines, the horses wild-eyed and stomping impatiently when reined back. Even in the gaiety of the parade, they looked fierce. Lucy rubbed prickly goose bumps from her arms, despite the warmth of the morning. Two wagons followed, with Delaware women in long wrap skirts and cotton blouses and children in clothes of leather or cotton.

Someone identified the next group as Shawnee. Like the Delaware, the men on horses were arrayed with feathers. They wore ornate necklaces of beads and animal claws. Some of the younger men wore little more than breechcloths. The women and children on the wagons behind them were dressed in clothing of muslin and brightly-colored calicoes, and many of the women wore necklaces with strands of beads and silver disks. Except for their jewelry, they were dressed like most of the women and children in Lawrence. Lucy glanced through the window behind her at the display of colorful beads and imagined an Indian family shopping in the store. What if a young man in a breechcloth came in?

After the Indians passed, spectators filled the street and followed the procession to the park for the speeches. Sam jumped down from the porch, landing on both feet in the dust. Joseph bent his knees and prepared to jump next, but Lucy grabbed the back of his shirt. "Oh, no, you're not going anywhere." He pulled to get away from her just as Mamma came back out to the porch.

"Stop that, both of you!" she scolded. "Come inside if you can't behave."

Lucy went to help Mamma in the kitchen. "The cakes smell wonderful."

"I barely saved them," Mamma said. "One was a little scorched on the edge. I've set them out to cool. By the time the men are finished with their speeches everyone will be nearly starved. We'll catch up with Papa at the picnic. Can you look for a basket to carry them? Joseph –" But Joseph had already vanished.

Mamma shook her head. "He wasn't helping, anyway. I'll pack some dishes for us to take to the picnic."

Lucy searched under the counter for a basket, but looked up when she heard voices. An Indian woman – one of the Shawnee from the parade – stood near the door with a boy who looked about Lucy's age. His dark hair was parted in the center and covered the bottom of his ears. He wore a muslin shirt, brown trousers, and moccasins. The woman carried a large cloth bundle, and the boy held several animal skins. Lucy looked back at the kitchen door, but Mamma had not seen their customers. Could she do this by herself?

"Hello," Lucy greeted them, hoping they would understand.

"Can I help you?"

The woman nodded, then set her basket on the counter. "You swap?"

The boy laid the skins next to the basket. "We want to trade for supplies."

Thank goodness they spoke English! "I'll get my mother," she said.

The woman looked at the boy. "She'll fetch her mother – *peatolah nekkaen*," he said. The woman nodded.

Lucy hurried through the door to the kitchen. "Mamma! Come out front. An Indian woman wants to trade!"

"Oh, my goodness!" Mamma wiped her hands on her apron and followed Lucy out front. "Hello," she said, approaching the woman.

The woman reached into her basket. She placed several newspaper-wrapped parcels on the counter. "Want swap," she said, pointing at the skins and her basket. "See. Good *pesicthey*." She glanced at the boy. "Deer skins," he said. She spread two pieces of hide on the counter.

Mamma stroked her hand across the skin and held it out for Lucy to do the same. It was soft as flannel. "Very nice," Mamma said.

The woman smiled. She opened one of the parcels on the counter and pulled back the newspaper to show Mamma the red berries inside.

"Raspberries." Mamma tasted one. She nodded and smiled. "Very sweet." The woman pointed to Lucy, then to the berries.

"You try," she said.

Lucy took one of the berries. She hadn't had a Kansas raspberry yet. It was springy between her fingers. When she closed her mouth on it, it exploded with a tart sweetness that made her mouth water. She smiled, and the woman smiled in return.

The Indian woman produced three more packets of the berries from her basket. Then she pulled out a pair of leather slippers. "*Mockeethena* – moccasins." They were sewn of soft rabbit skin and decorated on the top with tiny beads sewn in a geometric design. Lucy ran her fingers over the fringe that circled the ankles and imagined how the soft fur that lined them would feel on her feet. She looked at the woman and imagined her hands sewing them, carefully placing the beads just so. "They are beautiful," she said. "I've seen some of the Lawrence ladies wearing them." The woman smiled back, pleased with the compliment. "You swap?" she asked.

"What do you need?" Mamma asked.

The woman looked at the boy. He translated, "*Wehewayketuckawatah.*"

She nodded and spoke to him. "*Locana. Nepepemay. Thenamesay.*" She pulled three empty cloth sacks from her bundle.

"Flour, salt, sugar," he said. "One bag of each."

The woman next went to the shelf with the fabric. She pulled a bolt of green calico from the shelf. Lucy watched as she began to unwind the fabric, holding the end of the material between her fingers and stretching out her arm. She measured the calico along the length of her arm three times, then pinched the place where she wanted it cut. Mamma nodded and cut the fabric. "Lucy, you measure the dry goods while I help her with this."

The boy carried the sacks and followed Lucy to the back counter where she could weigh the flour, salt, and sugar on the scales. "I'm Lucy Thomkins," she said. "What's your name?"

"Levi Whitefeather." He gave her a sack. "Flour in this one, please."

Lucy took the bag and picked up the metal scoop from the bin. "It's nice to meet you, Levi. Do you live near Lawrence?"

"East of here. On Shawnee land."

Lucy scooped flour into the bag, but nodded across the room. "Is that your mother?"

"Yes. She doesn't come to town very often. She doesn't speak much English."

When the bag was nearly full, Lucy lifted it onto the scales. She looked at the weight and added one more scoop. "That's ten pounds." She cut some string and tied the top of the bag.

He handed her another sack. "Sugar in this one."

Lucy lifted the top of the sugar bin and reached for the scoop. "How did you learn English, if your parents don't speak it?"

"I went to the Shawnee Mission School. They taught us reading, spelling, writing, and arithmetic."

Lucy put the nearly-full bag on the scale. "You don't go to school there anymore?"

"No. The man who ran the school – Reverend Johnson – was no friend of the Shawnee. He helped make the treaty with the Shawnee, but he let settlers cut timber on Shawnee land anyway. Our fathers took us out of the school."

Lucy pointed at the needle on the scale. "That's eleven pounds of sugar. Do you want me to put any more in?"

"*Nekkaen*," he said to his mother.

She looked up from some muslin she was measuring.

The boy pointed to the bag of sugar, using his hand to show her how much it contained. "*Thenamesay.* Sugar. *Howay?*"

"*Howay* – enough." She smiled when the boy nodded. "Enough," she repeated.

Lucy tied the sugar bag with a string and picked up the third bag. "Salt?"

"Yes," he said.

When Lucy had filled the bag with salt, Mamma figured the prices to complete the trade. On one side of the page she listed the amounts of salt, sugar, flour, material, and the needles, buttons, and thread Levi's mother had chosen. On the other side of the paper, she made a list of the things they had brought to trade, and the prices she expected to be able to charge for them. She showed the paper to Levi and his mother. "For a fair trade, I still owe you about $2.50 in merchandise."

Levi translated for his mother. She nodded and looked around the store, then pointed at the beads in the display by the window. "*Welethee*," she said. "Pretty."

Mamma beamed with pride. "Yes, just right for moccasins."

Levi's mother smiled. She chose several colors and gave Mamma some small leather pouches to put the beads in.

Lucy packed the smaller things into Levi's mother's basket, and Levi carried the bags of salt and sugar out to the wagon. Mamma followed them to the door, with the sack of flour. "Thank you," she said. "I hope you'll come again."

Levi's mother smiled at Mamma. "You make good trade, *tootemat*," she said. "*Keewaylo* – we come back."

Levi placed the flour sack on the wagon. "Bye, Lucy," he said.

"Levi – wait," Lucy stopped him.

"What?"

The word your mother said to my mother, "Too-tay-ma –"

"*Tootemat*," he corrected.

"What does it mean?"

"It means 'sister,'" he answered.

Lucy smiled.

Levi helped his mother climb onto the wagon, then got into the driver's seat. "Maybe we'll see you at the picnic." He waved as the horse responded to his whistle. "Goodbye. *Nepaukechey.*"

Lucy waved. She watched as the wagon moved down the street. "*Nepaukechey*," she whispered. "Goodbye."

17

After the oration, the large assembly, numbering about 2,000 persons, gathered around the long and well loaded table for the first time in the wilds of Kansas, to partake of the good things of the land. Lemonade by the barrel, cakes, and meats appeared in great variety where we were. We did not, however, wait to see how many "baskets full were taken up" at last.

–Herald of Freedom, July 7, 1855

By the time Mamma was ready to close the store to go to the picnic, Lucy was so eager that she was nearly jumping in place. It was the biggest day Lawrence had ever seen, and she was missing all the excitement! Mamma fussed with the ledger book, she counted the money in the cash box at least a dozen times, arranged and rearranged the cakes in the baskets, and changed her mind three times about whether to take the better crockery dishes ("You know how Mrs. Harmon brags about her china,") or plain tin plates ("I'd hate to lose or break any of our nice ones,") before finally deciding on the crockery ones, despite the risk.

Lucy was looking out the window for at least the fiftieth time, when Mamma at last picked up the key to the front door and prepared to lock up. The streets of Lawrence were nearly deserted. As they walked toward the river, they could hear the music of the band and cheers from the crowd. Lucy walked ahead, then slowed to wait for Mamma, then walked ahead again.

"Lucy, for goodness sake, run along!" said Mamma. "You're making me positively nervous." She held out the basket. "Take the cakes – careful now – and set them out with the other desserts. I'll see you there."

As Lucy ran ahead, Mamma called after her, "Look for Papa and Joseph, and I'll meet you near the dessert table!"

At the edge of the grove, Lucy stopped in her tracks and stared. She had not seen this many people in one place since they'd left Pennsylvania. Noise and activity surrounded her on all sides. Wagons lined the streets, and horses flicked flies with their tails in the sun. Dogs slept in the shade of the wagons here and there, or darted for morsels of food dropped in the grass. Children chased each other through the crowd, and babies dozed on their mothers' laps. A table made of boards laid across sawhorses stretched at least fifty feet through the center of everything, and people milled around it, filling and refilling plates from the many platters and bowls lined up along its length. Laughter and shouts punctuated the steady cacophony of sounds. On the far edge of the grove, the river swept slowly and silently past.

"Lucy!"

She turned toward the voice and saw Levi coming toward her from the group of wagons where the Shawnee families were gathered.

"I need to put these cakes out," Lucy told him. "Come with me?"

As Lucy arranged Mamma's cakes in the middle of the other cakes, pies, and breads, the crowd fell silent near the wooden stage. A man at the table near the stage stood and raised his cup, sweeping it in the direction of the Shawnee and Delaware groups. "To our aboriginal neighbors," he announced. "Their presence and participation with us today is a mutual recognition of unity and good will. May we ever smoke the pipe of peace together."

Cheers and applause came from the crowd, and a tall Indian man stepped forward and raised his hand. The crowd again fell silent.

"Who is he?" Lucy whispered to Levi.

"He is our chief, Paschal Fish."

The chief spoke in a deep and powerful voice, but his words were Shawnee, not English. His hand swept around to gesture toward the land and the river as he spoke. His people nodded in agreement, but the settlers of Lawrence could only watch his face for signs of pleasure or anger.

"What is he saying?" Lucy asked.

Levi watched the chief and translated, one phrase at a time. "He says, 'I believe as strongly as you … of the wickedness of slavery … and I see before me … the good which comes from freedom … All these things … your hearty welcome … and my deep sympathy in your cause … makes me feel happy … I know I am among friends.'"

The chief finished his speech and stepped down as the

people applauded, even though they didn't know what he had said. Lucy joined the applause. "It was a wonderful speech," she told Levi. "Thank you for sharing it with me."

Lucy spied Papa looking over the food table. "Papa!" Lucy ran to him and hugged him. "You looked so handsome in the parade today!"

Papa laughed. "I'll bet you say that to all the soldiers." He nodded in Levi's direction. "Who's your friend?"

"Come on, I want you to meet him." She leaned closer and whispered, "He's Shawnee." Lucy pulled Papa by the hand. "This is Levi. He and his mother came into the store to shop this morning," Lucy said. "Levi, this is my father."

Levi held out his hand to shake. "Nice to meet you, sir."

Papa returned Levi's handshake. "A pleasure to meet you, Levi," he said. "Lucy, where's your mother? The food is disappearing fast."

"She should be here by now." Lucy looked through the crowd. "There she is." She pointed at a group of women clustered around Mrs. Marcum and her new baby.

"I should have known," Papa said. "Wherever there's a baby, no one else gets fed." He strode off toward the women.

Lucy looked for a spot where they could sit on the ground to eat and took out the tablecloth that had been in the basket with the cakes. When she began to unfold it, Levi helped her spread it on the ground.

Papa came back leading Mamma by the hand. "I just wanted to hold the baby," Mamma said.

"The rest of us are hungry, Maggie," said Papa, "and you have the plates."

Mamma smiled at Levi. "Nice to see you again, Levi." She set her basket down, took out the crockery plates and cups and set out forks and spoons. "Would you like to join us for dinner? I brought some extra plates."

Levi looked uncomfortable. "I don't know," he said. "I should go back to my family."

"You're welcome to stay if you'd like," Papa added.

Levi accepted a plate. Lucy smiled and handed him a fork and knife. Papa did not need to worry about a shortage of things to eat. Lucy had never seen so much food in one place in her whole life. Meats, melons, garden vegetables, breads, cakes, and pies. They filled their plates to overflowing and took their cups to be filled with lemonade. Once they returned to their picnic spot to eat, Papa dug eagerly into his plate of food.

Levi hesitated until Papa began to eat, then he carefully picked up his fork. Lucy spoke up. "Papa, Levi and his mother brought some beautiful deerskins to the store to trade today. And she sewed some moccasins with the softest fur inside you've ever felt."

"I'm glad to hear that," Papa said. "Was your mother pleased with her trade, Levi?"

"Yes, sir," Levi said. "She said she will go back to your store."

"Please tell her I'll be happy to see her again," Mamma said.

Levi smiled. "Yes, ma'am, I will."

They had barely begun eating when Joseph jumped onto

the edge of the cloth and sank into a cross-legged sit. He was red-faced and sweaty.

"Joseph!" Mamma scolded. "Be careful!"

"Boy, am I hungry! We've been running races," he said. "I almost won twice, but one of those cheatin' Indian boys beat – ow!"

Lucy's elbow caught Joseph in the ribs.

"What'd ya do that for?" Joseph noticed Levi for the first time. He looked down and saw the boy's moccasins, then looked up at his face and frowned. "I'm not eating with any Indians," he said.

"Joseph!" Papa scolded. "Mind your manners. This is our guest."

Without a word, Levi set his plate down, rose to his feet, and walked away in the direction of the Shawnee wagons.

"Levi!" Lucy called. "Please, wait!" He did not slow down or turn around.

Lucy turned to face her brother. "I hate you!" She stood up and threw her empty cup at him. "You don't deserve to eat with him!"

She ran through the crowd, but couldn't see Levi anywhere. She didn't see him among the groups near the Shawnee wagons, but she hesitated to go too close. How could Joseph be so rude and stupid? She wanted to apologize, but what could she say to excuse his behavior? Levi was the nicest boy she had met in the last four months, and Joseph had ruined everything. Her face burned with her anger, and she looked for a place to get out of the crowd before tears overtook her. She stepped behind one of the temporary outhouses set up at the edge of the grove and tried to ignore the smell. She imagined how she would feel if she sat with Levi's family and heard them talk that way about her.

"Lucy!" Annie stood there. She put a hand on Lucy's shoulder. "Are you all right?"

Lucy took a breath and swallowed. How could she explain it? Another breath. "I hate my brother."

Annie took Lucy's hand and led her across the street and around the corner of the nearest house.

"You didn't tell anybody, did you?"

Lucy shook her head. "I promised."

Annie put her finger to her lips, then whispered, "I told Pa what you said. He doesn't like it much, especially since your folks don't know." She looked around to make sure no one was near. "I told him you really want to help. Do you still?"

Lucy nodded.

"He said maybe you could help us with something today, and he'll see how you do."

Lucy took a breath. "What can I do?"

"We've got some new folks. Ruffians are watching our house, so we couldn't take them out there. They're here in town."

Lucy gulped. "You need me to hide them?" How could she do that?

Annie shook her head and glanced around again. She leaned her head closer. "We got friends to take them out of here tonight when the street is full of wagons, and no one will notice. But the folks are hungry. We need somebody to take them food. Somebody nobody suspects."

Lucy's heart beat fast. "Me?"

"Only if you want to."

Lucy nodded. "What do I do?"

Annie pointed to the grove. "There's plenty of food right over there. We need enough to feed four men."

"Where are they? Should I take it to them now?" Lucy whispered.

"No! If someone sees you, they'll be caught! Wait till dark."

"I understand. After dark," Lucy whispered. "Where do I go?"

"Take it to the stone barn on Mississippi Street. Go to the side door. Knock like this." Annie gently struck Lucy's arm with her fist as though knocking. One-two-three ... one-two-three-four.

The thought of walking alone after dark through the streets where Border Ruffians might lurk terrified her. "What if I forget?"

"Don't," said Annie. "Remember it this way. *Oh my dar ... ling Clementine.*" She sang softly while she tapped the rhythm of the secret knock on Lucy's arm again, holding out the third note to make the pause.

"I'll remember, I promise," Lucy said.

Annie looked into Lucy's eyes. "It isn't a game. Real people are depending on you."

Lucy nodded.

"If it goes well, we might use you again."

Before Lucy could respond, Annie was gone.

When she got back to their picnic spot, only Papa was there. "Your mother decided she needed to re-open the store," he said. "Joseph went with her. He has done enough harm for one day."

Papa took off his militia jacket and laid it on their picnic cloth. His white shirt was wet with perspiration. He picked up his rifle. "They're having a shooting contest over at the firing range," he said. "I think I'll see how my aim is today." Papa handed Lucy one of the dirty plates. "Can you take care of these things, Lucy Cat?"

"Yes, Papa."

Lucy began to pick up the plates. Levi's plate of food was still there. She picked it up, walked to the far edge of the grove and dumped the food in the grass, while she tried to make a plan. How could she carry enough food for four people away from the picnic without being noticed?

The grove was filled with activity. She heard a clang and a chorus of shouts from a group of men playing horseshoes in a shady area near the river's edge. In the distance, gunshots sounded from the firing range. Beneath the trees in the grove, babies slept on blankets while their mothers chatted in small circles nearby. In the dust of Ohio Street, the boys were still running foot races. The table of food had only a few people standing around now; nearly everyone had eaten, and cloths were spread over the remaining food to keep the insects away.

After she picked up the rest of the plates, Lucy pulled out the two extra plates in the basket. She put the clean plates into the basket that had carried the cakes and put the dirty ones in the other basket. If she was going to get food, this was the time.

She took one of the clean plates and went over to the table. She pulled the cloth cover back and forked several pieces of ham from one platter and some chicken from another. She added some green beans and potatoes and perched two rolls on the top. It was all she could fit on the plate. She was pulling the cloth cover back over the food when she looked up to see Miss Kellogg standing next to her, staring.

"Goodness, child, you have a healthy appetite."

"Oh! Miss Kellogg! Nice to see you, ma'am." Lucy looked down at the heaping plate she held. How could she explain this? "My mother is working at the store this afternoon …"

"On the Fourth of July?"

Lucy wanted to run. She gripped the plate tightly to keep her hands from shaking. "Yes, ma'am. She's coming later for the fireworks."

"So you're fixing her a plate for her supper?" Miss Kellogg smiled. "I'm sure she'll enjoy it. How's your poetry coming along these days?"

Lucy edged backward, away from the table. "Just fine, thank you. I wrote a new verse just last night."

"I'm glad to know you are still writing, even while school is out."

"Yes, ma'am. Well, I need to go now – I'll see you soon!"

"Yes. Tell your mother hello for me."

"I will, ma'am – thank you!" Lucy took the plate of food, set it in the basket and covered it with a napkin. Now what? Miss Kellogg still stood by the table, so Lucy walked with the basket toward the road, as though she were headed home. She smiled. Miss Kellogg must think Mamma had the appetite of an ox, but she was too polite to say it. Still, it wasn't enough food for four hungry people. She would need more. If she waited too long, people would come to take the food away.

She circled the block once, then looked around for Miss Kellogg. She went back to their blanket and pulled the other clean plate from the basket. She draped Papa's coat over the basket to hide the filled plate and keep the insects away. Once again, she approached the food table. She would be quicker this time. She reached for the things she could grab quickly: more chicken, some rolls, and several pieces of watermelon. That would have to be enough. She hurried toward the hidden basket, looking back at the table once. As she turned her head, she bumped straight into Sam Willis.

"Still hungry, *Lucky*?"

"Yes, I am." Lucy tried to step around him.

He stepped to the side to block her path. "Or maybe you're fixing a plate for your Injun boyfriend?"

"None of your business," she answered.

"Matt says you got a red-skinned beau," Sam sneered.

Lucy stepped back. "There's more to a person than skin color. Yours hasn't made you any smarter, has it?"

Sam stepped closer. "You calling me stupid?"

Lucy refused to budge "No. I'll call you Samuel, and you may call me Lucy. Please step aside, Samuel. I have more interesting things to do today than talk to you."

Sam didn't move, but he didn't stop her as she stepped around him. She did not look back. She held the plate and pretended to watch the horseshoes match.

When Sam ran off with some other boys, Lucy returned to their picnic spot. She moved Papa's coat and set the second plate in the basket, tucking the edges of another napkin around the plate to cover it. Her heart beat furiously, but she had the food she needed – the food *they* needed. Now, she just had to wait for dark.

18

We are credibly informed that the Abolitionists—operating through a secret organization—on some day not far off, have determined to run all the slaves out of Kansas Territory ... If anybody has to be driven out of Kansas, we know of none so deserving of such treatment as the Abolitionists themselves.

—*The Argus,* Platte County, Mo

The afternoon crawled by more slowly than any Lucy could remember in her life. She watched for Levi, but didn't see him. She tried to imagine what she might say to him, but she couldn't think of a single thing that could make up for Joseph's cruel words. More than anything, she thought of the errand she would do after dark and hummed, *Oh my darling, Clementine*, to herself. She stayed at their picnic spot through the afternoon and finally lay back on the blanket to stare up at the blue sky and light clouds that passed between the boughs of the trees overhead. The excitement of the day and the lazy warmth of the summer afternoon overtook her, and she drifted off to sleep.

She woke with a start and sat up. Some men were taking apart the wooden tables that had held the food. She looked around her. How long had she slept? Papa's coat was gone, but the basket was still there, covered with the napkins as she had left it. It was nearly dark.

Lucy walked slowly away from Pleasant Grove down Indiana Street. The basket was heavy on her arm. Her knees shook with nervousness and threatened to collapse under her. She wanted to run to the stone barn and complete her mission, but she knew she had to wait for full darkness. Voices and music still rose from the grove where hundreds of people waited for the fireworks to begin.

The storefronts that lined the east side of the street caught the last light of the setting sun. Lucy stopped in front of Woodward's Drug Store. She pretended to look in the window, but instead watched the images from the street reflected in the glass. Young men in militia uniforms made their way up the street toward Lykins' Hall where the dance would be starting soon. If she were only a few years older, she could be the belle of that ball; there were few young single women in Lawrence, and they didn't stay single for long. Even Miss Kellogg was rumored to have some "suitors" who vied for her attention. Lucy smiled. Miss Kellogg would certainly not make it easy for any man to gain her affection.

"Help you, miss?"

Lucy jumped and nearly dropped the basket. A man stood next to her, key poised to open the door to the store. "No!" She took a breath. "I mean … I was just admiring your window display."

"Well, you'd best be getting over to the grove, if you want to see the fireworks."

"Oh, I don't …" Lucy caught herself. "Thank you, I don't want to miss that!" She stepped down from the porch. As he watched, she hurried in the direction of the grove. When she was sure he had gone into the store, she glanced around, then ducked around the corner of the wagon repair shop. She leaned against the building, breathing heavily. Her hands were still shaking, and she decided to wait there for a few minutes.

Stars appeared in the clear Kansas sky like tiny lanterns seen across the prairie. First one or two at a time, then hundreds all at once. It was time.

Lucy kept to the shadows, staying close to the buildings. She looked for anyone who might be watching her. But the people who walked the streets of town barely noticed the girl with the basket on her arm.

Lucy walked the last block to the stone barn. She kept her face forward, but her eyes darted around again, and she listened for footsteps. She hummed the tune softly and said the words in her head, *Oh my darling, Oh my darling, Oh my dar … ling, Clementine, You are lost and gone forever, Dreadful sor … ry, Clementine.* A final glance around. She shivered. Goosebumps prickled her arms and made the hairs stand on end. She found the side door of the barn. Seven knocks: one-two-three … one-two-three-four; *Oh my dar … ling, Clementine.* The door opened, and Lucy stepped into the blackness of the barn.

"This way," a woman's voice said softly. The air was heavy with moist heat and the smells of hay and horse manure. A hand grasped her arm and led her through the darkness. As her eyes adjusted to the dark, she made out the silhouette of a wagon with two horses hitched to it. One of the horses snorted and shook its head, jingling its bridle. Lucy thought she recognized the woman who led her through the barn as someone she had met at the boarding house, but she wasn't sure. She led Lucy to a back stall where a closely-trimmed kerosene lantern hung on a hook. Lucy handed her basket to the woman.

"Here's food," the woman said, and four figures emerged from the darkest corner of the stall. Three men and a boy, probably about Lucy's age. The woman divided the food and gave some to each. Without a word, they huddled and ate, the silence broken only by breathing and chewing and swallowing. None of the men looked up from the food, but the boy's eyes caught Lucy's once, and he quickly looked away. The woman rose, picked up Lucy's basket and motioned for her to follow. She led the way back to the door. "God bless you," she said. She thrust the basket toward Lucy. "They haven't eaten in two days, and it may be two more before they will again." She nudged Lucy out the door. Lucy stood there for a moment. She had accomplished her mission, but she didn't feel proud; she felt only ashamed. She looked down at her empty basket. It was too little, not nearly enough to fill empty stomachs for two days. There had been food sufficient to feed a multitude today, but she had not taken enough for four hungry people. She had been too timid. She had only thought of her own discomfort and nervousness. Two days without food. She had never in her life gone two days without food.

An explosion startled her, and the sky filled with light. The fireworks! Mamma would be frantic. She ran all the way back, pausing only when the sky was lit with more fireworks. She stopped at the edge of the grove to catch her breath. Someone was watching her. She was certain of it. She peered into the shadows and saw no one, but she felt it as surely as she had felt it outside Annie's house that night. She slowed her steps to mingle with the crowd and made her way back to the picnic spot.

Mamma spotted her first. "There you are!" She frowned. "Papa is looking for you. Where have you been?"

"I was –" Lucy looked down, then raised the basket she still held. "I forgot your basket by the food table," she said. "I went back to get it, then I stopped to talk to Miss Kellogg, then the fireworks started, and –"

"Lucy Cat!" Papa put an arm around her shoulders. "You had us worried."

"I'm sorry, Papa." She returned his hug. "I didn't mean to stay away so long."

"Have you seen your brother?" Mamma asked.

Lucy shook her head.

Mamma frowned. "He ran off as soon as we left the store."

"He's probably with the Willis boy," Papa said.

As the last fireworks lit the sky, horses, wagons, and tired people filled the streets for the trip home. Lucy, Papa, and Mamma gathered their belongings and began the walk back to the store. Lucy looked around. Somewhere, in the middle of this crowd, another wagon would be heading out of town. Just one wagon, hiding in plain sight.

Hunger

Hungry stomachs growl for bread.
Hungry muscles ache for meat.
Hungry hands reach out for food
So hungry mouths may eat.

Hungry feet walk darkened roads,
Hungry hearts in bondage beat.
Hungry souls seek wings to fly
On the wind of freedom, so sweet.

19

Meeting of the Missouri-Kansas Legislature

... We regard them as a band of alien enemies, encamped in our midst. For our part, we repudiate and despise them and their authority, and hope the people of Kansas will spurn everything in the shape of laws they may attempt to impose upon us.

–Herald of Freedom

When Lucy came downstairs the next morning, Mamma was putting away the baskets from yesterday's picnic. "I'm sure we took six plates." She frowned.

The plates Lucy had taken to the barn! She hadn't waited to get them back. "Are you sure we took that many?"

"I'm certain we took six. I've counted the ones in the kitchen, and we're missing two. You don't know what happened to them?"

"Maybe I missed them when I picked up our things," Lucy said. "I could go see if they're still there."

Mamma shook her head, but her frown showed her irritation. "No, I need your help here this morning. I'm just angry at myself. We should have taken the tin plates."

"I'm sorry, Mamma. I didn't mean to forget them." That was the absolute truth.

"I'll check with Violet Jessup later," Mamma said. "Her blanket was near ours. Maybe she picked them up." Mamma pulled a dust rag from her apron pocket and held it out. "Will you wipe off the canned goods for me? Joseph has already gone off to the stable with Sam Willis. Papa is starting a fire for the wash kettle, and I need to take the clothes out."

Lucy lifted a jar of peaches from the shelf. What could she do about the plates? She wiped the jar. Mamma wouldn't give up easily. She'd ask everyone she could think of. If she kept asking, she might find out the connection between her plates and the Liberty Line.

Lucy couldn't let that happen. She had to think of something.

She put the clean jar on the shelf and picked up the next one. How could she have forgotten the plates? The more she wiped, the more she worried. Maybe Annie could help her get the plates. After she finished dusting the last jar of peaches, she reached for a jar of pickles. The bell on the door tinkled, and Lucy turned, the jar and the rag still in her hands.

Miss Kellogg stepped in, her shopping basket hanging heavy on her arm. "Good morning, Lucy. Did you enjoy the Fourth of July celebration?"

"Hello, Miss Kellogg." She thought of Joseph. "Well, mostly."

"Mostly?" Miss Kellogg raised her eyebrows.

"My brother insulted my new friend," Lucy explained.

"I'm sorry to hear that," Miss Kellogg said. "I hope it didn't spoil the day for you or your friend." She glanced around the store. "Is your mother nearby?"

"She's outside. Can I help you with something?"

"I hope so. I'm looking for the owner of some property." Miss Kellogg set her basket on the counter and removed a checkered cloth from it. Lucy stepped forward and looked in the basket. She gasped and dropped the pickle jar. It crashed at her feet.

Mamma's two crockery plates lay in Miss Kellogg's basket.

"Oh, my!" Lucy said, looking down at the mess. Glass, pickles, and pickle juice quickly spread to make a stinky stain on the floorboards. Her skirt and stockings were wet with the vinegary juice.

"Gracious, child," said Miss Kellogg, "I didn't mean to startle you."

Just then, Mamma hurried through the door. "What broke?" she asked. "Oh, good morning, Miss Kellogg." Mamma snatched up the dust pan while Lucy tried to mop the juice with the dust rag.

"I apologize, Mrs. Thomkins. I startled Lucy when I came in. It's my fault." Miss Kellogg lifted the plates from the basket. "I came over to see if these are yours."

"Oh, thank goodness! I was sure they were lost." Mamma passed the dust pan to Lucy and took the plates from Miss Kellogg.

Lucy scooped glass shards and pickles into the dust pan.

She desperately needed some explanation for the plates, but she couldn't think of a thing.

"I believe I must have picked them up with my things from the picnic," Miss Kellogg said. "I didn't notice them until this morning."

Lucy stared at her teacher.

"Careful, Lucy!" Miss Kellogg said. "You've cut yourself on the glass."

Lucy looked down. Blood dripped from a cut on her left thumb. She hadn't even felt it. Miss Kellogg pulled a handkerchief from her sleeve. "Let me help."

Miss Kellogg examined the cut then pressed her handkerchief to it. "It's a small cut," she said. "It will be fine."

"Thank you," Lucy breathed. "I …"

"Nonsense. It was nothing." Miss Kellogg looked straight into Lucy's eyes. "No need to say a word."

Lucy looked down at her hand and peeked under the handkerchief. "I'll wash your handkerchief and return it to you," she said.

"That will be fine." Miss Kellogg turned to Mamma. "Perhaps you can help me with a few items I need today."

As Mamma helped Miss Kellogg, Lucy went outside to put the handkerchief in the wash. Miss Kellogg knew exactly where those plates had been. So she was involved, too?

Lucy pumped some cool water to rinse the blood from the handkerchief. The wash pot hung from its tripod, and Papa piled firewood onto the small blaze below it.

Mr. Brown had come over from the newspaper office to talk. "The proslavery papers have been crowing about this legislature business since they threw out the Free State delegates," he said. "It's only a matter of time before they start writing new statutes to punish us for opposing their government. The Ruffians say Missouri has enough hemp to make nooses to hang us all."

Lucy let the wet cloth drip onto her shoes. She would be in the line for hanging if the Ruffians knew she was helping the Liberty Line. "Governor Reeder won't let them do that, will he, Mr. Brown?"

"He can't do a thing to stop them. The scoundrels ousted Reeder, too. They're packing up the whole convention to move it to the Shawnee Mission." He shook his head. "As close to Missouri and their real homes as they can get it. I'll put it all in the *Herald* this week."

Papa wiped sweat from his forehead and poked at the firewood under the pot. "But that's Indian land," he said. "It's not even in the boundary of the territory."

"Just one more reason why the whole thing is illegal. The Free State newspapers are already calling it the 'Bogus Legislature.'"

Lucy dropped Miss Kellogg's handkerchief into the wash pot. "If the legislature is illegal, does that mean we don't have to obey their laws?"

Mr. Brown shook his head again. "If the federal government gives them the authority to enforce them, then we're all in trouble. I've already had one subscriber send back his

216

newspaper because he didn't want to get caught reading it."

"But we're guaranteed freedom of speech!" Papa's voice rose, and it reminded Lucy of those arguments in Grandfather's house so long ago.

"We're not in the United States, Marcus. We're in Kansas Territory. Congress regards the Territorial Legislature as the legal governing body."

"We're going to have to do something," Papa said. "We came too far and worked too hard to let the Missourians take it from us now."

Mr. Brown nodded. "Let's talk to Robinson and see what he says."

Papa picked up the wash paddle and held it out to Lucy. "Are you taking over here?"

She nodded and took the paddle.

Papa followed Mr. Brown to the street, where they turned toward Dr. Robinson's house.

Lucy stood at the wash kettle. The job was hers now, but she didn't mind. At least it would give her a chance to think, and she certainly had a lot of things to consider. The cut on her thumb throbbed a little. She gripped the paddle and poked at the clothes in the kettle.

The Liberty Line was more complicated than she thought. Annie's family was in on it. Now, Miss Kellogg. There was the woman who had taken the plates from her last night, and there had to be others as well. And now, with the Bogus Legislature in power, they could all be in danger.

Would they really hang a thirteen-year-old girl? Would they go after Papa if she were caught? Had she put her whole family in danger?

The heat of the summer day, the steam rising from the kettle, and her own worry made Lucy's face drip with perspiration. She raised her arm to wipe her face on her sleeve and caught a glimpse of movement at the edge of her vision — someone at the corner of the house. Lucy let the paddle slide into the wash pot and hurried around the corner. It was Levi! He was walking away from her.

"Levi," Lucy called.

He stopped, his back to her. He was silent.

Lucy caught up to him, but stood behind him. "I'm glad you came."

"I didn't come to see you. I'm on an errand for my father." He started to walk away.

"Please don't leave."

"Your brother ..."

Lucy's voice trembled a little. "I'm not my brother."

"But he is your brother, your blood."

How could she say it? "Levi, I need your help."

He turned now, but he looked suspicious.

"I need to learn a Shawnee word." She looked into his face. "The word for 'sorry.'" He didn't respond. "Please," she added.

Levi's expression eased. "'*Matchelepo*'," he said quietly.

"*Mat-che-le-po*," Lucy imitated. She said it twice softly, then laid a hand on Levi's arm and spoke to him. "*Matchelepo,*

218

Levi. *Matchelepo.* My brother was wrong to speak that way, and I'm sorry. *Matchelepo.*"

Levi looked at her. He nodded and was quiet for a few seconds. Then he smiled, just a little. "I have another word for you."

"Another word? What is it?"

"*Neekanauh.*"

"What does it mean?"

"It means 'friend.'"

Lucy put out her right hand to shake. "*Nee-ka-na-uh.*"

Levi accepted her handshake, then laughed.

"What?"

"You smell like pickles," he said.

20

Lawrence Prices Current

Coffee, lb	.14, .16
Cheese, lb	.15, .20
Cornmeal, per bushel	$1.50
Tallow candles, lb	.12
Lamp oil, gal.	$1.25
Lard, lb.	.12

—*Herald of Freedom*, July 1855

The song of the crickets was deafening when Lucy stepped from the back door. A million stars lit the moonless sky, but no one seemed to be stirring nearby.

She looked back at the house for any sign of movement there. It, too, was dark. Everyone else was already asleep.

She placed the small parcel around the back side of the outhouse. Tonight, it was a few tallow candles. Two nights ago, a half-pound of cheese beside the back porch. Before that, some lamp oil in a jar hidden next to the pump.

This package would be gone by morning, just as all the others had.

It was the only work she could do for the Liberty Line, but

it was still stealing. And from her own family.

Lucy had not met any of the people who had passed through on their way to freedom.

"Soon," Annie had said.

Lucy hoped so.

21

If any person in this Territory shall entice, decoy, or carry away out of any State or other Territory, any slave belonging to another ... and shall bring such a slave into this territory, he shall be adjudged guilty of grand larceny ... The person offending shall suffer death, or be imprisoned at hard labor for not less than ten years.

–Section 6, *An Act to Punish Offences Against Slave Property, Kansas Legislature*, Aug. 14, 1855

A hot summer breeze blew in from the street, bringing a cloud of brown dust with it. It was inventory day. Lucy counted buttons and sewing notions near the fabric table. Joseph stacked and counted bars of soap, tallying the totals on a slate. Papa unpacked a box of brass hinges, locks, and keys, counting them as he emptied the crate. Mamma tapped her pencil and shook her head as she bent over the ledger books. "I just don't understand it," she said.

Papa looked up. "What's the matter?"

"According to our sales records, we seem to be coming up short on all kinds of things. It doesn't make sense."

"Don't blame me!" Papa said. "I haven't touched the books!"

"I know that, Marcus." Mamma's tone softened a little, but she still studied the totals and clicked her tongue. "I can't figure out these numbers."

Papa laughed. "If Maggie Thomkins can't figure out the numbers, then heaven knows her poor business partner can't."

"Don't make fun, Marcus," Mamma said. "We have a shortage. It's not a big shortage, but it's enough to worry me. I hate to say it, but I think someone might be stealing from us."

"Probably that Injun friend of Lucy's," Joseph said.

"Take that back!" Lucy snapped at him. "As long as you keep company with Samuel Willis, you have no right to …"

"Stop it, both of you. I won't have talk like that." Papa frowned and shook his head. "There must be another explanation. I can't believe our neighbors would steal from us."

Papa went to Mamma's side to look at the ledger. Lucy turned her back to the rest of the family and bit her lip.

Mamma had not missed any of it before now. Surely her parents would be glad to give the supplies, if they knew what they were for. But she couldn't tell them. If they knew, they could be accused of helping. If they went to trial in the Ruffians' court … it was too awful to think about.

Boots clomped on the front step, and they all looked toward the door.

Dr. Robinson, Mr. Babcock, and Mr. Brown crowded in. "Marcus, I'm glad you're here," Dr. Robinson said.

Papa reached out to shake his hand. "What can I do for you, Charles?"

"We're on our way over to the meeting house. We're making plans to organize against this Bogus Legislature."

"Can you do that?" Mamma asked. "They have Congress on their side."

Dr. Robinson took off his hat, as though he had only now noticed that Mamma was in the room. "Yes, ma'am, they do. But we hope that the congressmen are not completely blind. We want to convince them that we have both reason and sufficient numbers on our side."

"What's your plan?" Papa asked.

"President Pierce will have to send a governor to replace Reeder soon, and we need to show the new man that we are law-abiding citizens. Instead of just ignoring this false legislature, we want to set up our own Free State Legislature with some reasonable laws."

"Makes sense," Papa said. "How can I help?"

"We're making plans for a convention at Big Springs in three weeks. We'd like you to come as a representative from Lawrence."

Joseph jumped up. "Big Springs! Can I go, too? I'll drive the wagon and take care of the horses while you're at the meeting!"

Papa smiled. "A representative! What do you say to that, Maggie?"

Mamma did not look pleased. "Are you expecting trouble from the Missourians at this convention?"

Mr. Brown spoke up. "According to the proslavery papers, they don't consider us a threat. They plan to ignore us."

Papa picked up his hat from the hook by the door. "I'll see what it's about, Maggie. We'll talk about it later."

"Big Springs!" Joseph said. "I've got to tell Sam!" He went through the door and jumped down the steps.

"Joseph!" Mamma called after him. "You are not making that trip!" But Joseph was already across the street, on his way to Wyman's.

Mamma sighed. "I don't like it," she said. "A renegade legislature will surely bring trouble."

Lucy went to Mamma's side. "It can't be any more dangerous than sitting here waiting for the Ruffians to find an excuse to carry us off to jail – or worse," she said.

"I suppose you're right," Mamma said. "But we came here to run a business. I didn't expect to find ourselves in the middle of a war. And at the moment, it looks like we could lose both."

Lucy wanted to comfort her, but she could only feel guilty.

"Well, let's get back to work. With just the two of us, it's going to take a while."

Lucy and Mamma counted coffeepots, coffee grinders, skillets, Dutch ovens, and bread pans. When they were finished with the cookware, they counted dishes and cutlery.

Mamma became most worried when they began to check their stock of consumable supplies. Lucy nervously watched Mamma's expression as she counted bags of flour, sugar, coffee, and cornmeal. She tried to guess just how many times she had taken a pound here or there. It hadn't seemed like much, but maybe it added up to more than she thought.

Mamma was back at her ledger, adding numbers and shaking her head, when Annie came running through the door.

"Mrs. Thomkins," she said, and gasped for breath. "I need your help."

"What is it, Annie?"

"Ma is over at Miss Kellogg's house. She has a visitor from out of town with the ague. Do you have any quinine? Addison's drug store is all out."

Lucy pressed her lips together and tried to shoot Annie a look that said, "Not this time!" but Annie didn't meet her eyes.

Mamma examined the jars on the shelf behind the counter. "Yes, I have some. How much do you need?"

"Miss Kellogg sent me with fifty cents. She said to get as much as I could get for that." Annie held out the coins and set a small round tin on the counter.

Mamma scooped the powder into the tin. She put the coins in the cash box. "I hope Miss Kellogg's friend will be better soon."

"Thank you, ma'am, I hope so too." Annie looked at Lucy, then back to Mamma. "Can Lucy come with me, please? Miss Kellogg will need some help, but Ma and I have to get back to the house. Miss Kellogg would sure appreciate it."

Mamma frowned. "She's sure it's ague? I've heard there's been cholera in some areas."

"Yes, ma'am. She's sure."

"Well, I trust Miss Kellogg. If she's needed, Lucy may go." Mamma turned to Lucy. "Are you willing to help?"

Lucy looked from Annie to Mamma. She'd never cared for a sick person before. "I don't know what to do."

Mamma gave Annie the tin of quinine. "Just do what Miss Kellogg says, Lucy."

The girls hurried out the door. As soon as they were out of sight of the store, Lucy reached for Annie's arm to stop her. "What's really happening?"

"Just what I told your mother," said Annie.

"And the visitor is?"

"Exactly what you think. Now hurry!"

Annie knocked softly on Miss Kellogg's door. Three knocks, then four more. The door opened a crack, and Miss Kellogg peered out.

Annie stayed outside. "Today is your day to help." She slipped the tin of quinine into Lucy's hand.

Miss Kellogg closed the door behind Lucy. No one else was in the small kitchen, but a tattered dress was draped across a chair.

"Our patient is in the next room," Miss Kellogg said. "Did you bring the quinine?"

Lucy gave her the tin. Her hands shook with nervousness.

The kettle on the stove began to rattle. Miss Kellogg held the handle with a rag and poured boiling water into a teapot on the table. She spooned tea leaves into the pot and replaced the lid. She pulled a chair out for Lucy and sat across the table from her. "I'm glad you've come. Why did you decide to join this cause?"

Lucy's fingers traced the grain of the wood on the table top. "I read Mr. Whittier's poems, and I thought about what you said, that our struggle wasn't about the guns."

Miss Kellogg put the kettle back on the stove and sat down across the table from Lucy. "Whittier's poems changed your mind?"

She shook her head. "No, not just that. When I saw them," Lucy looked up, "the people, the poems made sense to me. I wanted to help."

"And you understand the danger?"

Lucy nodded. "Yes, ma'am. The new laws are hard."

"They are nothing compared to what our friends have suffered for years."

"My grandfather said that the stories were exaggerated just to give the politicians something to fight about."

"I wish that were so. I'm sure the young woman in the next room wishes her scars were imaginary." Miss Kellogg placed a small strainer over a cup. She lifted the teapot and poured the brewed tea into the cup, then stirred some of the quinine into it.

"Can I meet her, Miss Kellogg?"

Miss Kellogg placed the cup on a small tray. "Take this tea to her and help her drink it. She won't like it, but it will help with her illness."

"Aren't you coming?"

Miss Kellogg nodded toward the dress on the chair. "I need to mend her dress. You need to get to know her."

Lucy picked up the tray and entered the dark room, her

heart thumping. She set the tray on a table and knelt next to the bed. The young woman's shivering caused the bed to tremble. Lucy touched her shoulder. "I have tea for you," she said.

The woman turned her head and opened her eyes. Lucy put an arm behind her shoulders to help her sit up and placed a pillow behind her.

The woman extended a hand from beneath the quilts, but it shook violently, and she pulled it back. "Can't hold it," she said.

"I'll help you." Lucy lifted the cup to the woman's lips and tipped it slightly.

The woman took a sip and grimaced. "Bad," she said. She turned her head away.

"It's bitter, but it will help you feel better. Please drink some more."

The woman shook her head.

"You have to," Lucy said. "They can't take you any farther until you're better. If you stay here too long, someone will find you. They'll send you back."

The woman accepted another drink and struggled to swallow it. Lucy continued to offer the cup every few minutes for her to take another sip.

When she finished the tea, she sank back. She studied Lucy's face. "What's your name?"

"Lucy."

"Had a sister name of Lucy." She looked at the wall.

The woman's shivering had stopped. Lucy set the tea cup on the table. "What's your name?"

"Rose." She seemed to relax, and her eyelids fluttered.

"Roses are my favorite flower," Lucy told her. "My grandmother had lovely pink ones in her garden in Pennsylvania."

Rose dozed fitfully. Miss Kellogg came in to check on her. She brought a basin of water and a clean cloth.

"Will she be better now?" Lucy asked.

"She'll start up the sweats next. Put this cool compress on her head when the fever starts." She picked up the empty cup. "Sometimes the ague makes them do crazy things. Call out if you need me."

A few minutes later the woman's eyes flew open, and she sat upright. She threw off her blankets. "Where is this?" she asked. She tried to get up, but collapsed back on the bed.

Lucy picked up a blanket and tried to cover her with it. "You're in Lawrence. You're safe here."

"Got to go," she gasped. "Got to get out of here." She threw the cover away from her. "Hot. Too hot."

Lucy soaked the cloth in the basin of water. "Lie back. This will help."

The woman looked around wild-eyed, but accepted the cloth for her head. "Can't stay here," she said. "He'll come for me." She raised her right hand to the cloth on her head. Her arm was marked with scabbed lesions. "He'll kill me if he catches me."

"You're safe," Lucy told her again. When her patient seemed to calm, Lucy took the cloth away, dipped it again in the cool water, wrung it, and replaced it on Rose's forehead.

Outside, a dog barked. Rose sat upright, the cloth falling to her lap. "Dogs! They coming for me!" She thrust her feet to the floor, her head whipping left, then right, her eyes wide. "I won't go!"

Lucy reached for her arm, but Rose jerked free. "No!" She tried to stand, then fell to her knees. "I won't go!"

Miss Kellogg rushed into the room and pushed past Lucy. "Hush now, Rose!" she said. "You're in Lawrence!" She wrapped her arms around the scarred shoulders. Lucy helped Miss Kellogg lift Rose back on the bed. Once there, Rose passed once again into a fitful sleep, tossing and moaning.

"Is she dying?" Lucy asked.

"No, she's delirious right now. It will pass. She'll wake in a few hours and feel better."

Lucy looked at the sleeping Rose. "What will happen to her?"

"We had hoped to move her tonight, but I don't think she'll be well enough. Maybe tomorrow night." Miss Kellogg pulled the sheet over Rose's injured arms. "The ague will hit her again in a few days. There will be others to take care of her then."

"Where do they take them?"

"I don't know exactly where the Liberty Line leads, but they go all the way to Canada. There's a settlement there. It even has a school so that Rose can learn to read and write. She'll be safe."

"She said her owner would kill her if he caught her."

Miss Kellogg nodded. "He is a cruel man, but her freedom is worth the risk."

"May I stay with her a little while?"

"Not too long. You'll need to get back home before someone comes looking for you."

"I understand. Could I use a pen and some paper, please?"

Miss Kellogg returned with paper, pen, and ink. She laid Rose's mended black dress over the back of the chair next to the bed.

Lucy sat at the small table in the room with Rose. The scabby lesions and the scars from old wounds on her shoulders told her the story of Rose's past, but Lucy wanted to think about Rose's future. She imagined Rose in Canada, learning the alphabet and sounding out words.

Lucy picked up the pen and began to write. She would never see Rose again, but she could give her a gift. A simple poem Rose could keep until the day she could learn to read it. Lucy wrote a few lines on the paper.

Freedom's Rose

I see blue sky.
I breathe free air.
My life is mine,
When I get there.

No whips will cut.
No chains will bind.
I'm free at last,
Myself to find.

Lucy wished she could stay to read it to Rose. Would she smile when she heard it?

Lucy folded the paper and tucked it into the pocket of the dress. She secured it with a pin. She hoped it would make it all the way to Rose's destination.

22

Mr. G. W. Brown, Publisher of the *Herald of Freedom*—Sir:—By this mail I return you five copies of your paper without any inscription thereon. As there is a law now in force in this Territory prohibiting the circulation of incendiary publications, I most respectfully decline giving them a circulation. You will confer a favor by keeping your rotten and corrupt effusions from tainting the pure air of this portion of the Territory.

-Robert S. Kelley, Postmaster,
Atchison, K.T.

L ucy was standing near the door when Mr. Brown came storming in. The bell on the door nearly flew off.

He slapped the letter on the counter in front of Papa. "Look at this letter from the postmaster up in Atchison," he said. "He's refusing to deliver my newspapers!"

Papa read the letter aloud. He looked up. "The *Herald,* an 'incendiary publication'?"

"It's ridiculous!" Mr. Brown snatched back the letter and shoved it into his vest pocket. "If anything is incendiary, it's the rubbish they print in their *Squatter Sovereign* in Atchison! I've never seen such a nest of fire-eaters as populates that town!"

"What will you do, Mr. Brown?" Lucy asked.

"I'm going to publish this letter. I'll let the readers of the paper know what kind of men these are. It can only put more weight behind our purpose in Big Springs."

"Maybe we should work on a resolution to present at the meeting," Papa suggested.

"Good idea, Marcus," Mr. Brown said. "I'll get the other delegates together, and we'll meet here tomorrow afternoon. About one o'clock?" He stormed out the door without waiting for an answer.

Mamma came out of the kitchen. "Gracious! What was that about?"

Papa picked up several tin lanterns from a display on the counter. "Brown had a nasty letter from Atchison," he said. He put the lanterns on a shelf nearby. "He's calling a meeting of the delegates to write a resolution to present at Big Springs. We're meeting here tomorrow afternoon."

"Here in the store? What about our customers, Marcus?" Mamma put her hands on the countertop, as if trying to protect it. "Are you forgetting that we have a business to run?"

Papa continued to clear the counter. "It's just one meeting, Maggie."

"But you'll have half a dozen men in here, arguing about politics all afternoon!"

"It could be good for business, Mamma." Lucy said.

Papa smiled. "Lucy's got the right idea."

Mamma sighed. "I don't have much say about this, do I?"

By the next morning, Mamma had decided to make the

best of the situation. After breakfast, she kept the fire going in the stove. She mixed up dough and rolled it out, then opened three jars of canned peaches. She put a pot of coffee on the stove and had Lucy letter a sign that said, "Fresh-baked pie, 5¢ a slice."

All five Lawrence delegates came to the meeting. Mr. Brown was there to take notes for the newspaper. By the time the men arrived, Mamma had two pies in the oven.

Lucy filled the coffee cups and listened to the conversation.

"We need to present a strong resolution," Papa said. "Congress must know about the outrages of this Bogus Legislature."

"The proslavers are getting bolder every day," said Mr. Dobbs. "Newhouse said he was stopped on the Delaware Road last week and threatened when he was delivering lumber."

"Two barns belonging to Free State men have been burned in the last three weeks," Mr. Jacob added.

Mr. Farley held up his cup for Lucy to fill. "Sheriff Jones and his hoodlums up in Atchison have to be stopped. This business with Reverend Butler was the last straw."

"What happened to him?" Mr. Garrison asked.

"They beat the poor old man, called him a 'Republican,' and painted an R on his forehead," Mr. Farley said. "Then they set him adrift on the Missouri River on a raft with no rudder or paddle. He's lucky to be alive."

Mr. Brown pulled some papers from his pocket. "That's not the worst, gentlemen."

They all waited for him to continue. "I received this letter today from a farmer who lives near Atchison. He says that a female slave belonging to a man from that town had escaped, but was recaptured and returned. He says, 'She was inhumanely whipped by her master. With a just appreciation of her wrongs, and knowing of no other effectual means of deliverance, she committed herself to the waters of the Missouri. Her body floated down the river some three miles and was washed ashore.'" He put the paper down. "When they told her master what happened, he refused to even give her a decent burial. They left her body to the buzzards."

They were all quiet for a moment. Lucy thought of Rose and the scars that marked her shoulders and arms. Thank goodness Rose had made it to the Liberty Line.

"There's more," Mr. Brown said. He held a newspaper clipping. "Instead of recognizing the evil of her master, the *Squatter Sovereign* wants to blame the people of Lawrence, or as they call us, 'an organized band of abolitionists in our midst. We counsel our friends who have money in slave property to keep a sharp lookout, lest their valuable slaves may be induced to commit acts which might jeopardize their lives.'"

Mamma stood near the kitchen door. She put down the two plates of pie and shook her head sadly. "The poor woman. Her only relief was to take her own life."

"Are they sure she killed herself?" Lucy asked. She took Mr. Garrison's cup to refill it. "How do they know her master didn't beat her and throw her in the river?"

"The man who found the body found a note in her pocket," Mr. Brown said. "Actually, he said it wasn't really a regular note. It was a more like a poem, a little verse. Talked about freedom and heaven. I guess if she couldn't have freedom, she was ready to choose death."

Lucy's hand trembled, and she spilled coffee on the floor. She stared down at it, feeling dizzy. She set the coffeepot and cup on the counter.

"Lucy?" Mamma said. "Are you all right?"

"I need some fresh air. May I go out for a few minutes?"

"Don't be gone too long."

Lucy had to talk to Miss Kellogg. She ran the three blocks to her house and knocked on the door. When Miss Kellogg opened it, Lucy gasped.

"Rose …"

"I heard the news this morning," Miss Kellogg said.

Lucy sank into a chair. "How did she get caught?"

Miss Kellogg took her hand. "I don't know. They took her to the next stop. Maybe the ague made her delirious, and she ran out in the open and was captured. Or maybe the darkness was too much for her. The Liberty Line moves at night. After weeks of never seeing the sun, people become restless. Sometimes the dark makes them crazy."

Lucy began to cry. "I hoped she would learn to read that poem for herself once she was free."

"She found your note when she woke. She asked me to read it to her. It gave her hope, Lucy."

Lucy looked at Miss Kellogg. "I don't believe she killed herself. "

"I suspect you're right, but even if we could prove her owner was responsible, he would be tried in a court set up by the Territorial Legislature. They wouldn't convict him."

"What can we do?"

"The same thing we've been doing. Help others get away."

"But Rose didn't get away, Miss Kellogg."

"Some won't make it, Lucy. We can work our hardest, but some won't."

"Then why do we do it?"

"Because some will. "

<hr/>

Darkness
By Lucy Catherine Thomkins

Darkness takes you from all you have known.
A life not your life; a home not your home;
"Freedom" is only a word you have heard,
A life you can't dare to imagine.

In the dark you ride; in the dark you hide;
Dark skin, dark eyes, dark clothes, dark night.
Your friend is the dark; your betrayer is light,
And every strange face a new danger.

Darkness takes you where you will go.
A life in the light; a home of your own;
Where freedom will soon be a life that you know.
And chains you won't need to remember.

By the lamplight in her room that night, Lucy thought about darkness, and about Rose, and about the words she had just written. She wanted to believe them, but they described a future that Rose would never know. She had failed again. She took food for the fugitives at the barn, but it wasn't enough. She tried to help Rose through her sickness and give her hope, but now Rose was dead, killed by her own master. He would never be punished. Even worse, Lucy's poem had made people think that Rose had killed herself.

She raised the lid of her desk to place her poetry journal there. Under the scattered papers inside, she spied a corner of the brochure she had found in Papa's overcoat pocket so long ago, *Information for Kanzas Immigrants.* She slid it out to look at it again. The booklet had painted a picture, a promised land free of slavery, filled with "good men and true, who will maintain their own rights, and respect those of others." But the Ruffians and their Bogus Legislature were trying to turn Kansas into something far different: A Kansas where people could be put in jail for carrying a Free State newspaper. Where judges and juries supported laws made by men who were elected with stolen votes. What had happened to Kanzas, the one the brochure described?

The sleeve of her nightdress brushed the roughness of the carved words on the front edge of the lid. *The pen is mightier than the sword.*

She traced the letters with her finger. Papa had faith in the power of her words.

A poem wasn't enough, but what else could she do?

She couldn't vote, she couldn't change the laws, but she could tell the truth, even if the murderer would never face justice for his crime. If it would anger people enough to stand up against the Bogus Legislature, then Rose's death would have meaning.

She pulled out a blank piece of paper and began to write.

Dear Editor,

Your readers deserve to know the truth about a recent tragedy. The body of a girl, a slave from Atchison, washed ashore downriver from that town. The **Squatter Sovereign** claims that "abolitionists" influenced her to harm herself. Their evidence is a note found in her pocket.

But the proslavers have ignored one fact: She did not know how to write. That note in her pocket was not her own, but was given to her by a friend. It was an expression of hope, not despair. I know this is true. I wrote that note.

A witness says the whip marks on her body were fresh. Has no one considered that her killer may well have been the same man who so cruelly left her body to be devoured by buzzards?

No jury in the Territory would convict this murderer. Still, we must stand strong in our efforts to free Kanzas of the evils of slavery and this false government. We must make Kanzas free.

—A True Citizen of Kanzas

Lucy folded the paper. Mr. Brown and Papa would leave early for Big Springs. She didn't know if her plan would work, but it was all she could do.

23

Union is Strength!
Free State Convention!

Let no sectional or party issues distract or prevent the perfect cooperation of Free State men. Union and harmony are absolutely necessary to success. The proslavery party is fully and effectively organized. And to contend against them successfully, we also must be united. Without prudence and harmony of action we are certain to fail.

Let every man then do his duty and we are certain of victory.

— poster for Big Springs convention,
September 1855

Lucy awoke in the dark to the sounds of voices downstairs and the jingle of a horse's harness outside. Mr. Wyman had brought a buggy from the stable.

She crept to the top of the stairs and crouched in the shadows where she could see Mamma, Papa, Mr. Brown, and Mr. Wyman below. Papa held his rifle in one hand and his hat in the other.

"I don't like it," Mamma said. "The proslavery men could ride in and arrest you."

"I don't think we need to worry about that, Mrs. Thomkins," Mr. Wyman said. "They think the government won't recognize our movement, so we don't pose a threat to them. We're willing to let them think that – for now."

"And you don't worry about the rest of us here, with half the men away?"

Mr. Brown put on his hat and moved toward the door. "Ma'am, I worry more about that fool Lawson that I've left to finish this issue of the paper. If this meeting wasn't so important, I wouldn't be going."

Papa waited as the other men went out. Lucy grasped the stair railing to keep from tumbling over as Joseph rushed past her. "Papa – wait up! I'm coming!"

Papa shook his head. "I need you to stay here while I'm gone."

"But I can help Mr. Wyman with the horses while you're at Big Springs!"

Mamma pulled him back. "I'm sending one family member," she said. "That is enough representation."

Joseph looked at Papa. "Please," he begged.

Mr. Wyman came back to the door. "I'll tell you what, Joseph. You've been good help around the stable lately, and Sam will need some help with the rest of the horses while I'm away. If you'll feed and exercise the horses and clean the stalls, I'll pay you when I get back."

"Exercise them? You mean we can ride?"

Mr. Wyman laughed. "Yes, you can ride them. Any but Liberty, that is. Don't let anyone on that horse. And I'll expect to find them in good shape when we come back."

"Yes, sir!" Joseph smiled.

Papa kissed Mamma. "We'll be back tomorrow evening."

"I'll take that as a promise," Mamma said. "I won't be able to draw an easy breath until you get back."

"If we don't resist now, we will be at their mercy. It's the only way we can begin to work for a Free State constitution."

She nodded. "I know. But I will worry just the same."

Mamma retreated to her room for a while.

Joseph went back to bed.

Lucy went to her desk and lit her oil lamp. She pulled the folded letter from her desk and read it again. Would anyone believe what she had written?

Mr. Brown was gone to Big Springs. Mr. Lawson wouldn't arrive at the newspaper office for at least another hour. It seemed impossible to think that he would pay any attention to it. She had no proof. Perhaps he would discard it. Then again, Mr. Brown sometimes published anonymous letters. Especially if he thought people would talk about them. She remembered Mr. Whittier's words from Miss Kellogg's book:

> Shall Honor bleed?—Shall truth succumb?
> Shall pen, and press, and soul be dumb?

She had to try.

Lucy dressed quickly and tiptoed down the stairs, as if going to the outhouse just like any other morning. She slipped next door to the newspaper office, and she slid the folded paper under the door.

Mamma's worry made her shaky and distracted. Her hands were so fidgety she could hardly make breakfast. She dropped her spoon twice as she stirred the eggs. Then she knocked over a glass and broke it. Lucy offered to wash the dishes, just to get her out of the kitchen.

By the time the plates were put away, Mamma had decided to move everything in the store.

"We need to rearrange the displays," she said. "If the customers need to look around to find something, they may find more to buy." She considered the possibilities, then settled her gaze on some boxes near the wall. "Lucy, make a nice display of slates, slate pencils, pens, and inkwells in the front window where people will see them. School will start in a few weeks."

Joseph groaned. "School," he said, and let out a sigh.

She pointed to the wooden kegs of nails and the boxes of brass hinges. "Joseph, move those things across the room, next to the building supplies."

Joseph edged toward the door. "But Mamma, I need to go to the stable to clean out the stalls and help Sam exercise the horses."

"You can go to the stable when you've finished here."

"But if Sam does it all, he'll keep all the money."

"Then you'll want to finish your work quickly, won't you?"

Joseph grumbled, but he got to work.

The first week of September had brought little relief from the heat of summer. They opened the door to let in the breeze, but it brought more of the ever-present dust from the street in with it. Everything they moved also needed to be dusted. Mamma stopped giving them new chores only when customers came in, and today there weren't many. By mid-afternoon

Lucy had rearranged the bed linens and cookware twice to suit Mamma's satisfaction, and Joseph had polished every brass skeleton key and hinge in the store.

Lucy was dusting glass oil lamps when she heard hoof beats outside. She watched through the window as Levi slid from the back of a beautiful chestnut horse. He looped the reins over the porch rail, pulled a soft bag from the horse's back, and came in the door.

Joseph looked up from the clay smoking pipes he was arranging. He scowled.

Levi looked around. "Is your mother here? I came with some things to trade."

Mamma came out from the kitchen, wiping her hands on her apron. "I'm here."

Levi set the bag on the counter and reached into it. "*Nekkaen* sent some moccasins and two rabbit pelts."

"Oh, these are lovely!" Mamma said, as she turned the moccasins over in her hands.

Levi smiled. "Thank you, ma'am. I'll tell her you like them."

"What does she need today?"

"She has an order for a special project, and she needs more beads and thread." Levi looked around. "Do you still have beads?"

"Oh, yes, we've just moved things around a bit today."

"A bit," mumbled Joseph.

Mamma waved toward the sewing supplies. "The beads are over on that side now. Lucy can help you find thread, too."

Joseph stared out the front window. "That your horse?" he asked Levi.

"That's my horse."

"Where'd you steal it?"

"Joseph!" Mamma said.

Levi held his head high. "My father gave her to me, and I raised her. Her name is *Teakee*. It means 'Heart.'"

Lucy could see the jealousy in Joseph's frown. He put the last pipe in place. "I'm finished," he announced. "Can I go to the stable?"

Mamma nodded, and Joseph hurried out.

Mamma put a hand on Levi's shoulder. "I apologize for my son's rudeness. I'm afraid he is a poor reflection on us. You are always welcome here."

Levi said nothing, but pulled several small leather pouches from his bag. "Can we look at the beads now?"

Lucy helped Levi fill the pouches with the beads his mother wanted: dark blue, bright red, and some large iridescent pearl-tone white ones. Mamma helped him choose the right needle and thread for beading.

She wrote the transaction in her ledger book. "Is there anything else? You have some credit."

"No, ma'am. I need to get to the post office with a letter to mail for my father."

"Let your mother know she has three dollars credit and can use it anytime."

Levi put the beads and other things in his bag. "Thank you.

I'll tell her." He tied the bag shut.

Lucy wasn't ready to say goodbye yet. "Mamma, may I walk to the post office with Levi?"

Mamma nodded. "See if we have anything. I'm expecting a letter from Mr. Jenkins in Pittsburgh."

Lucy and Levi walked outside. A hot wind stirred up dust from the street, and the sun burned on the back of Lucy's neck. Levi untied Teakee and held the reins.

"She's beautiful," Lucy said, and stroked Teakee's velvety nose.

"I've had her since the day after she was born." Levi patted the side of the horse's neck, which glistened with sweat. "I need to find her some water."

"Mr. Babcock keeps the trough by the post office full," Lucy said.

As they stepped into the street, pounding hooves came toward them from the direction of the river. Two riders raced past the saw mill, whooping and urging their horses at breakneck speed. Teakee jerked her head and shied, but Levi held the reins and pulled her to the side of the street. Lucy jumped back, expecting a Ruffian invasion. But as the riders came closer, she recognized the red hair that stood straight up on the lead rider's head.

"It's Joseph!" she gasped. "And he's riding Liberty!" Sam rode a palomino that was at least fifteen feet back. He crouched low over the horse's neck, urging it forward, and the gap between the horses narrowed as they sped past. Lucy turned her head away from the cloud of dust that billowed in their wake.

A crowd of boys waited next to the Methodist church a block away. They cheered as Joseph sped by them, with Sam now close behind.

Levi shook his head. "It's too hot to be racing those horses. If my father caught me doing that, he'd take Teakee."

"They'll be in trouble if Mr. Wyman finds out they were racing Liberty."

Levi looked at Teakee and gently tugged her reins. "Let's get you some water," he said.

Lucy and Levi walked toward the post office. As they turned the corner by Mr. Fowler's law office, Levi stopped. When Lucy stopped too, he asked, "Do they hide slaves in the barn on Mississippi Street?"

Lucy's breath caught in her throat. She looked down at her dusty shoes. "I don't know what you mean."

He waited for her eyes to meet his. "You went there with a basket the night of the picnic."

Lucy didn't answer.

"You knocked at the door and went inside."

Lucy's voice shook. "You followed me?"

"You left the picnic with a heavy basket on your arm. When you came out of the barn, your basket was light. Then you ran away."

He knew everything. How could she have been so careless? Lucy looked around to be sure no one could hear them. "Please don't tell anyone!" she whispered. "I'd be in such awful trouble."

Levi shook his head. "I know the danger."

Lucy took a deep breath and relaxed. She looked at Levi. "Do you think I'm terrible for helping them?"

He shook his head. "Reverend Johnson had slaves at the mission." He paused. "It's good work you do."

Levi tied Teakee in front of the post office, where she could drink from the trough.

Mr. Babcock was sorting mail when they arrived. "Hello, Lucy," he said. "Want me to see if you have anything today?"

"Yes, please. Mamma is expecting a letter from Pittsburgh soon."

He looked through the tray of letters for last names beginning with T and checked for any addressed to Thomkins. "Not today," he said. "Check back on Friday." He looked at Levi. "Who's your friend?"

"This is Levi. He has a letter to mail."

Mr. Babcock nodded toward Levi, but looked at Lucy again. He leaned across the counter toward her and said softly, "Does he know he has to pay to mail it?"

Levi pulled coins from his pocket. "I have three cents for the postage." He put the letter on the counter with the pennies.

Mr. Babcock reddened. He looked at the address on the letter. "Yes ... that's right ... three cents." He took the coins. "I'll get this letter out for you with the next post."

"Thank you, sir." Levi smiled.

When Lucy was outside again, she giggled. "He was surprised you could speak English."

"So were you, remember?" He untied Teakee's reins.

As they started to go back toward the store, they heard shouting.

"Sam! Sam, come back and help me!"

Lucy knew Joseph's voice, and he sounded frantic.

"If that horse dies, I don't want to be anywhere around!" Sam yelled.

Lucy ran toward Vermont Street, in the direction of the voices. Levi followed with Teakee. Joseph was on his knees in the street. Liberty was lying on the ground, caked with dirt that had turned to mud on him.

"Get up, Liberty," Joseph wailed.

"What happened?" Lucy asked.

Joseph looked up. "He started pawing the ground. He was awful sweaty. He kept twisting around. Then he just dropped."

"You ran him too hard in this heat," Levi said.

Joseph wailed. "Mr. Wyman will kill me if anything happens to him." He looked desperately at Levi. "Please, can you help him?"

Levi handed Teakee's reins to Lucy and knelt next to Liberty's head. "What happened after the race?"

Joseph looked down at the horse. "Nothing. I let him loose to walk."

"Where did he go?"

"He went to the water trough. He drank for a while."

Levi stroked Liberty's head, then placed a hand at the horse's jaw, curled his fingers under it, and held it for a few seconds.

Joseph sniffed. "What's the matter with him?"

"You let him drink when he was too hot."

"Is he gonna die?"

"He won't die," Levi said. "His heart is steady, but his gut hurts."

Liberty snorted and rolled onto his back, then back again to his side. Levi tossed the reins to Joseph. "We have to get him up. He needs to walk."

Levi stood up and gave a soft whistle. Liberty struggled, but then collapsed on the ground again. "Help me," Levi said.

"We can't lift him!" Joseph said.

"We don't have to lift him. Just help him stay upright until he can get his feet under him." Joseph got on one side of the horse and Levi on the other. Levi gave a whistle. When Liberty tried to rise, both boys put their arms under him. He got to his feet.

Joseph held the reins out to Levi.

Levi shook his head. "No, you walk him. You did this to him. You have to help him now."

"How far should I walk him?"

"Walk him as far as you ran him," Levi said.

Joseph walked toward Eighth Street leading Liberty. Lucy had never seen her brother so miserable.

"Will Liberty be better now?" Lucy asked.

"Walking will help," Levi said. They stood in the shade of Hubbard's Carpentry Shop where Teakee could find a little grass in the side yard. They watched Joseph and Liberty walk the two blocks to Mosier's Hardware Store, where they turned around.

When Joseph came back to them, he slowed down. "Is that enough?"

Levi frowned. "Look at his gait. It's uneven. He still hurts. Walk him down to the levee, then back to the stable. We'll meet you there."

Joseph nodded and kept walking. He stroked Liberty's neck. "I'm sorry, boy," he said, as they walked away. "I'm so sorry."

Lucy and Levi sat in the shade a few more minutes while Teakee nibbled grass, then led her back to the stable to wait for Joseph and Liberty.

When they returned from the levee, they both looked better.

Levi reached out to pat Liberty's side. "He'll feel better now. Take him inside, brush him down. Give him a handful of feed and just a little water."

Joseph stood for a moment, not saying anything. He reached his hand out to Levi. "Thanks for helping me."

Levi stroked Liberty's neck. "I helped him."

Joseph let his hand fall. "Then, thanks for helping him." He turned and led Liberty into the barn.

Levi picked up Teakee's reins. "I stayed too long. *Nekkaen* will worry." He swung up easily onto her back. "Your brother has learned something about horses."

"I hope he learned something about people, too." Lucy smiled as Levi rode away.

Joseph was brushing Liberty when Lucy went inside the barn to check on him.

Lucy expected to start the conversation, but he didn't give her the chance.

"Sam dared me to race the horses. I thought it would be fun," he said, as he swept the curry comb in circles down the side of Liberty's neck. "I never meant to hurt Liberty."

"You're lucky Levi was there to help you."

"I know." Joseph moved the brush down Liberty's chest. "I thought Sam was my friend, but he ran off the minute there was trouble." He looked up at her. "I thought Levi was my enemy, but I was wrong about that, too."

She didn't say anything. She just watched as he continued to groom Liberty, brushing in circles over the horse's shoulder and down his back, using gentle strokes along his side.

When he was finished with the left side, Joseph ducked under the tie rope to begin on the other side. "Lucy, will you not tell Papa or Mr. Wyman what happened? If Mr. Wyman found out, he'd never let me work here again."

"What about Levi? You've been awful to him."

Joseph turned to face Lucy. "I know. He hates me, and I can't blame him."

"After the things you've said, I don't blame him, either." Lucy paused. "If you want me to keep your secret, you'll have to promise to treat Levi better."

"I will, I promise!" Joseph crossed his heart. "I'll make it up to Levi." He turned to begin brushing again. "I don't know how I'll do it, but I will."

"I hope so," Lucy said.

24

Resolved, That the best interests of Kansas require a population of free white men and that in the organization we are in favor of stringent laws excluding all Negroes, bond or free, from the Territory ...

– Big Springs Platform,
September 5, 1855

At breakfast on the morning after his return from Big Springs, Papa's red-rimmed eyes betrayed his lack of sleep. He had come home long after Lucy was in bed.

"Here's the new *Herald*," Mamma said. She held the newspaper out for him. "Mr. Lawson brought it by yesterday."

Papa glanced over the front page.

"Looks like Lawson did a respectable job with the newspaper," he said. "Look, Lucy, my name's in the paper."

She leaned toward him to see the paper. "Where, Papa?"

He pointed to a story near the top. "Right here. It lists the delegates to the meeting at Big Springs. See? 'Marcus Thomkins.'"

He sipped his coffee and continued to read. He chuckled. "The new governor, Wilson Shannon, arrived last week. I guess they took him to Westport, Missouri first. He thought he was in Kansas and told the crowd, all *Missourians*, he would uphold *their* laws." He shook his head. "The only thing funny about that is the truth of it."

Papa looked up from his newspaper. "Where's Joseph this morning?"

"He went to the stable early," Mamma said. "He wanted to check on the horses and clean the stalls before Mr. Wyman got there."

And check on Liberty, Lucy thought. Was he being responsible, or just making sure Mr. Wyman paid him?

Mamma brought a plate of fried ham slices to the table. As she put one on Papa's plate, she glanced at the paper. "What's that about the *Emma Harmon*?" she asked.

Papa looked at the page and read, "'The steamboat *Emma Harmon* ran aground on a sandbar on the Kansas River. The boat is stuck there, and no other boats will be traveling the river until the water rises.'"

"Oh, no!" Mamma said. "I was expecting a shipment tomorrow. We're low on some of our supplies."

Lucy took a slice from the plate. "Don't worry," she said. "Surely it will have to rain soon, and the boats will run again."

Mamma sat down next to Papa to eat her own breakfast. "Marcus, you haven't said a word about the meeting. What happened?"

Papa folded the paper and laid it on the table. "Most of the platform was what we all expected. They protested the illegal voting in the elections and the actions of the territorial legislature. They stated our intention to form our own government and elect a representative to Congress on our behalf. They declared our desire that Kansas be a free state."

"That all sounds good," Lucy said.

"Yes, it does." Papa stared into his empty coffee cup. "But, we came here to make Kansas a state where all people could live free."

Lucy looked up from her breakfast. "I don't understand. Isn't that what they put in their platform?"

"No. They got it in their heads that the only sure way keep slavery out was to forbid any Negroes to live within the borders of Kansas."

Mamma put down her coffee cup. "How could they pass such a thing?"

"It was Jim Lane," Papa said. "I never saw a slicker politician. He introduced the Black Law and sold it as a way to unify the party."

"Didn't the Lawrence men object?" Mamma asked.

Papa frowned. "When they talked among themselves they objected. But when it came time to vote, not one of them stood with me."

Lucy thought of Eliza's husband. He had worked so hard to buy their freedom, and he dreamed of someday owning land. "Does that mean that free Negroes couldn't live here, even though they can live free in other states?"

"That's right, Lucy Cat. Lane says that will keep them from accusing us of harboring runaways."

Lucy frowned. "But it's just wrong!"

"The constitution isn't final yet," Papa said. "We'll meet in Topeka on the 19th to plan the constitutional convention."

Mamma glared at Papa. "Marcus, another trip?"

"I have to go, Maggie. They'll be electing delegates to the convention. It's the only chance to get the representatives to strike that Black Law from the constitution. I have to get the others to stand up to Lane somehow."

Lucy wondered what would convince the Lawrence men to support the cause of freedom for everyone? Should she write another anonymous letter to the newspaper? If even one more delegate stood up with Papa, that would be two voices instead of just one. And if several men would support Papa, then they might be able to change the constitution. Lucy smiled as she thought of it. Maybe she had found her voice, just like Miss Collins said. She began to plan the letter she would write.

There was a rap at the back door. Mr. Brown stood there, red-faced, holding a newspaper. "Thomkins, have you seen the paper?"

Papa touched the paper that still lay on the table. "We're just looking at it."

Mr. Brown waved his copy in the air, then slapped it on the table. "That numbskull Lawson printed it after we left! I can't believe he'd do this!"

Papa rose and pulled a chair out. "Calm down, George. What's the matter?"

"That idiot! He put an anonymous letter right on the front page. It's an accusation of murder against the owner of that slave girl that drowned!"

Lucy pulled the paper closer. There on the front page, near the bottom of the center column, was the headline, *Cold-Blooded Murder.* The letter was signed "A Voice for Kanzas." It was her letter in the paper!

"I've already had a threat. It came in this morning – tied to a brick that crashed through my front window."

"What kind of threat?" Papa said.

Mr. Brown pulled a crumpled paper from his pocket. "A reminder of the laws of the 'true Kansas Legislature,' the laws that could provide me with 'secure lodging' for the next ten years." His hand shook as he read, "'Or if that doesn't suit you, Sheriff Jones would be pleased to bring some citizens from Atchison to build a gallows in front of the *Herald of Freedom* office to dispatch you more swiftly to your next destination.'"

Mamma gasped. "That settles it, Marcus. You cannot leave us here unprotected with men like this on the rampage."

Papa patted Mamma's hand. She pulled it from his reach. "What will you do, George?" he asked.

Mr. Brown put the note back in his pocket. "I'll write a retraction this week, of course. I hope that will satisfy them."

Papa looked at Mamma, who stood with arms crossed in front on her. "There you see?" he said. "The retraction will do it."

Mamma turned her back.

"I'll be on the lookout for any more letters like this. Josiah Miller over at the *Free State* is certain to make something of it. He never misses an opportunity to humiliate me in his newspaper." Mr. Brown hit his fist on the table, making all the dishes jump. "I've a score to settle with this 'Kanzas' fellow. At the very least I owe him a bloody nose in exchange for my window!"

Mamma and Papa were both watching Mr. Brown when Lucy slid the paper off the table. She rose from her chair, slipped from the kitchen, and climbed the stairs. In her room, she sat at her desk and looked again at her letter. It was right there, her letter in the newspaper. In the *Herald of Freedom* that was sent to subscribers as far away as New York! Who would read her words? She wanted to tell the world that Lucy Thomkins was "A Voice for Kanzas."

But she couldn't. She could never tell anyone that she wrote that letter.

Had the killer himself seen her letter? What if he came back with a mob and pulled Mr. Brown from his house and hanged him, right here?

She shook her head. Ink and paper, words on a page. She ran her fingers across the words inscribed along the edge of the desk. *... mightier than the sword ...* Her words *had* been powerful.

Everything seemed so wrong. They came to Kansas to make it free, but their votes meant nothing. The voices for freedom could be silenced in prison, or even by death.

Lucy opened her poetry journal and dipped her pen in the inkwell.

No Voice for Kanzas

In Washington they claimed the Kanza land.
They said the settlers would decide her fate.
The flames of strife this controversy fanned
Meant none who cared could dare to hesitate.
They came from East and South to stake their claims.
Election Day would take all doubts away.
But slav'ry's guardians cast their votes for shame,
And Freedom's voice was silenced on that day.

The United States was supposed to be the "Land of the Free", but the Liberty Line had to help people leave the country so they could be free. And now, the men who said they stood for freedom in Kansas wanted to keep some of their fellow American citizens, free citizens, out of Kansas because of the color of their skin. How could they deny freedom and still call themselves Free State men?

It seemed so hopeless. She didn't dare write another letter that would put Mr. Brown in danger again, but the Black Law was too important to ignore. She had to try.

How could she do it? She would be more careful this time. She must use a different signature, and her message must speak to the men who would go with Papa to the Free State meeting in Topeka. She wouldn't accuse anyone of anything, but she must remind the men of their reason for coming to Kansas.

Surely no one would threaten to murder someone for that.

She took up her pen and began:

Fellow Citizens of Lawrence:

We who are under the rule of outsiders, know the hunger for freedom. We now have the means to resist these outsiders as we work to form a new constitution for our future state. Did we not come to Kanzas to create a Free State? Did we not dream of a state which would be Free for All, including Negroes? Then why would we settle for a state which must only be free of Negroes? How can Free State men sit quietly and allow our new constitution to deny the very liberty that we sought? At Big Springs, only one man voiced a protest to the Black Law. We cannot let that man stand alone for freedom in Kanzas. If the delegates from Lawrence will stand together to strike this Black Law from our constitution, then we may realize the dream of Freedom that brought us here.

Stand up for Freedom in Kanzas!

She read the letter again. What could she do now? After her last letter, Mr. Brown would never print it. She would have to get it to Mr. Brown's rival, Josiah Miller, who published the *Kansas Free State.* She folded the letter and put it in her pocket. She would take it to Mr. Miller's office today. If she watched for a chance, she could surely slip inside and leave it without anyone seeing her.

25

Shooting in Lawrence

There is nothing connected with Lawrence that is so very disagreeable as a continual firing of pistols and guns ... Aside from the great annoyance, it is certainly attended with a great deal of danger. Balls have been seen and heard whistling about buildings along the streets, but luckily no human being has been injured yet.

–Herald of Freedom, Sept. 1855

Joseph set a fresh bucket of water on the floor, and Lucy dunked her mop into it. She moved the muddy water around on the floor in swirls.

Mamma stood at the store counter with her pencil and her ledger book. "With the river down, there's no guessing when the boats will start running again. We're nearly out of all our staple goods."

Papa pounded a nail into a loose floorboard and stroked his fingers across it to be sure it was smooth. "I'm sorry, Maggie," he said. "I just can't go to Westport for supplies."

"We don't have enough flour, sugar, or lamp oil to last through the week," Mamma said. "We'll lose our customers to

Hornsby and Ferril's. They have been making trips to town for supplies."

Papa stepped onto the floor board to test it. "The meeting in Topeka is Wednesday; I wouldn't get back in time."

Mamma closed the ledger book. "Our livelihood is at stake."

"The freedom of the territory is at stake," Papa replied. "Since the *Free State* ran that letter last week, four men have agreed to stand with me to protest the Black Law."

Lucy looked up from her mop. Her letter had moved four men to stand with Papa? At last, her words had worked the right way.

Joseph stopped on his way to the door with the bucket of dirty water. "I could go to town," he offered. "Mr. Wyman taught me how to hitch the wagon. He'd let me borrow it to go for supplies."

Papa shook his head. "It's too dangerous. The Ruffians have riders on all the roads to threaten the Free State settlers at every opportunity."

The jingle of the bell on the front door interrupted their conversation. Annie came in with a basket. Joseph lugged the bucket out through the kitchen.

"Hey, Lucy. Hello, Mrs. Thomkins." She set the basket on the counter. "Do you need eggs? Ma sent up three dozen."

"I certainly do," Mamma said. "I've been out for two days." She pulled a tin pan from the shelf and lined it with some towels.

Annie took the eggs one by one from her basket and put them into the pan. "Ma needs some flour, cornmeal, and coffee."

"Oh, dear," Mamma frowned. "We're low on flour. I can give her a little, but I don't know when I'll have more." She sent a look in Papa's direction.

"Are you sure? We're expecting some visitors. Ma wanted to bake some bread."

"I'm sorry, Annie. The river is too low for the boats to bring us supplies. I can give her some extra cornmeal, if that will help."

"I guess that will have to do," Annie said. She watched while Mamma scooped cornmeal into a bag. "Pa's going to town soon. Could he get your things for you?"

Mamma set the bag upright and smiled. "Do you think he would?"

"I could ask him, ma'am."

"It would be a great help to us if he could," Papa said.

"I'll ask him tonight and let you know tomorrow," Annie offered.

"Isn't he here with you?" Mamma asked.

Annie giggled. "No, ma'am. I walked."

"And you're going to carry these bags all that way? I don't like the idea of you walking that road by yourself."

Joseph opened the kitchen door. "Papa? How many more buckets of water?"

"That's enough for now," Papa said. "I have another job for you. Go ask if Mr. Wyman has a wagon we can use."

He turned to Mamma. "We could take Annie home and

276

ask John if he'll get our supplies."

Annie frowned. "I don't know if we should. Ma isn't expecting company."

"We won't stay long," Papa insisted.

Joseph ran off before Annie could object.

Mamma and Papa bent over the counter, making a list of the supplies they needed.

"Flour, sugar, cornmeal, lard," Mamma said.

"Don't forget coffee," Papa said. "We're nearly out."

Annie tugged on Lucy's sleeve and pulled her to the other side of the room. "You have to do something. Your pa can't go out to our house," she whispered. "We have *guests*."

"What can we do?"

Annie looked frantic. "I don't know, but we need to think of something."

A wagon clattered to a halt in front of the store. Joseph jumped down from the driver's seat and patted the rump of the dappled horse harnessed to the wagon. "Mr. Wyman said we could use Reuben today," he said.

"Good!" Papa said. "Come on, Annie, let's get those bags on the wagon."

Papa put Annie's sacks in the wagon bed and put out his hand to help her up.

"Can Lucy come?" Annie asked. "One of our cats had a litter last week. They're the cutest little things!"

Lucy looked at Mamma. "Go ahead." Mamma waved her on. "We're not getting any more work done here today."

Lucy climbed into the back of the wagon with Annie.

Papa sat next to Joseph. "Let's see how you handle this rig."

"Hyup!" Joseph snapped the reins. Reuben started forward, headed south on the road toward the Wakarusa.

"How many wagons does Wyman have at the stable?" Papa asked.

"Three good ones," Joseph said. "Seems like there's always a couple broken. He keeps the blacksmith busy fixing them."

He and Papa talked about horses, wagons, and harnesses as Reuben kept up an easy pace.

Lucy and Annie sat on top of a canvas tarp that covered a pile of hay in the bed of the wagon.

"What should we do?" Lucy whispered.

"I don't know. I just need to give them some warning before we get there."

As they neared the Wakarusa, the trees were closer together. Leaves rustled in the breeze and were beginning to change from green to gold and red. The abandoned claims Lucy and Annie had seen in the spring were now so overgrown with weeds that the logs that had marked the outlines of the cabins were nearly hidden.

When they were still a short distance away from her house, Annie tapped Papa's arm. "Mr. Thomkins, can we stop the wagon, please? I'd like to run ahead and let Ma know you're coming."

"Are you sure?" Papa asked. "We're almost there."

"You know how women are, sir. They don't like to be surprised by company."

Papa nodded. "Yes, I suppose you're right. You run ahead.

Come back and wave at us when she's ready."

"I will, thank you, sir!" Annie jumped from the back of the wagon and ran down the road toward the house.

While they waited, Joseph jumped off the wagon. He walked along Reuben's side to check the fittings on the harness.

He climbed back onto the wagon, just as Annie appeared at the side of the road and waved to them.

Joseph guided Reuben into the lane that led to the house. A new barn stood behind the dugout house, and a chicken coop huddled next to it. Annie stood next to the house, and Joseph stopped the wagon near her. Lucy handed the sacks of flour and cornmeal to Annie.

"Hello, Marcus!" Mr. Jacob emerged from the barn and walked toward them. "Good to see you."

He turned to Joseph. "I think you're half a foot taller than the last time I saw you!"

Joseph smiled.

"And I hear you're getting to be a pretty good with that Sharps!"

Papa looked at Joseph. "What?"

"No." Joseph shook his head.

"Nonsense, son, don't be modest." Mr. Jacob slapped Papa's shoulder. "Pritchard says your boy and the Willis boy have been practicing back behind the blacksmith shop. Says this one has a real knack for it."

Papa looked at Joseph again.

"Come on in the house," Mr. Jacob said. He led them toward the door.

Lucy pointed in the direction of the barn. "That's new, isn't it?"

Annie nodded. "Pa built it this summer. Ma's still mad about it, though."

"Why? Doesn't she like it?"

Annie giggled. "Oh, she likes it. She just says it isn't natural that the animals have a better place to stay than we have. She made him promise to build us a house above ground next year."

"One without snakes falling from the ceiling, I hope," Lucy said.

Joseph stopped. He looked from Annie to Lucy, then glanced at the house. "I'll stay out here and take care of Reuben."

"Nothing to worry about," Mr. Jacob laughed. "No snakes around today."

"No," Joseph said. "I should take care of the horse." He walked back to the wagon.

In the house, Annie's mother was setting cups on the table. "The dress looks nice on you, Lucy." She took the packages from Annie. "It's surely kind of you to bring Annie home, Mr. Thomkins, but I hate to trouble you. She would have been fine on foot."

Papa took off his hat. "No trouble," he said. "I came to ask a favor of your husband."

They all sat at the table, and Mrs. Jacob poured a cup of coffee for Papa.

"What can I do for you?" Mr. Jacob asked.

Papa smiled. "Annie said you're planning to make a trip to Westport soon."

"Yes, I have business there in a few days," Mr. Jacob said.

"With the river so low, the boats can't bring our supplies." He looked at Mrs. Jacob. "Maggie is sorry she couldn't give you as much flour as you asked for. We're nearly out."

Mr. Jacob took a drink then set his cup down. "When the river is low, we sure feel the distance from the States."

"I've agreed to go to the Free State meeting in Topeka, and I can't make a trip to town right now. It would be a great service to us if you could pick up some supplies for our store while you're there. Of course we'll send you with cash, and I'll give you some extra merchandise for your trouble."

"I'll make the trip for you, Marcus. We need your voice in Topeka."

That was all it took to start the men on a conversation about politics. Lucy and Annie sat at the table for a few minutes. Then Annie tapped Lucy's arm lightly. "Kittens," she mouthed. The two girls slipped outside. Reuben had his head down, tearing at the grass. Joseph sat in the shade by the wagon, his arms across his knees, and his head down, napping.

Annie put a finger to her lips. She took Lucy's hand and led her to the barn.

Hay dust swirled in the air inside the barn, illuminated by narrow beams of late afternoon sun that slanted between the boards. Annie paused and looked toward a darkened horse stall. "Here, kitty," she said. "I've brought a friend."

A rustling began, then a shadowy form came out from a horse stall. A Negro girl in a black dress stood there. She looked at Lucy.

"Phoebe, this is Lucy."

"Welcome to Kansas," Lucy said.

"Phoebe's been here three days," Annie said. "We need to move her on soon."

"I'm on my way to Canada." Phoebe smiled.

Annie led them back to the horse stall, and the girls sat in the hay.

"Where did you come from?"

"From Cass County, just over the state line," Phoebe said.

"When will you leave?"

Phoebe looked at Annie.

"We don't know," Annie said. "The sheriff's got riders out on the roads at night. They're making it hard for the Liberty Line."

Phoebe frowned. "I got to get far away. I never been away from Miss Evelyn's place before. They'll be looking for me."

"Was Miss Evelyn cruel?" Lucy asked.

Phoebe shook her head. "Miss Evelyn was the kindest woman I ever knew. She raised me in her house after my mama died. All three of us, Lula and Flossie and me, tended to her after her female sickness started. It warn't a year till she was just mostly bones and her swollen belly." Phoebe paused. "She passed last fall, poor thing."

"What happened when she died?" Lucy asked.

"She didn't have no family 'cept for a skunk nephew. He moved in with his whiskey and foulness. It warn't too bad at first. We did the chores and stayed out of his way. Then he turned mean. Took to gamblin', but not smart enough to ever

282

win. Came home mad and drunk all the time."

Lucy winced. "Did you tell anyone?"

"Who would we tell?" Phoebe shook her head. "He owned us. He lost Lula in a poker game to a slick riverboat man who sold her down to Georgia."

"What about you and Flossie?"

"He kept on losing. We knew the same thing could happen to us. Flossie wasn't having no part of it. That girl had some spunk, I tell you!" Phoebe grinned. "He got after her one day, blowing his whiskey breath in her face, and she jumped up and bit his earlobe clean through! Took off running while he was still yowling, and I never seen her again."

Lucy touched Phoebe's arm. "And you?"

"I heard that Flossie had met up with someone who helped her. That man was so mad – he had half the farmers in Cass County out combing the countryside for her. Never found her, but sure made life plenty hard on me. Figured I'd never be so lucky as Flossie."

Annie's eyes were wide. "What happened?"

"A handyman come to the house one day to fix our stove-pipe. Told me Flossie was safe." Phoebe reached into her pocket. "He give me this." She held a wooden disk, the size of a silver dollar. On one side, the letters LL were burned. "He said the folks in the farmhouse down the road would take me in if I showed it to them. I remembered Miss Evelyn's funeral dress was still in the house, and I thought it might make it harder to see me in the dark. That night, I was gone out of there." She put the token back in her pocket.

Annie stood up. "We need to get her out of here, Lucy, but the sheriff's men are watching Pa. Every time he takes the wagon out, they stop him and search it. When I told Pa you were coming with a wagon, he said maybe you could help us."

"But Papa and Joseph …"

"If we can get Phoebe to town, our people can take her north."

Lucy looked first at Phoebe, then at Annie. "How can we do it without them seeing her?"

Phoebe turned to Annie. "Her pa don't know?"

Annie shook her head. "I told Pa there was a tarp on the wagon. He said maybe you could hide under it." Annie glanced toward the barn door. "We didn't count on her brother sitting outside."

"I'd walk it if I thought I had half a chance of making it. I don't care how I get away, but I am not going back to that one-eared Otis!"

Lucy looked up. "Otis?" She shivered. *Otis.* The man who held her the day of the election. The man with the torn and scabbed earlobe.

She had to help Phoebe.

Reuben snorted and shook his harness. Lucy went to the barn door to look out. Joseph stood and stretched. He followed the path toward the outhouse. The door slammed.

Lucy took Phoebe's hand. "Come on. You're going to town."

"Wait," Annie said. "We'll run together. Stay between us, Phoebe."

They hurried to the wagon. Lucy climbed onto the wagon bed and lifted the tarp. She dug in the hay with both hands to clear a spot in the middle of the pile, close to the front wall of the wagon bed. Annie kept a watch on the outhouse.

Phoebe scrambled onto the wagon and lay crouched in the cleared space. Lucy pulled the tarp over her. "Stay still. We'll get you to town," she whispered.

"I'll go give Pa the signal," Annie said. "He'll send word to our folks in town." She hurried back to the house.

Lucy sat in the bed of the wagon, in front of the tarp where it covered Phoebe.

The door on the outhouse swung open, and Joseph emerged. He walked back to the wagon. "Time to go?"

"I hope so," Lucy said. "Mamma will be worried."

A moment later, Papa and Mr. Jacob followed Annie from the house.

"I sure appreciate your help, John," Papa said, as he climbed on the wagon.

"Glad to do it," Mr. Jacob said. "Talk some sense into them about that Black Law."

Papa nodded. "I'll do my best."

Joseph climbed onto the driver's seat and picked up the reins. As the wagon lurched forward, Lucy changed her position so she was not leaning on Phoebe.

Annie stood next to her father. "Bye!" She waved at Lucy.

Lucy waved.

The wind was cooler than it had been when they arrived.

Lucy lifted the edge of the tarp to give Phoebe a little air.

When Reuben's head pointed up the road toward Lawrence, Papa spoke. "Tell me about your target practice. You used my gun?"

"I used it," Joseph said.

"Did Sam Willis convince you to take it without asking?"

"He wanted to use it," Joseph said, "but I took it. It was my choice."

"Why?"

"I wanted to learn to shoot." Joseph's voice dropped. "I'm sorry I took it without asking. I knew you wouldn't let me."

A pause.

"And you learned to shoot it?"

"Yes, sir."

Papa let out a long breath. "It's probably for the best. The time may come when you'll need to use it."

"Will you tell Mamma?"

"I think that's for the best, too. Don't you?"

"I guess so."

They rode in silence after that.

Lucy had a while to think. What would she do with Phoebe when they got back to the store? How could she get her off the wagon? And then what?

She felt Phoebe shift a little under the tarp, and she slid a hand under it. Phoebe grasped her hand and squeezed.

26

We find the following in the *Frontier News* of last week, and believe it was copied from the *Kansas City Enterprise* of the week previous:

Lawrence K.T.—Stealing a Negro

By last advice from this grand depot of the underground railroad, we learn that a fugitive slave, belonging to a gentleman of this county, was being harbored by the abolitionists of that place, and that all efforts to apprehend the slave have so far proved unsuccessful.

—*Herald of Freedom*, Sept. 29, 1855

The sun was setting when they arrived home. Papa and Joseph jumped off the wagon.

"I smell supper," Papa said. "We stayed longer than I planned. Your mother is probably frantic." He placed a hand on Joseph's shoulder. "Our news about your shooting skills will not ease her mind, I'm afraid."

Lucy climbed out of the wagon, but stood next to it. "I'll be there in a minute," she said. "I need to use the outhouse first."

Joseph and Papa headed straight for the kitchen.

Lucy looked around. It was nearly dark, and the street was deserted. She lifted the edge of the tarp. Phoebe looked up, but didn't rise.

"Follow me," Lucy whispered.

Phoebe slipped out from under the tarp. Lucy went in the door first. She needed to be sure the rest of her family was in the kitchen.

"You stole your father's gun?" Mamma's voice rang through the store. "Oh, Joseph, how could you do such a thing?"

Lucy led Phoebe through the darkened store. They ducked along the south wall and tiptoed up the stairs to Lucy's room.

The corner on the far side of Lucy's bed was out of sight from the door. "Stay down, so no one sees you," she whispered. "I'll bring you some food as soon as I can."

She ran downstairs, then went outside and around the back of the house. She opened the outhouse door and let it slam shut. She pumped some water to wash her hands, then went in the back door.

Papa and Joseph sat at the table.

"It's done, Maggie," Papa said calmly. "The boy knows he was wrong. He apologized."

Mamma ladled stew into a bowl and placed it on the table with a thump. "I blame that Willis boy."

"No, Mamma," Joseph said. "I took the gun, not Sam. It was my fault."

Lucy looked at her brother. He was taking responsibility for his actions?

"I should have taught him to shoot," Papa said. "I knew how badly he wanted to try it. It was bound to happen."

Mamma set a bowl in front of Lucy. "And did you know about this?"

"I suspected it," she admitted.

"And you didn't tell us?" Mamma cried.

"It was only suspicion," Lucy said. "I didn't know for sure."

Mamma shook her head. "I don't know what to say."

Papa brightened. "At least we brought good news back with us. John said he would pick up our supplies."

Lucy stirred her stew. *That's not all we brought back with us.* If Mamma knew about Phoebe, she would fall over dead, for sure. She had to make a plan.

"When did Mr. Jacob say he planned to go?" Mamma asked.

"Wednesday morning," Papa said. "He'll come tomorrow for your list and the money."

"Can I go with him?" Joseph asked. "I could help him load the boxes on the wagon."

"I'm counting on you to keep an eye on things here," Papa said.

"When are you leaving, Papa?" Lucy asked.

"Before dawn," Papa said. "It's a long ride to Topeka. We want to get there while we can still get a room at the boarding house. The convention starts Wednesday morning."

Mamma set a plate of corn bread in the middle of the table, then pulled out a chair and sat next to Papa. "What if the pro-slavery men decide to ride into town?"

"I'll leave the rifle here," he said to Joseph. "But not for you to play with. No target practice. No showing off to your friends."

Joseph looked at his food. "I know."

Papa waited for Joseph to look up at him. "I want your word. You are not to pick up that gun unless you need it for defense."

Joseph nodded. "I promise, Papa."

When they finished eating, Joseph took Reuben and the wagon back to the stable. Lucy cleaned up the dishes while Mamma and Papa double-checked the list of things Mr. Jacob would buy for them. Lucy filled a bowl with leftover stew and poured a glass of water. While her parents huddled over the list, she slipped out of the kitchen and up the stairs.

"It's me," she whispered, when she came in the room. "I brought food."

Phoebe crouched against the wall, out of sight of the door. She gulped half the glass of water first, then dug the spoon into the stew.

Lucy lit the oil lamp while Phoebe ate. "Papa is leaving before dawn," Lucy whispered. "Mr. Jacob will come tomorrow. He'll know what to do. We have to hide you until then."

"Your folks don't know about the Liberty Line?"

Lucy sat on the bed. "No, I do it on my own. But I never brought anyone here."

"What'll happen if they see me?"

"We don't want to find out."

Phoebe looked around the room. "You got nice things. I couldn't see much downstairs. Is this a store?"

Lucy nodded.

Phoebe set the spoon in the empty bowl. "How long you been in Kansas?"

"Since spring. We came from Pennsylvania."

The bell on the front door jangled. "Joseph!" Lucy whispered. She extinguished the lamp. Mamma and Papa still murmured downstairs.

Lucy set the dishes aside. She would take them downstairs in the morning.

Joseph tromped up the stairs and went into his room.

Lucy pulled a blanket from her bed. She made a pallet on the floor for Phoebe. They arranged it next to Lucy's bed, on the side away from the door. They didn't dare whisper any more.

Lucy tossed and turned so much that it felt like she barely slept. Whenever she woke, she swept her hand next to the bed to be sure that Phoebe was still there.

27

Gov. Shannon passed within a mile of Lawrence, today, on his way to Lecompton—a little settlement some fourteen miles above here. It is also the place where Samuel J. Jones, postmaster at Westport, Missouri, and sheriff of Douglas County, Kansas Territory, has, in most wanton manner, burned down the houses of some free state settlers. Gov. Shannon passed by us entirely.

– Mrs. Charles Robinson,
September 14, 1855

Lucy's eyes sprang open when she heard glass crash on the floor downstairs. "Get out of my house!" Mamma yelled. "You little thief! Get out!"

Lucy sat up. She leaned over the edge of the bed. Phoebe was gone! She scrambled off and looked under the bed. No Phoebe!

Lucy nearly crashed into Joseph as she hurried from her room. Joseph was first down the stairs, but both of them stopped on the steps to watch.

Mamma had a broom in her hands and was running across the room. "Get out! Get out!"

Lucy looked all around, but didn't see Phoebe; just Mamma

running around in circles with the broom in front of her. A glass oil lamp lay broken on the floor.

"Mamma!" Lucy called. "What is it?" From the stairs she had a good view of the store. No sign of Phoebe anywhere.

"A mouse! He was in the cornmeal!" Mamma shouted.

The mouse skittered across the floor and under the flour barrel. "Oh, no, you don't!" Mamma tipped the barrel and poked her broom under it. "You've had one breakfast!"

The mouse dashed to a space under the corner of a crate near the front of the store, with Mamma close behind. "Joseph, open the door!"

Joseph ran a path around the glass shards and opened the door. Mamma watched the place where the mouse had gone and held her broom in front of her.

Lucy stood on the stairs, looking in all directions while Mamma pursued the mouse. Something brushed her bare foot. She jumped and looked down, expecting a mouse, but a hand came out from between the steps. It gave a quick tug on the hem of her nightdress, then disappeared. Phoebe! Lucy sat down on the steps to be sure no one could see between them into the storage closet beneath the stairs where Phoebe hid.

Mamma poked her broom under the crate and the mouse darted out. Mamma was quick. She batted the tiny creature with her broom in the direction of the open door. It jumped over the threshold and was gone.

"Close the door!" Mamma shouted.

Joseph swung the door shut.

Mamma looked into the cornmeal barrel. "I should have expected it, with the weather turning colder."

Joseph laughed. "You scared him, Mamma. He won't be back."

"He'll be back, and he'll bring his mousie wife." She replaced the lid on the barrel. "Before long we'll have a dozen of them, eating every last bit of corn, flour, and anything else they can find."

"We should get a cat," Joseph said. "We have four at the barn, and we never see a mouse – at least not a live one."

Mamma thought for a minute. "Better a cat than a nest of mice, I suppose."

"Mrs. Wyman's gray cat had a litter in the summer," Joseph said. "I'll bet she'd let us have one."

"I'll think about that," Mamma said. She knelt over the remains of the broken lamp. "At least only the chimney broke," she said. "I'd better sweep this up."

Lucy jumped up from the step. "I'll get the dustpan!" She hurried behind the sales counter, opened the door of the closet and peered inside. Where was Phoebe? She poked her head in farther. Phoebe crouched in the darkest corner. In her black dress, she was nearly invisible.

Lucy grabbed the dustpan and shut the door again.

Mamma swept up the broken glass. She emptied the dustpan into the ash can by the stove. "Your father left before daylight," she said. "I'll need your help around here for the next couple of days."

"I know," Lucy said. "We'll be fine."

"I'm going to the stable," Joseph said. "I'll ask Mrs. Wyman about that cat, if you want."

"You can ask," Mamma said, "but don't bring one home yet. I have enough to think about right now, with your father gone. I need to finish this list for Mr. Jacob."

Mamma stood at the back counter and opened her ledger. Phoebe was not five feet from her, still hidden in the storage closet.

Mamma looked up. "Well?"

"What?"

"Are you going to stand there in your nightgown all morning?"

"No, I'll go get dressed." Lucy climbed the stairs, trying to think of what to do. Phoebe would know enough to stay hidden in the darkest corner. Mamma wouldn't see her unless she poked her head all the way into the closet.

Lucy dressed quickly and picked up the blanket from the floor.

When she came downstairs, Mamma set her pencil down. "I think the list is ready," she said. "I need to go to Larson's smokehouse to have him put up some meat for us. Watch things for me?"

"I will," Lucy said.

Mamma picked up her handbag. "I left a pan of mush on the stove for your breakfast. Please clean up the dishes after you've eaten."

She put on her bonnet. The bell jingled as she walked out the door.

When Mamma was out of sight, Lucy opened the door of the closet. "She's gone."

Phoebe slipped out of the closet, but crouched behind the counter. Lucy crouched there with her. She brushed dust from Phoebe's sleeve. "How did you get under there?"

"I woke up when your daddy left. I had to go to the outhouse something fierce. I waited until the house was quiet again, but I just couldn't wait any longer. It was still dark, so I snuck out your back door. When I came back in, your mamma was moving around upstairs, so I ducked in here. She came down and took up figuring in her book, standing right where you are. I couldn't get out of there without running straight into her."

"When I heard her yelling, I was sure you were caught!" Lucy said.

Phoebe nodded. "What do you think I thought?"

"She won't be back for a while. Stay here. You're out of sight of the door. I'll get you something to eat."

Lucy went to the kitchen. She stirred the mush in the pan and picked up two bowls. She and Phoebe both sat on the floor behind the counter and ate. They left the closet door open.

"If you have to hide, be sure to pull the door closed," Lucy said. "When it's open, the light shows between the steps. As long as it's closed, nobody can see under there."

When they finished the mush, Lucy took the bowls to the kitchen. She had just put them in the wash pan when the bell on the door jangled.

Lucy hurried out front. She glanced behind the counter as she passed it. The closet door swung shut.

Two men pushed their way in. One was tall and lanky, the other shorter and heavier. Both were unshaven.

The short man spit a stream of tobacco juice onto the floor, then wiped his chin with the back of his hand. "Your pa Marcus Thomkins, like the sign says?"

"Yes, sir. Can I help you with something?"

"We got business with your pa," the tall man said. He scowled and narrowed his eyes, looking around the store.

Everyone in Lawrence knew Papa was in Topeka. Lucy saw no need to tell this stranger anything. "He just stepped out. Is there something you need?"

"We come to talk to him," the tall man said. "We'll wait."

"He might be a while," she said. "I can tell him you were here, Mr.?"

The shorter man shot his hand out and gripped her arm above the elbow. "We ain't got all day. We didn't come to talk to some half-growed girl." He pulled her toward him and spoke right at her face. "Go. Get. Your. Pa. "

Lucy flinched at the man's foul breath and turned her head.

The tall man stepped up and put a hand on his companion's shoulder. "Let her go, Jeb."

Jeb released his grip, and Lucy stepped back.

The tall man stood next to the shelf of cookware and squinted at Lucy. "I'm sure we can trust this young lady to give her pa a message." He reached into his shirt pocket, pulling the edge of his jacket back far enough to reveal a pistol stuck into the waistband of his trousers. He dug in his pocket with his right hand, then pulled out a wood-stemmed pipe and a leather pouch.

As he did, Jeb moved behind Lucy.

The tall man spoke casually as he dipped his pipe into the pouch. He waved it toward a copy of the *Herald* that lay on the counter. "You folks in Lawrence must think you're the only ones can read a newspaper."

Lucy didn't move. "I don't take your meaning, sir, but please, my mother doesn't allow anyone to smoke inside our store."

He laughed. "Your ma said so, did she?" He pulled a wooden matchbox from his pocket. "I hear your pa was the only one at that Big Springs meeting who protested Lane's Black Law." He opened the matchbox and removed one.

Lucy watched the match in the man's hand. "Please, sir, don't –"

"You worried about this little match?" He frowned. "You're right to be worried. Accidents happen." The lamp Mamma had broken that morning sat on a shelf. Its chimney was gone, but the base was still half-full of oil. He swung out his elbow, and the lamp crashed to the floor. The thick glass of the base did not break, but the metal neck popped off. Oil poured onto the floor. "Accidents do happen," he repeated.

Lucy moved forward, but Jeb grabbed her arms from behind and held her.

The tall man kicked the glass away, leaving a small puddle of oil on the wood floor. He struck his match on the bottom of a cast iron skillet and lit his pipe, puffing on it until smoke rose from it. He bent down and placed the match into the puddle of lamp oil. The tiny flame from the match nearly disappeared, then it glowed and danced across the surface of the oil.

He exhaled a long puff of smoke. "Someone has called me a murderer. And he tried to steal my slave, my rightful property. They put it in your paper."

The muscles in Lucy's throat tensed. Rose's owner! The man who killed her! She didn't dare to look toward the closet where Phoebe hid. The flame on the floor grew. Panic rose in her chest. She struggled, but Jeb tightened his grip.

"I think that same person wrote another letter, asking his friends to help him protest that Black Law," the man continued.

"My father didn't write that letter," Lucy said.

How could she have caused all this trouble? The tip of the flame reached a little higher, now burning in a circle around the match. Two metal cans – kerosene – stood just inches from the growing flame.

"Let go!" she pleaded. Jeb's hands squeezed her arms even tighter.

The tall man looked at the flame on the floor. "These frame houses, they can go up in the wink of an eye."

Lucy could no longer hold back tears. "Please! This is our livelihood!"

The tall man's smile disappeared. "And I have my livelihood.

Tell your pa – from Kanzas with a Z – to mind his business if he expects to keep his."

He turned and strode toward the door. Jeb released Lucy with a shove and followed him.

Lucy rushed to the fire. "Fire, Phoebe! Oil fire!" She spun around, looking for something, anything, to extinguish it.

"Salt!" Phoebe called. "Use salt!"

Lucy ran to the fire and threw handfuls of salt on the puddle of burning oil. The flame snuffed out. She held her skirt up and stomped on the salt, but the flame was already extinguished.

Phoebe's voice came from the storage closet. "Is it out?"

"It's out."

Lucy dropped to her knees and brushed the salt aside. Most of the oil had already soaked into the wood. The fire had seemed so large as she watched it, but the mark on the floor was smaller than the palm of her hand.

This was all her fault. Using "Kanzas" in her signature had seemed clever. But now her letters had led the Ruffians straight to their house. She wrote those words, she helped the Liberty Line, she brought a slave under their roof. She had to get Phoebe out of this house. For her safety and theirs.

She didn't know how soon Mamma would be back – too soon. She didn't know when Mr. Jacob would be here – not soon enough. Miss Kellogg was visiting a sick friend out of town, so Lucy couldn't even go to her.

But this. This was too big to handle by herself.

The bell on the door jangled. Joseph rushed in. "Mrs.

Wyman'll give us a kitten!"

Lucy rose slowly. She wiped her face with her hand. "That's … that's good."

"What's wrong?"

He looked down at the burned spot on the floor by her feet. "What happened?"

Her voice shook. "Some men were here. They threatened Papa and nearly set fire to the store."

Joseph squatted and ran his hand across the dark spot. "Why would they do that?"

She struggled to keep her voice steady. "They think Papa is stealing slaves and helping them escape."

"Papa wouldn't steal slaves!" Joseph said. "Why would they think that?"

"Because of me," she said.

He looked at the floor again. "I don't understand."

"I wrote letters to the newspaper. I thought it would help, but it made things worse."

He shook his head and stood up. "Lucy, I don't know what you're talking about, but this is bad. Really bad. We need to tell someone."

"No!"

If she ever needed her brother's help, it was now. Two months ago she wouldn't have dared to trust him. Had he changed? What choice did she have?

"I kept your secret about Liberty. I need you to keep one for me," she said.

He hesitated.

"You have to promise."

"What kind of secret?"

"Please, Joseph. Promise."

"I promise."

She looked at the floor. "I helped them. I've been helping the slaves."

Joseph's eyes grew wide. "Lucy!"

Lucy put a hand on his shoulder. "I mean it, Joseph. No one can know." She dropped her hand. "Remember, I've kept a secret for you."

"No one threatened to burn down our store for my secret."

"There's more."

She led him behind the counter and opened the door to the closet. They waited a few seconds. Phoebe moved in front of the open door, but didn't come out.

Joseph took a step back and shook his head. "You shouldn't be here." He didn't take his eyes from Phoebe.

"Her name is Phoebe," Lucy said. "She's going to Canada."

"Where did she come from?"

"Never mind that." Lucy touched his arm to get his attention. When he looked at her, she went on. "I'm going to help her. You can't tell anyone about her."

"But," Joseph looked at Phoebe again. "I don't want to be part of this."

"Our friends will take Phoebe out of town, but it may be a day or two. I just need your help to keep Mamma from finding out."

He looked at Lucy. "She can't stay here! What if those men come back and find her?"

"He's right," Phoebe said. "As long as I'm here, you're not safe."

"They'll come for you soon," Lucy said.

Joseph looked from Lucy to Phoebe and back again. "No, Lucy, you've got to think about it. If she gets caught here, who would the Ruffians hang? You? No! They'd hang Papa! We have to get her out of here."

"We don't have any place for her to go."

"Well, your so-called friends need to find someplace and quick!" Joseph glanced out the front windows and back to Lucy. "You need to tell them."

"I can't," Lucy whispered.

"What? Why not?"

"Because it's a secret organization. I don't know who they are!"

Joseph was quiet for a minute. "Then we'll have to find somewhere to hide her. Someplace outside of this house." He took a deep breath. "Just a day or two?"

Lucy nodded. "They want to get her moving as soon as they can."

"Mr. Wyman went to Topeka with Papa. They won't be back until Friday." He turned to Phoebe. "Maybe you could stay in the tack room at the stable. I'm the only one who'll go in there while Mr. Wyman's gone."

"What about Samuel?" Lucy asked. "We can't trust him."

"He's helping his folks cut grain. He won't be at the stable all week."

"How do we get her there?" Lucy asked. "I don't think we can wait until tonight. I told those men that Papa just stepped out."

"She sure can't go in the daytime," Joseph said. He looked at Phoebe. "You couldn't walk a yard outside our door without someone spotting you."

"I can give her a sunbonnet to cover her face," Lucy said.

Joseph shook his head and pointed at Phoebe's dress. "With that black dress, the first woman she meets will want to hurry over to find out who died."

Lucy gasped. "That's it!" she said. She grabbed Phoebe's hand. "Come with me."

Lucy looked to be sure no one was within sight of the windows and let Phoebe go up the stairs first.

When they were safely in her room, Lucy opened the bottom drawer of her bureau and pulled out her old blue gown. "I knew there was a reason to save this dress. I sure didn't think this would be it."

Lucy unfastened the buttons on the back of the blue dress. At least she had washed and mended it. It didn't look too bad. She held the dress in front of Phoebe.

Phoebe shook her head. "I walk outside in that, and everybody west of the Mississippi is going to be looking at me."

Lucy could hear Sam Willis' voice. "You get lost on the way to the ball, Cinderella?" She nodded. "You're right. But what else can we do?" She looked down. Her Kansas dress? It was the only way. "Wear my dress," she said.

Phoebe shook her head. "I'll need the black one to travel at night."

"Take the black dress with you and leave mine at the stable when they take you on," Lucy said. "I'll get it later."

Lucy unbuttoned her calico dress and gave it to Phoebe. When Phoebe was dressed, she helped Lucy with the hooks on the back of the blue dress.

"Now the bonnet," Lucy said, as she tied the ends under Phoebe's chin. "Let's see what Joseph says. I'll wait while you go downstairs."

Joseph was sweeping up the salt. He glanced up when Phoebe was halfway down the stairs. "We need to do something quick. Did you figure out what to do about her dress?"

Phoebe stood still, but didn't speak.

He looked again. "Lucy?"

"Guess again." Lucy stood at the top of the stairs. She held Phoebe's black dress. "See? She can walk across town, and no one will suspect a thing."

Lucy reached under the counter for a basket, put the black dress in it, and covered it with a towel. "Hold it with your hands under the basket to hide them." She glanced out the front windows. "Now, hurry, Mamma will be home soon!"

"I don't like it, but we need to get you out of here. Let's go." Joseph held the door. "I'll walk fast. Stay with me."

Lucy gave Phoebe a quick hug. "I'll come to the stable to see you. Please be careful, Phoebe."

Joseph and Phoebe stepped out of the door. Joseph moved

quickly, and Phoebe followed him.

Lucy watched them through the window until they cut between Mr. Oakhurst's law office and Mrs. Jameson's herb garden. She prayed they would make it safely.

28

Resolved, That our true interests socially, morally, and pecuniarily require that Kansas should be a FREE STATE; that free labor will best promote the happiness, the rapid population, the prosperity and the wealth of our people; that slave labor is a curse to the master and the community ... and that we will devote our energies as a party to exclude the institution and to secure for Kansas the Constitution of a free state.

—First Free State Platform, 1855

Once Joseph and Phoebe were out of sight, Lucy hurried around the store to put things back in order before Mamma returned. She washed the mush pan and dishes and put them away.

The burned spot on the floor was another matter.

She would have to tell Papa what had happened. He needed to know about the threat. But Mamma had plenty to worry about right now, and Lucy could not think of one good reason she could give for a burned spot on the floor that would not send Mamma into a frenzy.

She scrubbed it with water, but it didn't lighten at all. She moved a box of door knobs to sit there, but it just looked out of place. No matter how she arranged things, it only put an obstacle in a place where people needed to walk. It was a small spot, but Mamma would certainly notice it. She walked from one end of the store to the other looking for something that would cover that spot.

As she walked past it one more time, she bumped into the table that held the school supplies. A small glass bottle of ink toppled over, and Lucy caught it before it dropped to the floor. That was it! She loosened the cork in the bottle a little and pushed it off the edge of the table so that it fell near the burned spot. The bottle didn't break, but ink began to spill from the neck of it. She rolled the bottle with her finger until the leaking ink spilled in the right spot, then watched for a few seconds as the dark liquid made a puddle on the wooden floor. When it had covered the spot, she took a rag from the sales counter. She was kneeling and mopping the ink when the bell on the front door announced Mamma's return.

"I'm sorry I was gone so long," she said. "Mrs. Larson is quite the gossip. I thought I'd never get out of there. I was afraid I'd kept Mr. Jacob waiting."

She was taking off her bonnet when she noticed Lucy crouched on the floor. "What happened?"

"I bumped the table, and the bottle fell off." She held out the ink-soaked rag. "I tried to clean it up, but it made an awful spot."

"Oh, my. That will never come up." Mamma knelt to

examine the spot. "Well, I guess we can live with it."

She rose and looked curiously at Lucy. "I didn't expect to see you in that dress again."

"I got my dress wet when I washed the dishes, so I changed."

"Where's your brother?"

Lucy dropped the ink-soaked rag into the ash bin. "At the stable."

"He spends so much time there." Mamma frowned. "He didn't take the gun, did he?"

"No," Lucy said. "I don't think he'll be doing that again." She smiled. "He talked to Mrs. Wyman. She promised us a kitten!"

"Ah, a mouth that will find some of its own food."

A wagon clattered out front. Lucy looked through the front window as Annie jumped to the ground.

Mr. Jacob came through the door first. "Mornin', Mrs. Thomkins." He took off his hat. "I'm here to see about your order."

"Thank you for helping us out, Mr. Jacob." Mamma went to the back counter and pulled some papers from her ledger book. "I'd like to go over this with you, if you have a few minutes."

While her father walked to the back of the store, Annie pulled Lucy aside. "Where is she?"

"The livery stable," Lucy whispered.

"Is she safe there?"

"For now."

"Pa," Annie said. "Lucy and I are going over to the livery stable."

Mr. Jacob looked up.

"We're going to see a friend there."

He nodded. "Don't be long. We need to go soon."

"Bring your brother back with you," Mamma said. "I have work for him here."

The girls hurried out the door.

"Let's cut between the houses," Lucy said. "It'll be faster."

"Why is she at the stable?" Annie asked.

"We had to get her out of the house," Lucy said. "Some men came to the store this morning. Proslavers."

"How did you get her there?"

"I gave her my dress and a bonnet. Joseph walked her there."

Annie stopped. "Lucy, no! Are you sure you can trust him?"

Lucy nodded. "He doesn't like the whole idea, but he knows what could happen if we got caught. He wants to get Phoebe out of Lawrence as much as we do."

When they got there, Joseph was shoveling manure from the stalls in the barn into a wheelbarrow.

"Mamma wants you to come back to the store," Lucy told him.

"Let me finish cleaning up," he said. "I'm almost done." He threw another shovelful into the wheelbarrow. He looked around, then lowered his voice. "You can go in the tack room if you want."

Lucy and Annie went to the back of the barn. They opened the door a crack.

"Phoebe, it's us," Annie said.

They opened the door, and Phoebe rose from a corner behind some saddles.

Phoebe grinned. "I walked over here in the daylight, and nobody suspected a thing!"

"We've got a plan," Annie said. "We're going to get you across the river and on to the next stop tomorrow."

"In the daytime?" Lucy asked. "Isn't that dangerous?"

"The way they're watching the roads at night, Pa thinks we've got a better chance of getting her out in the day."

"I'm ready," Phoebe said.

"Pa will be heading out toward Kansas City at first light tomorrow. He thinks the riders will follow him. Just to be sure they do, I'm going with him, but I'm going to be in the back of the wagon, looking like I'm hiding under a blanket. Pa's hoping they will follow us pretty far up the road before they decide to stop us and investigate." She turned to Phoebe. "Where's your black dress?"

Phoebe picked up the basket. "Right here."

"I'll get it before we leave today. If I let a corner of it peek out from under the blanket, it might help them think I'm Phoebe."

"But I'll need my dress back," Lucy said. "Mamma will ask questions."

"She needs a regular dress," Annie said. "Her owner knows that one."

"Can't she wear your dress, then? At least you wouldn't have to explain it to your mother. And you still have material for another dress."

Annie looked down at her dress. "Ma used that to make clothes for somebody else. Some of the folks who came through."

Phoebe looked at Lucy's face, then Annie's. "Maybe I best keep the black one."

Lucy looked at Phoebe. Her Kansas dress. She had waited for that dress so many months. Endured the looks and teasing as she wore this blue gown. When she put it away, it was like she put away that prideful and silly girl who had left Pennsylvania. Now, here she was, wearing it again, and all she could think about was her dress, not the girl in front of her whose life was at stake. "No," she told Phoebe. "You wear that one," she said. "I'll think of something to tell Mamma."

"Mr. Newhouse is taking his lumber wagon across the river and up the road to the north tomorrow. Phoebe's going to be on that wagon. If the Ruffians follow us, then she should have a clear road to the next stop." Annie touched Phoebe's sleeve. "I'll have Pa tell Mr. Newhouse to come here. Be ready. He'll come before daylight."

Phoebe spoke quietly. "Lord. Someday, I'll learn to write, and then I'll make a story about this."

Lucy smiled. "Maybe I'll write a poem about it."

Phoebe's eyes crinkled at the corners. "Miss Evelyn loved

poems. She wouldn't teach me to read, but she said poems to me and had me remember them so I could recite for her when she wasn't feeling good. They were like little plays for her, and they made her feel better."

"Say one for me," Lucy said.

"I don't know the whole thing, but this one's my favorite," Phoebe said. She sat up very straight and made her face serious as she intoned, "*Once upon a midnight dreary, while I pondered weak and weary,/ Over many a quaint and curious volume of forgotten lore …*" She continued with the first stanza of the poem and made her voice deepen as she recited.

Lucy smiled. It was one of her favorites, too.

"*Ah distinctly, I remember, it was in the bleak December,/ And each separate dying ember wrought its ghost upon the floor./ … vainly I had sought to borrow/ From my books, sur –*" she paused, "*sur –*"

"*Surcease,*" Lucy offered.

"*Surcease of sorrow – sorrow for the lost Lenore –/ For the rare and radiant maiden whom the angels name Lenore –*" Phoebe paused for effect. "*Nameless here forever more.*"

Phoebe whispered. "I'll shorten it up some. Here comes the best part."

"*And the silken sad uncertain rustling of each purple curtain –/ Thrilled me – filled me with fantastic terrors never felt before …*"

Annie and Lucy leaned forward as Phoebe talked faster. "*So that now, to still the beating of my heart, I stood repeating,/ 'Tis some visitor entreating entrance at my chamber door,*

Some late visitor entreating entrance at my chamber door."
Phoebe skipped ahead to the chorus, *"Quoth the raven,"* and
she croaked like a parrot, *"Nevermore!"*

"Sshh! Sshh!" Annie hissed, trying to control her giggles.

Lucy took a deep breath and looked at Phoebe.

Phoebe saw that Lucy was watching her. "You want to ask
me something, don't you?"

Lucy nodded. "I was just thinking. I'm sorry Miss Evelyn
died, Phoebe. And I'm sorry that Otis came there. But in a way
I'm glad, too."

Phoebe frowned. "Glad?"

"Because ..." Lucy looked down. She felt selfish. "If Miss
Evelyn had lived, you wouldn't have run away. And then I
wouldn't have met you."

"Even if Miss Evelyn had lived, I would have probably
found my way through here."

Lucy looked up, surprised. "You would have run away anyway? Even though Miss Evelyn was kind to you?"

"Slave is slave."

"I'm sorry, Phoebe," Lucy said. "I should have known that."

"You always been free, so how could you really understand?"

A knock, and Joseph put his head in the door. "We'd better
go back."

Lucy nodded, "I wish we'd had more time. I will be wishing
and praying with all my heart for you to get to Canada."

"I'll find some way to let you know I made it," Phoebe said.
"I promise."

Farewell

Your destination calls to you,
　　And I must let you go.
I wish that you could linger here,
　　But you and I both know
That freedom's call is stronger than
　　The strongest friendship's pull.
And I must let you take that road
　　Though now my heart is full
Of feelings that seem opposite—
　　Great joy, but sadness too.
I'll celebrate our sad farewell;
　　Your freedom calls to you!

29

Kansas will probably be the first field of bloody struggle with the slave power. In this country Freedom or Slavery is to predominate. Both cannot live upon an equality, and he who cries Peace, Peace, is only waiting for stronger manacles to be played upon his own limbs and the limbs of his children.

—*Massachusetts Spy* (quoted in *Herald of Freedom*)

Lucy woke with Joseph shaking her shoulder and whispering her name. "Lucy, get up."

"What is it?" Lucy sat up. All she could see through her window was dark gray sky.

Joseph leaned close and kept his voice low. "Something's wrong. I went over to feed the horses, and Phoebe's still there."

Lucy rubbed her eyes. "What happened to Mr. Newhouse?"

"I don't know, but she's nearly crazy with worry. She wants to see you."

Lucy got out of bed. She reached for her clothes. "Where's Mamma?"

"Still in her room," Joseph said. "I'll wait for you out back. Hurry."

The wind swept up the street, and Lucy put her left hand up to keep the dirt out of her eyes as she ran to keep up with Joseph. Dark clouds were blowing in from the west.

As they turned at the corner, they could see the stable. "Maybe Mr. Newhouse came right after you were there," Lucy said. "I hope they're already on the road. This looks like a storm coming."

The blacksmith shop was still closed up, but the wooden sign that hung by the front door swung on its chains and banged against the side of the building.

There was no activity at the stable and no sign that Mr. Newhouse had been there. Joseph led the way into the dark barn. When Lucy opened the door to the tack room, Phoebe was pacing restlessly. "That wind is howling like demons from Hades," she said. "I'm near to losing my mind."

"Mr. Newhouse should be here by now," Joseph said. "Something's wrong."

"Let's go to his house." Lucy took Phoebe's hand. "We'll come back to tell you when he'll be ready."

They hurried down the alley behind the blacksmith shop and cut between Mrs. Lewis' hen house and the Congregational Church. A rumble of thunder rolled through the clouds overhead.

The painted sign on the side of the sawmill advertised, "Newhouse wood for your new house." Mr. Newhouse's big lumber wagon stood in the side yard between the mill and the house. Two large draft horses, one black and one dappled gray, were hitched to it. Lumber was piled on the wagon, but a dozen boards lay scattered on the ground. A folded canvas tarp and a coil of rope lay on the seat of the wagon.

Lucy knocked at the door. The window curtain moved aside, and Mrs. Newhouse peered out. When she saw them, she opened the door. "Sawmill's closed today," she said. She had her hand on the door to close it.

"Please, Mrs. Newhouse," Lucy said. "Is your husband here? We have a friend who needs to travel."

Mrs. Newhouse swung the door open. "I've been expecting someone would come asking. Come in out of the street."

"Who is it, Alma?" came a man's voice from the bedroom.

"Some children," she said. "About your passenger."

"Bring them in," he said.

They followed Mrs. Newhouse into the bedroom. Her husband lay on the bed, his leg wrapped in sheeting and propped up on pillows. Sweat beaded on his forehead. He tried to raise himself up, winced in pain, and sank back on the bed. "Busted my leg," he said. "Wind slammed a shutter on the house and spooked Betsy. She jumped, Hector sidestepped, and a pile of boards slid off on me."

"Oh, that's awful!" Lucy said. "Is the doctor coming?"

"He should be here soon," Mrs. Newsome said.

"What can we do about Phoebe?" Lucy asked. "She needs to go, and the plan was to move her today."

"I'm real sorry," he said. "I can't."

It was true. He couldn't. But what about Phoebe? Lucy stepped closer to the bed. "What if we take the wagon, sir? My brother could do it."

Joseph grabbed Lucy's arm, but she shook free of his grip.

Mr. Newhouse frowned. "You know how to drive a wagon, boy?"

Joseph hesitated.

"He's been working at the stable for three months," Lucy said. "He takes the wagons out all the time."

"Hmmm ..." Mr. Newhouse looked at Joseph. "I'd ask Parker to take her, but he's gone to Topeka." He squinted at Joseph. "You really think you can handle those horses? Betsy, that's the gray horse, she's young and a little skittish. Hector is pretty steady, though."

Joseph grabbed Lucy, pulled her to the side of the room and turned away from Mr. Newhouse. "The only horse I've ever hitched is Reuben!" he whispered. "Not some nervous draft horse!"

Lucy bent her head close to Joseph's. "What else can we do? Take Phoebe back home with us?"

"Mr. Wyman won't be back for two more days," Joseph said. "She could stay at the stable."

Lucy shook her head. "Mr. Jacob is already gone. We don't know when we'll get another chance. Then what happens to Phoebe? And Papa?"

Joseph glared at Lucy, then nodded. He returned to Mr.

Newhouse's bedside. "I can do it, sir."

Mr. Newhouse shook his head. "I don't like it much, but I don't see another way. Here's the plan: Take the wagon up to Baldwin's ferry, and tell him you're making a delivery for me. Alma will give you money for your passage. As long as you pay him, Baldwin won't ask you any questions."

Mr. Newhouse looked at Lucy. "They won't be looking for your passenger in the daytime. Does she have something to cover her head, so no one can get a good look at her?"

"Yes, sir," Lucy answered. "And she has a blue dress, not black."

"That's good. Pretend like she belongs to you. Come up with a story ahead of time, in case you get asked. Tell her to sit quiet and act natural and keep her face turned."

Lucy's thoughts filled with visions of disaster, and she struggled to keep down the panic.

"Once you're across the river, head up the old Delaware Road toward Leavenworth. You'll have to cross Walnut Creek. There's no bridge, but the horses can make it across. It's a rocky little stream, but not deep. Once you're past the creek, look for the third homestead on the left side of the road. Martin should have a blue bandanna tied to a post by the road. He's expecting the lumber and your friend. You think you can remember all that, young man?"

"Yes, sir," Joseph said. "I'll remember."

Mr. Newhouse pointed to the corner of the room, where a rifle leaned up against the wall. "You know how to handle a Sharps?"

"Yes, sir," Joseph answered. "My papa has one."

"I don't expect you'll have any trouble, but I wouldn't go out on the road myself without it. Cartridges are in the bag next to it. You can bring it back when you return the wagon. If you go now, you can make it back by nightfall."

Joseph nodded. "Yes, sir, I will."

"Good luck," Mr. Newhouse said, as they turned to go.

Joseph picked up the gun and the bag of cartridges. Mrs. Newhouse gave Lucy a small leather pouch. "This is enough for passage on the ferry." As she let them out the door, her husband called from the bedroom. "Be sure to tie the tarp down tight over that wood. You don't want it sliding off when you're crossing the creek!"

Lucy and Joseph hurried to the wagon in Mr. Newhouse's yard. Thunder rumbled in the distance.

"Let's load this wood and go," Joseph said.

He picked up one of the fallen boards. Lucy picked up the other end. In a few minutes, they had it all on the wagon. Joseph picked up the folded tarp and the rope from the wagon seat. Lucy helped him spread the tarp on top of the wood. Joseph stretched the rope across the wood and tied both sides as tightly as he could. "That will make it easier to ride back here," Joseph said. "You and Phoebe can sit on top of the tarp."

"I've never been on the other side of the Kaw," he continued. "I'm not sure I'll know the way to Walnut Creek."

"I guess we'll just have to hope there's only one road," Lucy said.

Joseph checked the horses' harnesses and traces to see that they were secure and climbed onto the driver's seat. "Wait," he said.

Seated on the bench of the wagon, Joseph pulled the Sharps rifle across his lap and loaded it. Then he lifted the front end of the tarp and slid Mr. Newhouse's gun under it, hidden, but easy to reach from the driver's seat. Lucy climbed onto the back of the wagon on top of the tarp, behind the seat.

Joseph picked up the lines. "Git up!" The horses jerked forward at the sound, and Lucy grabbed the wagon seat and held on. They left the mill yard and turned east down Sixth Street toward the stable.

"When we get there, I'll stop outside, and you run in to get her," Joseph said. "We need to get moving before this storm hits."

When they arrived at the barn, Lucy jumped off the wagon. She ran around the barn and stopped. A horse stood next to the door. Teakee. She hurried to the door and barely avoided colliding with Levi. He held a fancy beaded bridle in his hands. She recognized the beads – the red, white, and blue ones he'd gotten from her two weeks ago.

He smiled. "Lucy. I didn't expect to see you. Is Mr. Wyman here?"

"He's gone to Topeka, won't be back until Friday," she said.

"Oh. He ordered this bridle." He held it up so she could see it.

"It's beautiful, Levi, but he's not here." She looked past him, into the barn. "Did you see anyone inside?"

Joseph came around the barn. "Lucy! What's the holdup?" He stopped short when he saw Levi.

"Levi brought something for Mr. Wyman," she said.

"He'll be back Friday." Joseph looked at Levi. He looked at Lucy. "We have to go now."

Joseph looked at Levi again. "I'm sorry," he paused.

"I'll come back on Friday," Levi said. He looked away.

"No. I mean, yes. Come back Friday. No, I mean –" Joseph looked down at his feet, then back up at Levi. "I'm sorry, Levi. I'm sorry for everything. I was wrong about you."

Levi stood silent.

Joseph took a breath. "You helped Liberty, helped me, when I didn't deserve your help."

Lucy stepped next to her brother and nudged him with her elbow.

"*Matchelepo*, Levi," he said. "If I could be your friend, I'd like that."

Levi nodded. "I'd like it, too."

Lucy smiled.

Thunder rumbled again, and Betsy snorted.

"We need to go," Joseph said.

Lucy turned to Levi. "Do you know the road on the other side of the Kaw?"

"I know it."

"Do you know how to get to Walnut Creek?"

"Yes, but there's no bridge there. How will you cross?"

"Mr. Newhouse says these horses know how," Joseph said.

Levi looked at the team. "You'll have to lead them." He paused. "That gray one isn't going to like it. She's nervous. She'll fight you."

"Would you help us?" Joseph asked. "You know horses. I trust you."

Levi nodded. "I'll help."

Lucy went to the tack room. "It's me," she said. Phoebe raised her head. "Are we ready?"

"Mr. Newhouse can't go."

"Can't go? What do you mean?"

"We're taking you," Lucy said. "Joseph and me … and a friend."

Phoebe shook her head, but didn't seem too surprised when she saw Levi. Joseph told Levi their plan. "We only have enough money to pay our own fare across the river and back," he said.

"There's a shallow place two miles upriver," Levi said. "Teakee and I will cross the river there and meet you on the other side. Once you're across, head up the road. I'll catch up with you."

Phoebe climbed into the wagon and sat on the tarp next to Lucy. They watched as Levi rode west up Sixth Street, to follow the river.

"We need to work out our story," Lucy said. "If anybody asks, we all need to say the same thing about who we are and why we're traveling together."

Joseph guided the horses toward the river as thick clouds darkened and hovered lower over them.

30

BALDWIN'S FERRY

Crossing the Kansas River at Lawrence

The undersigned, having built a good and substantial ferryboat, would inform the traveling public, that they are prepared to carry over all passengers and teams who may desire to cross at this point. We will always be at our post and ready to wait on all who may need our services.

—advertisement, *Kansas Free State*

The wind had calmed, but the air felt thick and close. As they neared the river, insects swarmed around them. The horses' ears twitched, and even calm Hector shook his head to shoo the flies that buzzed around his face.

They were still half a block from the ferry when they saw a horse and rider board the boat. The rider dismounted and stood by his horse. As they watched, the ferryman stepped on board to release the loop of rope that held the boat to the Lawrence side of the Kaw River.

"Hurry, Joseph, he's leaving!" Lucy said. "We'll have to wait for him to come back across."

"Mr. Baldwin!" Joseph called. "Please wait!"

The ferryman looked up when he heard his name and stepped ashore to wait for them. When they were near enough for him to see them better, he frowned.

"You children taking that wagon across the river?" He frowned. "I'm running a business here. You'll have to pay."

"Yes, sir," Joseph said. "Mr. Newhouse broke his leg. I told him I'd make his delivery for him. He gave me money for the fare."

Mr. Baldwin looked at the girls. Phoebe kept her head turned so that the wide brim of the bonnet would hide her face.

"Hmmph, Newhouse don't usually take passengers when he makes a delivery. He know you got riders with you?"

"Yes, sir," Joseph answered. "He knows."

"It's fifty cents for wagon and driver." He looked at the girls again. "I'll have to charge you extra for your passengers."

Joseph looked at Lucy.

She opened the pouch Mrs. Newsome had given them. Inside were four quarters.

"How much extra?" he asked Mr. Baldwin.

"Ten cents each."

Lucy leaned close to Joseph's ear. "We won't have enough to get back," she whispered.

"We have to get across," he whispered back. "Maybe the Martins will give us the extra when we get to their house."

The ferryman looked impatient. "I got a paying passenger here," he said. "You got the fare, or not?"

"We have it," Lucy said. She handed him three quarters.

Joseph jumped down from the wagon. He stayed closest to

Betsy and walked the horses slowly down the wooden ramp to the deck of the boat.

Lucy and Phoebe walked beside the wagon. Lucy kept a hand on it for support. The boat had no railings, and the muddy water of the Kaw splashed up against the side of the boat that faced the current. One false move, and she would find herself in the water.

Phoebe grabbed Lucy's arm and held on. She squeezed it so tightly that Lucy could feel her trembling. Phoebe must be as nervous about this boat as she was.

"Come on," said the horseman ahead of them on the boat. "Storm's coming. Let's go!"

That voice! Lucy looked up and knew why Phoebe had ducked behind her. It was Otis!

They both turned to face away from him. "I got to get off this boat," Phoebe whispered in Lucy's ear.

But it was too late. Mr. Baldwin had already unhooked the rope that held them to the loading ramp. They drifted into the river, secured only by the ropes that looped through the large pulley that rolled along the cable which stretched across the Kaw.

"Stay next to me," Lucy whispered. "Keep looking the other way."

Mr. Baldwin set to work, pulling on the rope that attached the ends of the boat to the pulley. As he pulled the rope tighter, the end of the boat that faced the far shore angled upstream, and the pulley began to move on the cable. The current pushed against the side of the boat, and they started across the river. Mr. Baldwin held the rope tight with both hands.

Lucy turned, pretending to look at the opposite shore, but watched Otis. Joseph stood in front of the two horses. He talked softly to them and stroked Betsy's head. The thunder had grown louder and was now a steady rumble.

Otis looped the reins over the saddle horn and stepped nearer to Joseph. "Big storm coming up," he said. "Where you headed?" He glanced at Lucy.

Lucy looked down and pretended to brush some dust from her skirt. If Joseph could keep the conversation going, maybe Otis wouldn't take any notice of Phoebe.

Joseph raised his fist with thumb pointed at the wagon behind him. "Taking this wood to a farm up the road."

"You live in Lawrence?"

"Yes, sir," Joseph said.

Otis looked back across the river toward the town. "I s'pose your pa's one of them abolitionists."

Joseph hesitated. "He's a storekeeper, sir."

"Yep. I just bet he is."

The boat rocked a bit. Phoebe grabbed the side of the wagon. Lucy tried to block Otis' view of Phoebe's hands, but she was too late. He had already seen them.

"Say, boy, you got a darky with you! What're you up to?"

Joseph looked at Lucy. He hesitated.

"She's with me, sir," Lucy said. "We're on our way to Atchison. This boy is giving us a ride home."

333

His eyes narrowed. "She belong to you?"

"Yes, sir," Lucy said.

He looked from Lucy to Phoebe, who still kept her face turned away from him. His eyes narrowed. "Keep a watch on her. Slave stealers are thick around here. Lost a girl myself a week ago." He spat over the side of the boat. "Thought maybe I'd find her in Lawrence."

He looked again at Phoebe. "Is that right, missy? You belong to this girl?"

Phoebe still looked away. "Yes, sir," she said, her voice high and tinny. Lucy looked at Mr. Baldwin. He was holding tightly to the rope, but he was also listening.

Otis was silent for a moment. Then he moved closer to Joseph. His voice became a snarl, like an animal. "You won't get away with it."

Joseph's eyes got big. "With what?"

Otis took hold of Joseph's arm and pulled him close. "We know all about it."

"Sir?"

"That big meeting up in Topeka. They think they can make Free State laws! I went to help elect that legislature myself last March …" His voice trailed off, and he turned. He looked across the boat toward Lucy. "Say, I know you …"

He released Joseph and paced around to the side of the wagon where Lucy stood. She stepped back, but Otis took hold of her by both arms, just as he had on Election Day. "I remember that fancy dress."

Otis pulled her close, his mouth next to Lucy's ear. "You was supposed to be my dancing partner. I was looking forward to having some fun with you."

Lucy looked around frantically.

Phoebe still faced away. She couldn't help without revealing herself.

Joseph looked both frightened and confused. He was backing away, moving behind Hector, inching toward the wagon.

"Let her go!" Mr. Baldwin said. He glared at Otis, but he couldn't let go of the rope or the boat would whip around, and they would all be thrown into the river. "What's the matter with you? She's just a girl!"

Otis grinned. "That's right, she is." He pulled her closer and pressed his body up against hers. "And we still got a chance to …" He glanced at Phoebe.

"Wait a minute," Otis snarled. "If you're that abolitionist's girl, then she must be …"

"Let her go, mister," Joseph said.

Otis looked up, straight into the barrel of the Sharps rifle. Joseph crouched on the wagon, sighting down the barrel, his finger on the trigger.

Lucy held her breath. The gun was shaking in Joseph's grasp. Would he be able to use it?

"Back away!" The look in Joseph's eyes was all business. "I don't want to kill you," he said. "But I haven't had much practice with this gun. If I try to miss your ugly head, I can't guarantee that I will."

Otis kept his gaze on Joseph and stepped backward. As he did, Mr. Baldwin released the rope for an instant and grabbed it again. The boat pivoted, then lurched. The sudden movement caught Otis off guard, and he stumbled.

Lucy grabbed the edge of the wagon to keep from falling overboard. In that instant, Phoebe stepped toward Otis and aimed a kick at the back of his right knee. It buckled, and he went down on the edge of the deck, then tumbled into the river with a splash.

They watched as Otis disappeared below the murky ripples of the Kaw.

Seconds later he surfaced, spluttering.

Phoebe watched as the current carried Otis farther down the stream, forgetting to turn her head away.

His face showed his recognition. "Lousy slave stealers!" he yelled, as he struggled to keep his head above the waves.

Phoebe was silent for a few seconds, then "*Get thee back into the tempest,*" she said. "*I shall see thee … Nevermore!*"

Mr. Baldwin stared at Phoebe, open mouthed. He shook his head and looked at Lucy. "That man should be in jail for the way he treated you, miss, but I can't be taking part in such business as this. I'll let you all off on the other side of the river, but I don't expect to see you coming back across this way."

Lucy looked downstream. Otis was no longer in sight. "Do you think he could catch up to us, Mr. Baldwin?"

Mr. Baldwin shook his head. "I know this river. He won't get his feet on the bank for another quarter mile or so, I reckon."

He smiled. "And I still got his horse. I wouldn't put a man's horse on shore where it might get stolen." He paused. "Yes, sir. This horse will just have to ride with me till his owner comes to claim him. By then that scoundrel will probably owe me fare for four or five trips across the river for his horse."

Joseph slid the rifle back under the tarp. He looked up and caught Lucy staring at him.

"Good work, little brother," she said.

By the time the boat touched the north bank of the Kaw, rain was coming down in big, slow drops.

"I hope you don't have far to go to find shelter," Mr. Baldwin said, as Joseph led Hector and Betsy from the boat. He looked at the sky. "It'll get worse before it gets better."

A whistle came from across the river. A wagon waited on the opposite bank. "Got to head back," Mr. Baldwin said. "When that snake comes through here again, I'll do my best to slow him down." He looked at Phoebe. "But he's seen you. You all best get your story straight. On this side of the river, you're bound to meet lots more like that one."

Joseph climbed onto the wagon seat, and the girls took their places on top of the lumber. The rain was coming faster now.

"How far is it to the creek?" Lucy asked.

"I don't know. Maybe five or six miles."

Lucy touched Joseph's sleeve. "What time do you think it is?"

"I don't know. I can't even guess without the sun. Why?"

"I was just thinking about Mamma. She's probably stopped being angry by now, and she's worried sick."

"Don't worry," he said. "By the time we get home, she'll be plenty mad again."

31

It is well known that on Independence and Walnut creeks, within a few miles of this place, a great number of freesoilers or abolitionists are settled, whose thieving propensities have been well known for some time past. We honestly believe that an organized band of these outlaws exists whose objects are to rob us of our property, incite our slaves to rebellion and afford them facilities for escaping.

—*Squatter Sovereign*, Atchison, K.T.

Joseph flicked the lines. "Git up!"

The rain was deafening. It pounded the road, the wagon, and the canvas tarp. The silk fabric of Lucy's dress clung to her skin. The wet brim of Phoebe's bonnet drooped over her face. Joseph's clothes were as wet as if he had swum the Kaw. Water pooled on top of the tarp that covered the lumber, and soon the girls were sitting in a puddle.

"Help me pull this tarp loose," Lucy shouted over the storm. "We can hold it over us."

She and Phoebe tugged the edge of the canvas fabric and inched it out from under the ropes. They struggled to keep their balance against the swaying of the wagon while they worked at freeing the tarp. When they finally pulled it loose, they held the edge of it over their heads so they could see out.

"That's not much better, but at least we're covered now," Lucy said.

On the open landscape there were few trees and no shelter in sight.

The heavy rain soon filled the ruts in the road, and the mud pulled at the wagon wheels. Betsy still lurched at every crack of thunder, and Joseph struggled to control her. For the next hour, they made their way up the Delaware Road. The rain sometimes eased for a few minutes, only to lash at them with new fury with the next cloudburst. "We have to stop," Joseph shouted. He pointed up the road. "I see a barn. Stay under the tarp until we know if anyone's home."

Joseph pulled the line in his right hand so the horses would follow the short lane that led to the barn. The wind and rain was blowing from behind them now. The only house nearby was dark. Lucy peered out from under the tarp and watched her brother walk near the house and look in the window. He ran through the driving rain back to the wagon.

"No one here. I'm going to pull the wagon around to the other side."

Joseph led the horses to the side of the barn out of the wind and away from the road. "Make a dash for the barn!"

The girls threw back the tarp and ran inside.

The noise of the storm was even louder inside the barn, as

rain pounded the roof and the west wall in waves as the wind gusted.

Joseph unbuttoned his shirt and took it off.

"What did you see in the house?" Lucy asked.

He twisted the shirt, and water dripped from it onto the floor. "No one's been here for a long while. Not much in there."

Phoebe untied her dripping bonnet and shook it. "How far we got to go?"

"Could be five miles. Could be ten," Joseph answered.

Lucy looked out the barn door toward the road. "What if Levi passes by while we're here?"

"I'll watch," Joseph said. "You stay out of sight."

Lucy moved away from the door and sat on the floor. She couldn't imagine anything much worse than this. Otis would be after them. Probably soon. Probably with others. And they didn't even know where they were going. She was cold and wet and frightened. But she had to do something.

"What was in the house?"

Joseph turned from the barn door. "Not much. Whatever was left by the people who lived here has been picked through."

"Why don't you go in there and look around anyway?" Lucy said. "Maybe you can find some clothes, or a blanket or something. If we can dry off a little, that'll help."

Joseph ran out the barn door.

Phoebe sat down beside Lucy again. "You knew Otis already?"

Lucy nodded. "Just like he said. On Election Day. He

grabbed me. I thought he would …"

"I know," Phoebe said. "And he would if he got half a chance."

"When you called him 'One-eared Otis' I knew," Lucy said.

Joseph came back through the door, his arms full. "I found some things. No dresses, but some old shirts and trousers and a blanket." He dropped the bundle of clothes on the floor.

Lucy pulled out a flannel shirt and a worn pair of denim pants. She held them out to Joseph. "Try these. They're pretty big, but at least they're dry."

Joseph put on the shirt. He rolled up the sleeves and fastened the few buttons that remained. "Better," he said. The girls turned while he took off his wet trousers and put on the denim pants. He laughed. He held out the large waistband. "Good thing I've got suspenders."

Joseph went back to the barn door and turned away from the girls.

As soon as she was out of the wet blue gown, Lucy felt better.

Some of the clothes were little more than rags, but Phoebe pulled one worn shirt and a pair of trousers from the pile.

"That would make a good disguise for you," Lucy said. "Those men will be looking for a girl. If anyone we pass thinks you are a boy, that might help. You could wear Joseph's hat."

"Good idea," Phoebe said. She took off Lucy's calico dress and put the clothes on. "How will I keep these pants on?"

Lucy pulled at a torn corner of the blanket she'd wrapped

around herself. "I'll tear a strip off this, and you can tie it around like a belt."

Within a few minutes, the rain slowed to a steady drizzle. "I think that's the worst of it," Joseph said. "At least for now. I'll get the wagon ready." He picked up a shirt from the pile of clothes.

Lucy put on the calico dress Phoebe had taken off and left the old blue gown behind. One less thing she'd need to explain later.

The girls watched from the door of the barn as Joseph led the horses and wagon around so they faced the road. He used the old shirt to wipe as much rain from the horses' backs as he could. He wrung out the shirt and wiped the seat with it, then lifted the edge of the tarp to allow the pooled water to roll off the side. He called into the barn, "Ready?"

Phoebe pulled Joseph's hat on. "Ready."

The girls ran out to the wagon and climbed back on top. Joseph checked to be sure the Sharps was still in its place. "I hope we meet up with Levi soon."

The road was muddy, but passable, and the horses plodded their way along.

"Can't they go any faster?" Lucy asked.

"Not with this mud," Joseph answered. "The load of wood is heavy, and the mud is pulling at the wheels. If the horses slip, they could sprain a leg."

The flooded fields on either side of the road looked like lakes. The landscape now was mostly flat and bare of trees, with the few farmhouses they passed set back from the road.

There was no sign of Levi anywhere.

Lucy guessed they'd been traveling about an hour when the rain finally stopped. The landscape had changed from prairie to low hills. Solid dark gray sky still hung overhead, and another front of deep blue clouds crawled up from the west.

When Joseph pulled the lines to stop the wagon, they could hear running water.

The road crossed a ravine here, and a swift stream cut across it.

"Is this it?" Lucy asked. "Walnut Creek?"

"Must be," Joseph said.

Lucy looked at Phoebe. "Then we're close!"

"We've still got this creek to cross," Joseph reminded her.

He jumped down from the seat and walked past the horses to examine the obstacle in front of them. Lucy and Phoebe climbed down from the wagon to look, too.

The water hissed and gurgled as it rushed past and splashed along rocks that stood in its way. The road continued straight into the water and came out on the other side. The deepest area in the middle of the rushing water looked only about one or two feet deep. It was about twenty feet from one side to the other.

"It's not as rocky as I thought it would be," Joseph said. "It looks pretty soft there in the middle."

"Can we get across?" Phoebe asked.

Joseph squatted at the edge of the water. He reached his hand into it to feel the strength of the current. "I think so," he said. "But it might be tricky."

He looked at the incline on the other side.

"Get back on the wagon," he told the girls. "I'll lead the horses across. If I can keep Betsy calm, Hector will follow."

Joseph grasped the lines where they connected to Betsy's bridle. He gave a soft click and tugged gently as he stepped into the water, pulling Betsy. She pulled her nose back at first. "Git up, Betsy," Joseph said sharply. She stepped forward into the water, and Hector stepped in with her.

They were halfway across when the current swept Joseph's feet out from under him. He went down.

"Joseph!" Lucy screamed.

Betsy tossed her head back. Joseph still grasped the bridle, and Betsy's movement jerked his arm up. He got to his feet and splashed toward the road on the other side. When the front wagon wheels crossed the deepest part, Joseph walked faster to get the horses across. The current pushed at the wagon wheels, and the horses strained against the crosswise movement of the wagon.

When the rear wheels reached the deepest water, the current pulled the back of the wagon to the side.

"H'ya!" Joseph pulled on Betsy's bridle, but the weight of the wagon continued to pull against the horses' harness.

The wagon tipped sideways. The lumber shifted.

"Hold on!" Joseph called to them.

Lucy and Phoebe both grabbed the back of the driver's seat. As the front wheels began to pull out of the stream, the back wheels slipped in the mud.

"Git up!" Joseph said again, and urged the horses forward.

The horses pulled, and at last the wagon was on the road on the other side.

Joseph stopped the wagon, and Lucy and Phoebe climbed down.

Joseph still held Betsy's bridle with his left hand. He was pale and shaking.

"Sorry I screamed, Joseph." Lucy said. "I didn't mean to scare Betsy. Are you all right?"

"It's a good thing you did. If she hadn't jerked her head up, I'm not sure I could have gotten my feet under me." He rubbed his shoulder. "It sure hurt, though."

A whistle on the other side of the stream.

"It's Levi!" Joseph said.

Levi pointed Teakee at an angle upstream, and they splashed through the current to join them on the other side.

"We stopped during the storm," Lucy said. "I was afraid we'd missed you."

"The Kaw was higher than I thought," Levi said. "I had to go upstream two more miles to find a place to cross."

"We had some trouble on the ferry," Lucy said. "We may have someone after us."

Levi nodded. "I passed two riders on the road. One with half his ear cut off."

"That's Otis," Phoebe said.

"They stopped me to ask if I'd seen you. They described you, but I pretended that I couldn't speak English. I just listened as they made plans."

"How far back are they?" Joseph asked.

"They don't seem to know people around here. They said they would stop at every farm along the road."

"We haven't passed many farms," Joseph said. "They may not be far behind."

"They're looking for a white girl in a fancy blue dress and a slave girl," Levi said. "They know this wagon, though."

Joseph rubbed his shoulder again. "Mr. Newhouse said Walnut Creek wouldn't cause us any trouble," he said. "It was harder than we thought."

Levi looked at the flowing water they had just crossed. "That's not Walnut Creek," he said. "It's just high water from the rain. Walnut Creek is another three miles ahead."

"Then we'd better get going," Joseph said. "We don't know how close those men are."

Levi watched as the girls took their places on top of the boards in the wagon. He frowned and tugged on the rope tied over the lumber. "That's too loose."

Joseph came around to look. Together the boys pulled the ropes tighter and retied them. Lucy watched Joseph's face as he tugged on the rope. Every time he used his left hand, his face twitched. Beads of sweat dotted his forehead despite the cool air and his wet clothing and shoes.

He pulled himself into the driver's seat with his right arm. His face scrunched with pain when he reached out with his left arm for balance. He held both lines in his right hand.

They would definitely need Levi's help when they got to

Walnut Creek.

Lucy's stomach growled. They had left home before breakfast. It must be late afternoon now. What must Mamma be thinking?

The clouds continued to sweep toward the east, and the darkest part of the cloudbank was nearly overhead. Jagged flashes of lightning cut through the dark sky, with sharp crashes of thunder close behind. Betsy began to toss her head again. Levi and Teakee stayed near her, and Hector's steadiness on one side and Teakee on the other seemed to help.

When rain began again, the girls once more pulled up the tarp. With the ropes tightened and the road a little smoother, the boards beneath them felt more stable. It couldn't be far to the creek.

Then the storm truly hit.

They were headed northeast, and the stinging rain chased them and lashed at them from behind. It drummed on the tarp over Lucy's head. Phoebe leaned against her, and Lucy was glad of the warmth. The falling rain seemed to drown out all sound – at least until they heard the rushing water ahead.

"Walnut Creek," Levi shouted to Joseph. Joseph pulled on the lines with his right hand. "Whoa!"

Lucy lifted the front of the tarp to look. Slender trees lined both sides of the creek. Water nipped at the roots of those trees as it tumbled over the rocks and rushed past them.

"It's high and fast," Levi shouted.

Joseph jumped down from the wagon. "How deep is it?"

"I'll see," Levi said. He rode Teakee to the edge of the creek and urged her to step into the water. It swirled around her legs and splashed high enough to touch her belly, but she could still walk across and didn't seem frightened.

"Can we get the wagon across?" Joseph asked.

Levi bent down to look under the wagon bed at the under-carriage. "I think so," he said. "As long as the water doesn't pick it up off the bottom. The rocks will be easier than the mud you had at that gulley." He looked at Hector and Betsy. "These are strong horses. They can pull it across."

Joseph walked toward Betsy. "Should I lead them?"

Levi shook his head. "The horses can keep their footing, you can't. The water's too fast. I'll ride next to Betsy."

Joseph climbed back on the wagon. He turned to the girls. "Let go of the tarp and hold on to the back of my seat!" He looked at Lucy. "And don't scream!"

The rain lashed at their backs as they neared the creek. Levi and Teakee stayed close to Betsy. It looked like Levi was talking to her.

The horses went in slowly at first. As the front wheels entered the water, the wagon tipped forward. The boards shifted under them. Lucy bit her bottom lip.

They inched forward, and the rear wheels entered the water. Waves lapped at the upstream side of the wagon and splashed water over the edge. Lucy felt the hair on her arms rise.

A blinding light and thunder split the thick air in an explosion.

Betsy bolted. Something broke.

The wagon flipped sideways. The rope holding the lumber snapped as the wagon tipped to the side.

Boards tumbled, and Lucy tumbled with them. Something crashed against her head so hard her teeth felt the jolt.

Then, only water. Water in her mouth, cold water. No air. No top or bottom. Rocks scraped her back. Where were her feet? She tumbled into darkness.

Something had her. Pulling, dragging her arm. She heard yelling and rushing water. Her face scraped on rough, hard rocks.

Joseph yelled at her. "Lucy! Lucy! Wake up!"

She opened her eyes.

Joseph knelt next to her. "Can you hear me?"

She could hear him, but she couldn't find her voice. She choked.

Phoebe stood behind Joseph, looking at her over his shoulder. "Lucy ..."

Her head hurt.

Levi stood by Phoebe. He took her arm. "Come –"

"No," Phoebe said.

Lucy choked again. Joseph pushed Lucy to her side.

Creek water ran from her mouth. The rain had slowed. The overturned wagon lay in the creek. The two horses, Betsy and Hector, stood calmly beside the creek.

She remembered. The wagon ride. Phoebe. Otis! She shook her head. "Phoebe ..." she said.

Phoebe pulled loose from Levi. She dropped to the ground next to Lucy. Lucy struggled to speak. "Go …"

"But …"

"Go." It was all Lucy could say.

Joseph turned. "If you don't go, it's all for nothing!"

Levi had Phoebe's arm again. And this time she went. Levi and Phoebe on Teakee. Creek gravel flew past her head as Teakee's hooves dug in.

And everything went black.

⟫◆⟪

"Gone! Whaddya mean, gone!"

Lucy opened her eyes. A strange man stood near her.

She recognized the shouting voice … Otis! He had Joseph, shaking him. "You know where she is! That gal's my property!"

"I don't know where she went," Joseph said. "Our wagon crashed when we crossed the creek! That girl," Joseph looked at her, "she's hurt. I think she's hurt bad."

The man next to her leaned over and looked in her face. "Her eyes are open," he said. "She ain't dead yet."

"I pulled her out of the creek," Joseph said. "I thought she'd drowned. When I got her out, the other one was gone. I don't know where she went."

The stranger looked at her and frowned. "This the same one, you was looking for, Otis? Thought she had some fancy dress."

"That's her," Otis growled. "Different dress, same girl. Slave

352

stealer." He stomped across the gravel and put his boot next to her head. "Where is she?"

Lucy shook her head, then winced at the pain.

Otis lunged over her and grabbed her shoulders. "You know where Phoebe is! Tell me!" He shook her. "Now!"

"Stop it!" Joseph yelled. "She's hurt!"

Otis put his face just inches from hers. "Tell me!" he shouted.

A shot fired. Lucy heard the rifle ball zip past Otis' head. He dropped her.

"Let her be!"

Lucy tried to lift her head, but couldn't. Who was that?

"Hands up and back away!"

Lucy didn't know the voice.

Otis and his companion both put their hands up.

A big man jumped from a wagon. His heavy boots crunched in the gravel. "What's going on here? A rider came to my house and said there was a wagon accident."

"These slave stealers took my property!" Otis said. "They know where she is!"

The big man kept his rifle leveled at Otis. "I don't see any slave here," he said. "I see a busted wagon, two injured children, and two grown men threatening them." He turned to Joseph. "I heard his side of it. You want to tell me yours?"

Joseph looked at Lucy, then at the man with the gun. "I was delivering this load of lumber for Mr. Newhouse. This girl and her slave needed a ride." He pointed at Otis. "That man took hold of this girl on the ferry. He said terrible things to her – indecent things. Mr. Baldwin saw it all."

The man came closer to Lucy. "The slave belonged to you?" he asked.

She nodded.

"That's a lie!" Otis shouted. "She ran away from my place a week ago!"

"Calm down and keep your hands up."

The man addressed Otis' partner. "Did you see this slave?" He shook his head.

He turned to Otis. "Anybody else see this slave?"

"Baldwin saw her!"

"And does Baldwin know her identity?"

"Well, no, but …"

The man turned to Joseph. "What happened to the slave?"

Joseph pointed to the wagon. "When we turned over, this girl fell off. A board hit her in the head. I jumped in to save her. When I pulled her out of the creek, the slave was gone."

Lucy moaned and turned her head. "Manda … Manda's gone?"

Joseph looked at her. "Yes, gone."

Otis fumed. "Liars and slave stealers! Sheriff Jones will hear about this!"

The man looked at Otis. "Looks to me like you got a pretty flimsy case. You got no slave, no witnesses who'll vouch for you, and several folks who have seen you abuse and threaten these children." He tipped his hat back on his head. "Now, we could ride on over to Baldwin's ferry and get his account. Or we could ride up to Atchison and see what Sheriff Jones has to say about a man taking indecent liberties with a young white girl. What do you want to do?"

Otis cursed. He shook his head. "Come on," he snarled to his companion. They mounted their horses and rode off in the direction of Atchison.

The farmer bent down to look at Lucy's face. "Can you see me all right?"

She nodded.

He put a hand behind her head. She winced.

"You got a pretty good knot there, but I think you'll live." He smiled. "Let's get you on the wagon." He looked at Joseph. "Help me?"

Joseph reached toward Lucy. He grimaced when he put his left arm out.

"Never mind, son. You're hurt, too." He lifted Lucy gently and carried her to the wagon. "I'll come back for the horses later. Let's get you two home now."

Joseph followed. "Thank you, Mr.?"

The man smiled. "Martin. Zachary Martin. Third house past the creek."

Lucy looked up at him. "Phoebe?"

"Safe."

———⟫◆⟪———

Levi was waiting at the Martin farm when they arrived, but

Phoebe was not there. "They took her to the next stop," Levi said. "In case those men come looking for her again."

Mr. Martin took Lucy to the back bedroom, and Mrs. Martin gave her a warm nightgown and put her in bed.

When she was settled, Levi came in to see her. "You look better, *Neekanauh.*"

She smiled. "Thanks for taking Phoebe."

"It wasn't easy," he said. "I had to convince her that you weren't dying, and I wasn't too sure about that."

Mr. Martin laid a hand on Levi's shoulder. "Do you know where these two live?"

Levi nodded.

"I have a letter for their parents. Will you take it?"

"I don't have money for the ferry," Levi said.

"I'll see to that," Mr. Martin said.

"What did you tell them?" Lucy asked. "They don't know about the Liberty Line."

"I told them their children are safe," he said. "That's what they want to know."

Lucy imagined Mamma standing by the window, watching for them all day. "I feel so awful for Mamma. She must be frantic."

Levi rose. "If I go now, I'll get there before dark." He took the letter and ferry money from Mr. Martin.

He nodded at Lucy. "*Nepaukechey.*"

"Goodbye," Lucy said.

Mrs. Martin wrapped a sling around Joseph's neck to hold

his left arm. "Bad sprain, but nothing broken," she pronounced. "It'll need some rest."

"I'm sorry I lost the lumber," Joseph told Mr. Martin.

"No harm, son. The important part of that shipment was safely delivered."

Lucy smiled at her brother. "You made me proud today, even if I do hate to say it."

"We both did something to be proud of today," he said. "But we nearly got killed doing it."

"You saved my life," Lucy said. "I don't remember much, except that I couldn't get out of the water. I felt you grab my arm and pull me out."

"Not me," Joseph said. "I had to catch the horses."

"But you said …"

"I said a lot of things." Joseph smiled. "It was Phoebe."

Lucy exhaled a long breath. She shook her head and laughed.

"What?"

"And all this time, I thought I was saving her."

32

School Notice

The citizens of Lawrence and vicinity are respectfully requested to meet in Union Hall on Thursday evening next, at 7 o'clock to make the necessary arrangements for a winter school.

Per order School Committee,
Sam Tappan, Clerk
Lawrence, Oct. 6, 1855.

Mr. Martin rode out to the abandoned farm to retrieve Joseph's clothes, and Mrs. Martin washed them together with Lucy's calico dress. After two nights' rest, Lucy and Joseph were ready to go home. Mr. Martin placed Lucy in the wagon bed on a cushion of blankets. Joseph sat next to Mr. Martin on the wagon seat.

Mamma rushed out the front door to greet them. She was smiling, but Lucy's heart ached, knowing how much Mamma had worried about them.

Joseph still wore the sling, and Mamma hugged him gently.

"I hope you won't be too hard on them," Mr. Martin told Mamma. "They shouldn't have gone off without telling you, but they just wanted to help Mr. Newhouse with his delivery. Nobody could have guessed how mean that storm would get."

"Thank you for your kind care of them," Mamma said. "And thank you for sending word to me. I was worried out of my mind, especially with my husband gone to Topeka."

"Yes, ma'am," Mr. Martin said. "We'll hope for good news from that meeting." He lifted Lucy gently. "You'll need to let this one rest a few days," he said. "She took a hard bump to the head."

Mamma led Mr. Martin up the stairs to Lucy's room. He placed her on her bed.

"Thank you – for everything,"

"I'm glad I was there to help," he said.

Her bed never felt better to Lucy than it did at that moment.

When they left her, she looked around her room. She had whispered with Phoebe here. The bureau drawer was still open from when she had pulled the blue silk gown from it. Her poetry journal and Miss Kellogg's book lay on top of the desk.

In the last six months, she had written poems about so many things: books, home, guns, slaves, and even friendship. Mr. Whittier's poems had helped her understand about the slaves. And yet, she still wondered if she had found her own voice in all that.

As soon as Papa came back from Topeka that evening, he came upstairs to see Lucy.

He hugged her and held her a few seconds longer than usual. "Lucy Cat," he said, "we nearly lost you."

"I'll be all right," she told him. "How is Mamma doing? We worried her so much."

Papa raised his eyebrows. "Let's just say that your injuries – and your brother's – probably saved you both from a lot worse trouble."

"Tell me about Topeka," Lucy said. "What happened with the Black Law?"

He smiled. "We stood, Lucy Cat. We stood up to Jim Lane and his men. I read that letter from the *Free State*, and then more stood with us."

"And did they strike the Black Law from the constitution?"

"They didn't omit it, but they have agreed to put the matter to the Free State voters. When they vote on the constitution, the voters of Kansas will decide whether the Black Law will be part of it. It's not a victory yet, but at least the people will decide."

Lucy hugged Papa again. "That's wonderful!"

———◦◦◦———

It was nearly a month until school began again, and by then, Lucy was ready. The weather had turned cool, and it didn't feel right to not be in school. She also wanted to return Miss Kellogg's book and talk to her about what had happened. Miss Kellogg would be proud that they had helped Phoebe.

The day before school started, Annie came to the store. When Mamma wasn't looking, she slipped an envelope in Lucy's hand. "This came through the Liberty Line. It's for you," she whispered. Annie pulled at the door handle. She waved.

"See you at school tomorrow, Lucy." Lucy slid the envelope in her pocket.

When Mamma sent her outside to pump water, Lucy pulled it out and opened it.

Dear Lucy
I'm free! I hope you are not dead.
Give this to someone who needs it.
Your friend,
Phoebe

Lucy looked in the bottom of the envelope. There was the wooden disk with the letters LL.

Phoebe had made it.

That night Lucy opened her poetry journal. She leafed through the pages of poems she had written. Each one seemed like a part of a journey she had made during her time in Kansas.

She turned a page to her poem, *No Voice for Kanzas*. She had been so disappointed when she wrote that poem. The Ruffians had stolen the election and filled the legislature with proslavery men. They had threatened Mr. Brown. Even the Free State legislature seemed set on the Black Law.

But now, it all felt different. They would vote on the Black Law at a Free State election. And Phoebe was free.

Lucy looked at the poem again. All of it was true, but it only told part of the story. Now was the time to tell the whole story of Kansas.

She counted the lines of the poem: eight so far. But that was only about half-done.

When she finished the poem she extinguished her lamp. She would show it to Miss Kellogg tomorrow.

The day began with introductions. New children had moved to Lawrence since the last school session, and several young ones were coming to school for the first time. As soon as she had taken attendance, Miss Kellogg passed out the copies of *Town's Readers*. By noon, she had assigned all the students to their proper reading groups.

She dismissed them for lunch, but added, "Miss Thomkins, I'd like to speak to you, please."

Lucy waited as the others ran outside.

Miss Kellogg closed the door.

She turned away from Lucy and looked out the window. "I know about your trip across the Kaw," she said. She turned to face her. "That is perhaps the most foolish thing I can imagine."

"Ma'am?"

"You heard me. What on earth were you thinking? You could have all been killed."

"Mr. Newhouse –"

"I'm aware of his accident. Nonetheless, this was not an errand for children to undertake. You should never have tried it, and he should never have agreed to it."

"But Phoebe –"

364

"Would have been taken to her next stop by one of our people." Miss Kellogg took a sharp breath and stood stiff. "The Liberty Line has a responsibility to both the people we serve and the people who serve with us. Your actions could have caused many people to be exposed. Considering the current laws that govern us, you might have endangered lives."

Of course Miss Kellogg was right. Once again, she had risked others' welfare by her own actions. "I'm sorry, Miss Kellogg. We only wanted to help Phoebe."

Miss Kellogg relaxed. "I understand that." She reached out to put her hands on Lucy's shoulders. "You must promise me that you will never undertake another risk like that."

"No, ma'am."

Miss Kellogg's eyebrows raised.

Lucy looked at Miss Kellogg. "I can't make that promise. I had to help Phoebe, and I would do it again. She made it, Miss Kellogg."

"Yes. She made it."

Lucy reached into her pocket. "And I have something for you." She unfolded the paper and handed it to Miss Kellogg. "It's a sonnet. A sonnet about Kansas."

Miss Kellogg took the paper. She moved to her desk, picked up her spectacles and read.

Lucy waited. It seemed like a very long time before Miss Kellogg looked up.

Miss Kellogg smiled. "You have finally found your voice, Lucy Thomkins."

A Voice for Kansas

By Lucy Catherine Thomkins

In Washington they claimed the Kanza land.
They said the settlers would decide her fate.
The flames of strife this controversy fanned
Meant none who cared could dare to hesitate.

They came from East and South to stake their claims.
Election Day would take all doubts away.
But slav'ry's guardians cast their votes for shame,
And Freedom's voice was silenced on that day.

But human hearts cannot be held by chains,
Though legislature's laws may threaten death.
Now Freedom's voice speaks loud and clear again,
While secret forces work with ev'ry breath.

For Freedom's voice is Kansas' voice now heard!
And all who share this land shall know the word:

FREEDOM

Author's Note:
On Story and History

This story is set in a historical time period that contained many rich elements of story in characters and conflict as Kansas struggled toward statehood. Some of the events in this story are historical and are depicted much as they were described in the newspapers and journals of the day. Other events are partially based on actual happenings, but have been dramatized and woven into the stories of the characters in the novel. Still other events are entirely fictional and come from my own imagination. The introductions to the chapters are excerpted from actual documents of the era.

Likewise, some of the characters in this book were real people who lived in and around Lawrence, Kansas. Their participation in the events of this story are mostly fictional, and their dialogue is mostly invented, except for some instances such as the speech of the Shawnee Chief on the Fourth of July, which was given in translation in the newspaper. Other characters, like Lucy and her family, are creations of my imagination, although they have often seemed very real to me as I wrote the story.

In any case, I hope that this work of fiction will give readers a fairly accurate sense of the history of Kansas Territory in 1855. Living conditions were harsh, and the settlers' lives contained both joy and sorrow, mixed with the fear that comes from living in a place where both man and nature add danger to everyday life.

Acknowledgments

I am indebted to so many wonderful people who have helped and encouraged me as I worked on *A Voice for Kanzas* that it is impossible to list them all.

I was blessed to have the opportunity to study in the MFA program at Hamline University in St. Paul, Minnesota. This book has benefitted from the workshops with my classmates and from the guidance of my instructors Jane Resh Thomas, Liza Ketchum, Claire Rudolf Murphy, and Gary Schmidt. I will always remember my Hamline time as "golden days" in my development as a writer.

My dear friends and fellow writers at the Mainely Writing Workshop encouraged me to take the leap of faith of moving from nonfiction writer to novelist. Amy Coombs, Theadora Gammans, Ann Mack, Mary Beth Lundgren, Tessa Elwood, Karyn Everham, and others who have joined us through the years have been sisters of the craft and cheerleaders. Special thanks to our mentor, Louise Hawes, who has provided us with so much love and wisdom for many years.

Thanks to editor Kira Lynn at Kane Miller, who has been

a joy to work with and whose suggestions have improved the book. You have made this journey a pleasant one.

I would not be a writer today without the love for stories shared with me by my parents, George and Norma Roberts.

And I thank my husband and my children who always believed in me. They ate a lot of take-out Chinese food and delivery pizza and did their own laundry for the past several years without much complaining. I noticed.

Notes on Sources

The following sources are used in *A Voice for Kanzas*:

An Act to Punish Offences Against Slave Property, Section 6. Kansas Legislature, Aug. 14, 1855. *Territorial Kansas Online*. Web. 16 Dec 2009.

"Big Springs Platform," September 5, 1855. *Annals of Kansas*, p. 76. *Territorial Kansas Online*. Web. 16 Dec 2009.

Denny, Ebenezer. *Denny's Vocabulary of Shawnee*. Bristol, PA: Evolution Publishing, 1999. [Reprint of 1860 edition].

Emerson, Ralph Waldo. "The Rhodora." *Ralph Waldo Emerson Texts*. Web. 15 Dec. 2009.

"First Free State Platform." August 5, 1855. In William G. Cutler's *History of the State of Kansas*. Territorial History, Part 19. *KanColl.org/books*. Web. 16 Dec 2009.

Notice of elections on August 25, 1855 for delegates to a Free State convention at Big Springs on Sept. 5, 1855. *Territorial Kansas Online*. Web. 16 Dec 2009.

Robinson, Sara T. L. *Kansas: Its Interior and Exterior Life.* 1856. Kansas Collection Books. *KanColl.org/books.* Web. 16 Dec 2009.

Stewart, John E. "Experience of John E. Stewart." c. 1856. *Territorial Kansas Online.* Web. 15 Dec 2009.

Webb, Thomas H. "Information for Kanzas Immigrants." [Circular] Boston: Alfred Mudge & Son, 1855. *Internet Archive.* Web. 15 Dec. 2009.

Newspaper excerpts have been taken from the newspapers *Herald of Freedom* and *Kansas Free State.* Both newspapers published in Lawrence, Kansas, between April and October 1855. Available through the Kansas State Historical Society, Topeka, KS.

Additional sources used for reference:

Caldwell, Martha B. *Annals of the Shawnee Methodist Mission and Indian Manual Labor School.* Topeka, KS: Kansas State Historical Society.

Dean, Virgil, Ed. *Kansas Territorial Reader.* Topeka, Kansas: Kansas State Historical Society, 2006.

Dick, Everett. *The Sod-House Frontier, 1854-1890.* Lincoln, NE: University of Nebraska Press, 1954.

Goodrich, Thomas. *War to the Knife: Bleeding Kansas, 1854-1861.* Mechanicsburg, PA: Stackpole Books, 1998.

Nichols, Alice. *Bleeding Kansas.* New York: Oxford University Press, 1954.

Phillips, William. *The Conquest of Kansas by Missouri and Her Allies.* Boston: Phillips, Sampson, and Co., 1856.

Sheridan, Richard B., Ed. *Freedom's Crucible: The Underground Railroad in Lawrence and Douglas County, Kansas, 1854-1865.* Lawrence, KS: University of Kansas Press, 2000.

Stratton, Joanna L. *Pioneer Women: Voices from the Kansas Frontier.* New York: Simon and Schuster, 1981.

I have also referred to artifacts and information from historical sites and collections such as the Steamboat Arabia museum in Kansas City, Missouri; Missouri Town 1855 (Jackson County, Mo Parks), and the Shawnee Indian Mission in Shawnee, Kansas.